I0522985

A Sugarverse Novel

Arm
Candy

Written By

Marlayna James

Friends With Pens Author Group

Previously published in part as: Sugar Daddies: Spencer Series by Marlayna James

Published by Friends With Pens Author Group

www.friendswithpensauthorgroup.com

Copyright © 2013 Marlayna James

www.marlaynajames.com

All rights reserved. This book or any portion thereof may not be reproduced or used in any manner whatsoever without the express written permission of the publisher except for the use of brief quotations in a book review.

Cover Art © 2022 by Nicole Farrer

PRINT ISBN 978-0-9918512-2-5

EBOOK ISBN 978-0-9918512-3-2

Printed in U.S.A.

This complete work is **Fiction** > Romance > Contemporary

Any names, characters, places, and incidents which align are used fictitiously and/or are the product of my overactive, under-caffeinated imagination. Any resemblance to actual persons (living or dead), businesses, companies, events, pets, cars or locales are entirely coincidental.

The voices I hear aren't relaying your stories to me.

Second Edited Edition, 2022

Friends With Pens Author Group

Dedication

*Jade Greenberg, for being a sounding board
for all my crazy, insane ideas.
www.jadegreenberg.com*

*Ashley Marie, for being my alpha,
my beta, my ten draft reader.
www.ashleyhempelphoto.com*

*All my author friends who inspire,
support, and encouraged me to write every day.*

...Thank you

CHAPTER 1

How Much for the Night?

JUNE

If anyone was unwell, it was her—his best friend, Gwen—she was delusional.

She'd read an article and informed Aurick that he suffered seven of eight signs of mental illness. According to her, his reclusive lifestyle was unhealthy, and she was worried.

Cranky. Who wouldn't be when inaccurate inspections, missed deadlines, government red-tape, and financial audits had slowed his current acquisition?

Tardiness. At thirty-two, shouldn't the boss enjoy certain perks?

Tired. Who wasn't after sixteen-hour days?

Forgetful. He'd forgotten her birthday the previous month. With their grueling travel schedule flying between several cities in a day only to repeat it the next, he'd lost track of the date.

Unsociable. Pardon him for allowing her space during the few free hours they had.

Illness and red eyes. She was grasping at straws. Him crying? No. They were allergies and/or caused by chlorine. From the chlorine pool, where he exercised, so he wouldn't gain weight—the eighth sign.

If Gwen only knew how he spent his alone time,

she'd be disgusted. When he *chose* to; he frequented nightclubs where he could handpick someone willing to engage in the meaningless sex a one-night stand would offer. Relationships, long-distance or otherwise, were out of the question when his businesses took him around the world without warning. No woman would put up with it.

Although exhausted, he was content with his uncomplicated, business-driven life. The last thing he needed was to spend the night guarded and uncomfortable while entertaining a stranger.

She'd played him well—waiting until they were alone in the hotel's elevator before springing the 'scheduled relaxation' on him. He flatly refused. But her pitying gaze and patronizing tone goaded him. Fine! He punched the lobby level button with his thumb as she withdrew. He'd prove her concerns were misguided and appease her.

Through the dimly lit restaurant's privacy glass, Aurick scanned the hotel lobby. The cream-colored marble floor seamlessly molded into the benches circling the elaborate planters filled with exotic lush trees and flowering bushes, not native to the Canadian city of Edmonton.

It was utter chaos. Guided by a guest relations supervisor, several concierge staff negated the long check-in line by personally seeing to the needs of more prominent guests. They snapped their fingers to flag bell staff, hospitality staff, food service advisors, and valets to take care of their very specific eccentricities. Running children weaved through the busy crowd, avoiding near accidents with carts, bags, and other obstacles. Though he couldn't see the public elevators, he knew when another landed as a small burst of people flooded from its hallway on their way elsewhere. Soon, it would be abandoned for the evening and the excess staff would exit, leaving a skeleton crew to deal with the few stragglers checking in late or the odd request.

As he sized and measured the unaccompanied females, he wondered where Gwen had found his expected companion.

But it was forgotten when a yellow-clad blonde pushed through the revolving glass door.

Examining her friends' artistry, Mercy Haggins turned in the mirror, surveying the damage.

"I look ridiculous," she blurted, not caring if she hurt their feelings. "These bangle bracelets and cheap beaded necklaces are chipped and peeling." She leaned closer, scowling at the profusely caked makeup. "I look like Ursula, the sea witch."

Stepping into her, Carmen feigned primping the girl's long, curly blonde hair as she hid her grin. "You look nothing like her. Don't be *so* dramatic. You only feel that way because you're unaccustomed to poorly made clothing and drugstore makeup. Be careful, you may offend me."

"I've never seen you wear any of this, including this canary sundress. The top might as well be nonexistent for how little it covers." Mercy's spine was entirely exposed except for the tie at her neck and her cascading curls. The fabric plunged the valley between her breasts, then squeezed every curve to her mid-thigh.

Carmen eyed the third girl in the room. "See how much attention she pays me?" She turned back to fidget with the curls. "I wear it all the time. It's semi-casual."

"I don't know. I feel naked and there's little left to

the imagination." She batted her friend's hands away as she faced them.

"You look like you're going to the lake instead of dinner." Beverly studied her, preferring more flash in her own clothing choices.

"Look at the time. You'll be late if you don't leave now. Relax and enjoy yourself." Carmen ushered her out the door. Not feeling the least bit guilty for sabotaging Mercy's final date.

Once the taxi driver pulled away from the curb, Mercy withdrew her small compact from the small clutch. Hoping to lighten the heavy-handed makeup, she dampened a tissue with saliva and wiped her eyelid, but it was infallible. What was it made of? Glue? It was going to take more effort, tissue, and spit than she had right now.

At least, she could relax the tight dolly curls, her hair hated to hold any style. Flipping her head forward, she combed her fingers through and watched the strands loosen.

Short of leaving Carmen's bracelets and necklaces behind, she had no choice but to wear them.

With an optimistic eye, she checked her reflection again. Her now tousled hair looked halfway decent—nearly sexy.

She shrugged and returned the items. What difference did it make, anyway? She was done. This dating experiment was over. And, after the first two disastrous dates, there was no telling how much worse this one was going to be.

Her glance bounced to the buildings, landmarks, and street signs. Within a couple of minutes, she'd arrive at her destination. She settled into the leather, focusing on the street ahead. In the rearview mirror, she caught the driver's creepy, interested eyes boring into her.

Ugh! Men were all the same. Cheaters, users, and schemers with dirty thoughts and designs. *No, thank you!*

To Aurick, she appeared overwhelmed and meek as her eyes swept the interior. The lobby's bustle stopped and gawking patrons stood straighter and lifted their noses as if the very sight of her offended them.

Busted, a security guard blocked her passage as the guest relations supervisor marched to his side. Discreet but obvious by their posture and hand gestures, they were eager to help her, then see her leave. Her mere presence diminished the hotel's sophisticated atmosphere.

All she wanted was to slip inside unnoticed and find a washroom. She wasn't so lucky—as security blocked her path and a pompously clean-cut, well-groomed manager rushed forward. From the flip-side, she'd witnessed this before, staff maneuvering undesirables out. As herself, she could scurry them by mentioning her real name. But tonight, she wasn't Mercy Haggins, the millionaire's daughter. She was Mercy Richards, a poor, unknown orphan.

"Pardon me?" The security guard's uncomfortable, guilty eyes bounced off of her.

Waylaying her until the other man reached them, he was merely doing his job.

The stiff manager checked his cuffs and tie, ensuring no minuscule detail was out of place. "Are you a hotel guest?"

Her presence had drawn the unwanted attention of bystanders. With a sweet smile, she played dumb. "Isn't anyone who comes inside?"

"You know very well what I'm asking. Have you purchased a stay here?"

Embracing the outrageousness of the situation, she slowly sashayed as she spun around, giving everyone an eyeful. "No, what gave me away?" She rested her palm on his immaculate sleeve and leaned forward. "Relax. I'm not headed for the elevators. I'm having supper in the restaurant. You do serve food, right?"

"*Dinner*," he corrected. "Unfortunately miss, the restaurant is only seating reservations."

She straightened. "Then it's *fortunate* I have one. Under Spencer."

Apparently, the name held clout, which both recognized and, as the security guard retreated with an apologetic look, the skeptic manager's brows narrowed. "Am I to believe–"

"There's only one way to prove it." She squared her frame with perfect posture and shouldered past him, done playing the sweet, dumb blonde and answering his questions. Regrettably, if she headed for a washroom now, there'd be more staff waiting when she came out and she may not get another opportunity to prove her claim.

Right after her girlfriends were done laughing at this story, she'd kill Carmen. Mercy knew she looked outrageous, but interrogated and barred by the hotel staff? It was too much.

Disliking the elite's practice of ostracizing those deemed unworthy, Aurick set his drink down, intending to offer his assistance. However, whatever her response, the guard left, and she shouldered past the supervisor unchecked.

Now, governing herself with an intense assertiveness—she was exceptionally hot, if you could ignore her getup. He could. He'd happily volunteer to strip her of the costume and soap her entire body clean. Naked and natural, tangled in satin sheets, she'd be more than any man's fantasy.

With purpose, her round breasts thrust higher and her full, curved hips swung as her high heels clicked across the floor to the reservation desk. Several hotel staff stood at the restaurant's entrance as she followed the hostess through the tables.

Damn Gwen's meddling! Few things were unattainable when he set his mind to them. And, if he weren't waiting on another, he'd have her tonight, no matter who she was destined to meet. He'd knot her hair in his fingers while her blue eyes sparkled with the ecstasy he gave her.

Before the night was through, she'd thrill someone to exhaustion. His knowing eyes met hers with a wicked chin-dimpling grin. Hers bounced away as she passed.

Except—as she walked by, the hostess stopped at his elbow. "Your table."

Mercy was thankful for the dimly lit restaurant. Most tables were engrossed in their immediate surroundings while they ate and conversed as hovering wait staff fluttered from guest to guest.

Her eyes scanned the single occupant tables. In his

photo, he sat on a brown leather sofa and with a day's growth, he was an athletic, business-suited man with bronzed skin, gorgeous jaw-length black hair, and piercing blue eyes. According to his profile, he was thirty-two and over six feet tall. But soured by experience, she knew he could be pushing fifty, fat, short, and bald.

At first glance, her eyes disregarded him, then they darted back, fixating. Her pulse quickened when she measured his features against the image. His sexy bottom lip. His hard, defined jawline. His intent, icy eyes—traveled upward, lingering on every curve of her body. Under his scrutiny, her skin tingled as though he'd physically caressed her. She expected when his blatant eyes reached hers, they'd hold an apology. They didn't. Self-satisfied with amusement, he smiled and her eyes rolled away.

Herein lie the problem with Apollo-looking men —they knew they were and brazenly felt licensed to act any way whatsoever as long as they wore a seductive expression.

As if he didn't recognize her, he looked almost startled when the hostess stopped and addressed him, but he recovered quickly.

When he stood, his frame dwarfed Mercy and under his jacket, his dress shirt strained against the sinewy muscles rippling down his chest. As if his appearance wasn't intimidating enough, he exuded coiled power and primitive sex appeal.

Wow. Good looking was an understatement.

"Mr. Spencer?" She stammered. "I'm Mercy Richards. Please call me Mercy, everyone does." The slight tremble in her voice betrayed her anxiousness as she extended her hand and he engulfed it in his.

"Allow me." His husky voice was intimately sexy as he rounded the table, withdrew her chair, and signaled for her to sit. Her skin burned and her stomach fluttered when his hand brushed her naked spine as he pushed the chair under her.

"Please call me Aurick." He sat and poured a glass of white wine for her from the decanter.

"Such an unusual name," *and so fitting*.

"It was a gift... From my mother." His cleft chin dimpled when he chuckled and watched her cheeks flame with embarrassment.

"I'm sorry, that was rather rude. I'm nervous." She balled her hands in her lap. *What's wrong with me?* She asked and answered. *Because his gaze, his mouth, his voice—makes me want to surrender to his animalistic magnetism.*

"There's no need to apologize or be nervous. Very recently, Gwen told me I spend too much time alone and need to relax. She arranged this." He paused. "Exactly, how did she set this up?" Disturbingly, his eyes roamed to her mouth, then lingered on her neck and naked shoulders.

"She used an app—I'm on an app." She stammered, feeling like an idiot. Could she have said anything more awkward? Who was Gwen? Her tongue moistened her parched lips.

"Tell me about yourself." He relaxed against his chair, draping his arm over another.

Her agitated fingers ran lightly over her wineglass's rim, then recited. "I'm originally from Vancouver and moved here six months ago. I've no immediate family—other than a few aunts, uncles, and a dozen cousins. I live with my cousin Carmen in the city's north end." She prayed it sounded plausible.

He smiled. "That sounded rehearsed." He accused, noting her movement.

"Does it matter?" Defensively, she blurted. Then, uncomfortably, she blushed and commanded her fingers to stop.

"I suppose not." He dismissed with a disinterested

shrug, then bluntly asked. "What do you do?" His mind clouded with images of men touching her. A smattering of jealousy disturbed him and he chided himself for the uncharacteristic and uncalled for emotion.

His unexpected, hard tone distracted her. "I'm an office assistant to a project manager."

He growled with contempt. "I didn't mean your day job. How much for the night?"

Indignant, she stood abruptly, nearly knocking her chair over. "Excuse me?" *Of all the... What have I gotten myself into?*

"Look around." He paused, letting her eyes roam the room. His voice was calm and calculating. "We're in a hotel and I don't like games. If Gwen has already paid you, then I'm ready to leave. If not, tell me how much and we can go upstairs." He rose and threw a couple of bills on the table. "I don't normally wine and dine hookers—no matter how top-shelf they are." He seized her elbow, and she was momentarily stunned as he propelled her from the restaurant.

The check-in line was empty, and only a handful of employees remained at their stations. At the sound of footsteps, they looked up, but with recognition and ingrained discretion, they averted their gaze and returned to their tasks as the couple crossed the lobby.

At the first door on the left, he swiped his keycard and pushed open the heavy door, granting them access to a narrow private hallway reserved for the hotel's ultra-elite guests.

Speechless, Mercy found herself standing before a small elevator as he punched the button.

Finally alone, Aurick used his broad chest to pin her naked back to the cold wall as his muscled thigh settled between her legs and his arousal pushed against her abdomen.

She tried to protest, but his mouth crushed hers. Masterfully, his tongue dragged over her lips, then swept and massaged her tongue. His devouring, lengthy kiss drugged her. His hunger felt dangerous, felt thrilling—it was carnal, and never knowing it, she wanted it.

Every sensation heightened when she gave in. Desirous embers fueled, then blazed in her center. Her delicate hands traveled under his jacket, up his sinewy ribs, over his wide chest, and onto his neck. Her long, manicured fingers tangled in his long waves and tugged, encouraging him to be bolder and demand more from her.

Her skilled roleplaying was astounding. If he didn't know otherwise, he would think her inexperienced and untried—as if he would be her first and, that drove him. He couldn't be close enough or satiate his all-consuming appetite. He tunneled his strong arm along her naked back and walked them backwards into the elevator.

Without interruption, he pressed his floor, delighted the rickety box climbed slowly. He slouched against the side and pulled her shapely body between his carved thighs. His large hand kneaded the soft, naked flesh of her spine, while his other hand fingered and traced the contour of her rounded breast.

To him, it didn't matter if there were cameras watching. He'd pay to have the recordings erased. When her hands balled in his shirt and yanked him forward, the minuscule part of his brain still functioning stopped.

Third... The strength of her pull propelled them across the floor and they crashed against the opposite wall. He preferred it this way as his hands settled on her waist.

She was dizzily breathless, but powerless to end their thirsty embrace. Under her palm, she felt his heartbeat galloping, nearly as loud as her own. As if he sensed her need for air, his mouth slowly traveled off of hers and her throat released a small, resistant cry. Her face turned into his hair. His warm masculine scent intoxicated her and with quick, deep breaths she buried her nose, wanting more.

The roughness of his tongue's tip trailed a scintillating route along her cheek to her earlobe where his lips seductively nibbled and tugged. Breathing raggedly against her neck, she felt his skilled hands rush down her tailbone and his fingers bunched the tight skirt's material upwards. Firmly, he gripped her lacy-clad ass and lifted her pliable frame. His hips pinned her to the smooth wall, his arousal brushed against her fabric-covered nub.

Sixth... Instinctively, her legs encircled his thighs, anchoring herself in the air as her hungry mouth found his. She hunted for what would quench her unfathomable need. She became the aggressor. Her hands, her touch, her body drove her to discover what he could offer—shedding her inhibitions.

The sundress's halter let go, and he pulled the material down, removing the barrier. His hand curved around her exposed breast and lifted it as he tore his mouth from hers and latched over her pointed nipple.

Eighth... Her pleasured moan goaded him and wanting to hear more of her excited sounds, his other hand ran up the length of her silky thigh, then disappeared under her as his fingers sought to touch her. She quivered and pressed her breast into his mouth as her hands raked his hair and she tongued his ear.

His thumb pulled the damp lacy fabric aside as two of his calloused digits rolled her slick button. At their touch, her legs clenched against him as her wanting sigh sounded in his ear. His thumb replaced his digits and his two fingers slipped into her hot, tight center. Her back arched away from his mouth and he watched her passion-drugged eyes roll and close as she purred with ecstasy, grinding her heat against his hand. Her head lolled and soft, whimpering pleas escaped her as she licked her lips.

A distant bell sounded, and he sheltered her exposed chest against him, nuzzling her ear as he whispered. "How much?"

As if doused in cold water, reality returned with her societal-inflicted ethics. Her gaze darted past him. Thank God, no one was there. Her thighs let go and her hands pushed his chest, forcing him backward. The immediate hot to cold startled his expression, and the doors attempted to slide closed behind him. He held out a hand to stop them, then turned, reaching for her. In the short span, she had already righted her skirt and was fastening the material around her neck.

When he grabbed her hand, she shook free, then arched her palm and propelled it hard across his jaw. Before he recovered, she forcefully heaved him into the hall. She drummed her palm on the button to close the door as she kicked his discarded jacket out.

The doors slid, but his hand snaked through, imprisoning her wrist as she took a step backward. His eyes swept her expression, considering her swollen lips and bright watery eyes.

"It's not for sale." Breathlessly, she retorted, as her icy eyes condemned him. She shook off his hand and brought her hair forward to cover her shoulders like a shawl as the doors closed.

Frustrated, Aurick picked up his suit jacket and balled it in his fist as he walked to his room. What kind of game was this? What had ended, what promised to be a good time? He raked his hand through his hair and fought to regulate his breathing. He glanced down to pull his hanging tie off and found his dress shirt gaping open. Apparently, he hadn't been the only one wanting to remove the barriers between them.

The scent of her perfume clung to his skin, and the taste of her mouth lingered on his tongue as the shower's cold water washed over his muscular body. He couldn't believe his loss of control or the fierce emotions the evening had uncovered. Maybe his best friend's concerns weren't so far off base. Perhaps this lifestyle was unhealthy. Self-loathing, he cursed his forceful behavior—never had he broken his rule to allow his companion to set the pace. And by her violence and expression, he knew he'd lost control and crossed the line.

As he shut the water off, his mind recalled her lustful eyes, her breast's weight in his palm, and the silkiness of her muscles as they tightened around his fingers. Then he imagined her entirely naked and tangled in satin sheets.

"Fuck." He muttered, turning the knob back on. Cold water doused his body as desire swept through him again.

CHAPTER 2

You Don't Have to Go Home

THREE MONTHS EARLIER...

Mercy had dated the entire gamut of bad choices; the cheater, the user, and most recently, the schemer.

And the morning after a breakup was always the worst—no amount of April's morning sunshine would improve her disposition as she ran the brush through her long, wavy, blonde hair. The odd tear caught on her waterproof mascara and trailed down her cheek. She coated her still quivering lips in a beet red lipstick.

It was pointless. The makeup couldn't hide the effects of the emotional, sleepless night. She checked her length in the mirror as she swept past. The floor-length ivory V-neck dress hugged her slim waist, then flared down beyond her hips to dance around her ankles. The black cover-up, belt, purse, and shoes completed the outfit. She was unaware that the haunted, vulnerable impression she exuded made her seem much younger than her twenty-six years.

"Last night, while having a nightcap with my parents, he announced how happy it would make *me* if my father promoted him to President in the L.A. office." Animated, Mercy's voice grew in volume as she paced the office-turned furniture graveyard. "He patted me on the knee, and said 'your dad needed to know, *honey*'. And then, he winked at me!" She threw herself down on an old couch, utterly sickened by Roger's behavior.

"Oh, my god." Beverly choked, her brown straight hair cascading about her shoulders as she shook her head and reclined in her seat.

"Your father couldn't have been too pleased?" Carmen asked from behind a desk. Her long, red fingernails ceased their incessant drumming, totally blindsided by her friend's confession.

"On the contrary, he was extremely pleased! He thought it very fitting that his future son-in-law take over the most prestigious office in the company, since he himself cannot leave Edmonton." Mercy stated, then bit her lip. "I really thought Roger was different. I mean, we dated for a year before we were engaged and he was very understanding why we've waited so long to be married." *How could I have been so gullible again?* Her mind reeled.

"What happened next?" Beverly needed to hear the rest, like when someone yells *train wreck* and everyone goes to see it, even though they probably shouldn't.

Mercy stood, towering over the girls where they sat, and began pacing the room again. "I was shocked... Speechless at first... I let the charade continue. I couldn't very well start an argument with my mother there. She could have had a seizure. I listened while my father and my fiancé planned my life in L.A. and feigned interest until it occurred to me that my interest didn't enhance the discussion." She walked to the wall of windows, her eyes blurring as raindrops skipped on the sidewalk, her misery as dreary as the day outside. Her pained eyes looked at the girls. "I listened for another forty-five minutes then whispered to Roger I had a headache, which at that point, wasn't a lie. He excused himself, and I walked him out, where I waited for him to put his coat on, playing the doting bride-to-be. He leaned in for a goodnight kiss and I slapped him. My hand burned from the force I used."

"I'd have loved to see his reaction?" Carmen stifled a laugh behind her hand, her jet black hair bobbing about her chin.

Numbed, Mercy continued. "I stunned him... I think? As I took off my engagement ring and bawled his fist around it, he never said a word. He just stood there looking at me. One second, it was a look of contempt because I was stealing his opportunity. The next, indignation that I thought I could do better. Like he was a god, and I was more than lucky to be marrying him. I opened the door, told him to use it, and went to my room."

"Has he reached out? Have you told your parents?" Beverly asked.

"I haven't talked to Roger directly, although he left several messages with the house staff, and he's texted, emailed, and called my cell. My mother understands I want to marry for love. I want someone who wants me. She gets it." Mercy sighed, walking back to the couch to sit. "My father doesn't understand. He had talked at length with Roger this morning before I got to the breakfast table. He was angry. I could tell, but he refrained from yelling because it would upset my mother. He spoke of me getting too old to be choosy. How it's natural and expected for any man I marry to take a powerful position in the company. Then he ordered me to reconcile with Roger. He compared it to a dowry! Can you imagine?" She buried her tear-streaked face in her hands as she whispered. "I'm to be a trophy wife. The icing on someone's cake. It's so humiliating."

The overwhelming defeat in her voice struck both girls. Beverly's green eyes welled as she rushed to the upset girl's side and draped her arms around her.

Normally optimistic, Carmen said. "Give it a few days. Your dad will get over it. Maybe he didn't use the right words, but I think he's worried about you. Your mom is getting sicker, and he's not getting any younger. His mortality is catching up with him. You'll see he's not focused on you, you're just easiest to lash out at."

Mercy straightened from her friend, and Beverly helped to blot her running makeup and tears.

Beverly didn't know what to add and was aware their lunch break was ending. "I agree. Chin up and all that. Let's get back to work."

The girls cleaned their makeshift lunchroom, which was actually no more than a glorified storage closet with windows. The girls began using it shortly after Carmen was hired when a shift in offices occurred and upper management designated it for overflow furniture and files. It gave them privacy to speak freely without others intruding, and because Mercy was the boss's daughter, no one questioned them using it.

Mercy worked diligently at her desk, attempting with little success to stay focused on the details of another charity event her father had planned for the fall. He delegated projects to Connie Dover, one of his project managers. She oversaw the flowery projects—decorating new hotels, designing landscapes, planning company functions, and charity events. And as one of Connie's assistants, this project had Mercy cursing. These were things her father saw as women's work. Pretty and beautifying were fluffy jobs a woman could handle.

Mercy realized Connie loved her job and thought one day the role of Project Manager would take her farther. However, Mercy knew this was probably the end of the corporate ladder for her here. She respected her and in return received the respect of an employee. When trouble rolled downhill, Connie never spared her. When she gave praise, it was genuine, not brown-nosing the boss's daughter. These were traits Mercy admired and respected.

"Mercy, your father wants a breakdown of costs for the charity event assembled for his nine am appointment tomorrow. Do you have the staffing figures finished?" Connie's voice sounded through the intercom system.

With a finger, she responded. "Almost, but I've run into a delay. The bartenders are requesting we add an automatic gratuity into the drink prices. So I just finished with Josh Frankford. The guy you set up to do the pricing on the drinks and merchandizing. He worked on them, so now the bartenders have agreed to our original quote plus three percent." She removed her manicured nail from the button.

"Don't bother. Three percent will not cut it. Our budget can't afford it. Let me call Dale, from the bartender service, myself and talk this out with him. For god's sake, this is for charity. At this rate, they'll leave no money for the children's hospital." Connie lectured.

She had known it would be unacceptable. Three percent was her best, however, her boss would probably get it down to one or two percent.

Although her support staff handled all details, Connie routinely changed everything. In negotiations, she proved herself shrewd and cunning—better than any man in the business world.

Mercy strode from her desk with the budget in

hand to Connie's office, placing it quietly on the desk while the woman bartered on the phone. Silently, she left the room, closing the door behind her.

Like a circus, an energetic whirlwind invaded the lobby office Mercy occupied, breaking the professional stillness. Its name was Carmen, and it exhausted her to watch her rambunctious friend. The ever-perfect Beverly followed her.

In a big booming, off-key, off-tune, and off-tempo voice, Carmen exploded. "You don't have to go home..."

"Shh! She's on the phone." Mercy hissed and darted a look at the closed door, worried her friend's outburst had interrupted her boss's phone call.

Quieting her voice, Carmen added. "Ooh, let's tiptoe out before she notices you're gone, then. It's Friday night and I can't wait for our weekend to begin!"

"I can't leave yet. I have a few things to finish up, but I'll see you tonight. Are we still on?" She sighed, wishing she could leave now.

"Of course, we need a Friday night of pampering. We'll pick up snacks. Come over when you're done." Beverly said and entangled her arm with Carmen's, pulling her out.

As it often was in spring, the breeze was cool, and although it was barely seven pm, the sun had set. What remained of the winter's snow lined the streets in dirty piles heaped by plows. Children forewent playing outside for the warmth of their homes and their devices.

Beverly and Carmen lived in a small two-bedroom apartment in Castle Downs. The rundown building desperately needed repair. Granting access to the upper floors, staircases zigzagged its exterior. Its discolored paint peeled, and the railings were missing or broken. It was in shambles, but between the city's near-zero vacancy rate and the reasonable price, the girls had been fortunate to find it.

As Mercy climbed to the third floor, she thought about the two girls who had become like sisters to her. What a feeling it must be to be free from their parents, free to come and go with whoever they pleased. No one had grandeur expectations of them, and high society and tabloids didn't scrutinize their every step. They were individuals, not someone's daughter or prize. If only she could be so lucky.

A loud shout greeted her as she closed the door and carried through into the living room, where the two girls lounged on futons. Making room for her, Beverly scooched over.

As she came in, Carmen barely took a breath. "Well, I think it sounds fun. Can you imagine how many lonely old men are out there, waiting to spend money on a younger woman just for the pleasure of her company? It's literally a match made in heaven."

"Really? You aren't thinking about who these men would be. They're probably geriatric perverts and *have* to pay money or no woman would go out with them." Beverly turned to explain to the newcomer. "It was a commercial on TV. Girls can sign up on an app to date 'sugar daddies'." She air-quoted with her fingers, then turned back to the other girl. "Someone you don't know—might not even like? Come on... It's ludicrous."

"It's not as bad as you make it sound." Carmen pleaded with Mercy. "She's making it sound obscene. You build a profile on their app and they send your profile to hand-selected men. If they're interested, they give you permission to view their profile and ask you out to dinner. If you're comfortable with each other, you set guidelines between yourselves. Like; how much time you spend together, how romantic the relationship will get, and how much he'll pay to keep you at his beck and call. It's a win, win situation. Women provide the company the men are seeking and the girls earn money."

"It sounds really, for a lack of a better word, cold. Other than that–" Mercy shrugged as the doorbell rang.

"Pizza's here." Beverly straightened.

"I'll grab it. I'll be your *sugar momma* tonight, ladies." Mercy air-quoted with a laugh.

Wood crackled in the fireplace as flames licked at the freshly placed logs. The hearth and fixtures emitted a soft glow through the formal dining room. A long mahogany table for sixteen was set with silver candlesticks and fine china. The windows were framed by heavy Victorian drapes of chocolate brown and covered by tan, sheer material. Mercy's heels clicked on the near-black tile as she entered.

Her mother was dressed in a pantsuit of deep lavender with a purple lilac printed camisole underneath. Now faded with age, her blonde hair was a sea of dull brown and silver, but not a strand was out of place, swept atop her head. She'd applied makeup to appear she wore none.

Her father, Keith, was seated at the table's head, his broad stature commanded respect. His disheveled business suit proved he worked hard and had recently arrived. Sharing an intimate moment with his wife, he whispered to her seated on his right. As Mercy walked in, he stood up, his ingrained manners still impeccable.

"You look lovely this evening. How do you feel?"

Mercy bent to kiss her cheek before taking the place directly left of her father.

Briefly, her mother smiled. "Today was a good day. What about you?"

"I'm fine." She wished to avoid an argument and negate her mother's worry.

She squeezed her husband's hand, drawing his attention as he sat back down. "How's business?"

"There's new money driving prices up on a few properties I want to acquire." His eyes flashed with excited anticipation over the new challenge. "But we've faced more and older money before. I'll ensure there are insurmountable obstacles placed in their path, then they'll flee."

For the rest of the meal, Mercy stayed silent, not wanting to cause an argument over her broken engagement or have a conversation about the numerous expectations the shareholders, society, and her parents had of her. As soon as her father finished eating, he shut himself inside his study.

CHAPTER 3

It Could Have Been the Whisky

As Carmen teetered atop the living room table, her blue, glassy eyes and her goofy smirk were exaggerated by the alcohol-induced euphoria. She danced and shook her black short hair to the rhythm of the obnoxiously loud music. She held center stage—no matter the situation.

Mercy staggered as she danced to the window and opened it wide. The crisp but refreshing June air rushed in, cooling and aiding to dry the sweat on their exerted bodies.

Off-key, Carmen amplified the twang as she sang. *"... who knooowwws–"*

Beverly's tipsy voice chimed in louder as she tossed her long brown hair over her shoulder. *"How'da treat a hoooeee..."* The girls bubbled with laughter.

"New song?" Mercy yelled over the surround sound system's volume as she stumbled back into their dancing circle.

In unison, the other two shrieked. "New song!"

The girl on the tabletop fingered the remote in her hand, and a bouncy pop song played.

Immediately, Mercy sang, *"lie here in this..."* the girls giggled as she grabbed Beverly's hand, and sent her into a spin. "This is *our* song!"

Carmen listened to the music as she danced. "It's not *my* song!" She shouted to be heard.

Mercy swayed toward her and patted her arm. "No, not *our* song. *Our* song—Roger's and mine."

Beverly hiccupped. "Does he know it's your song?"

"Oh my God, that's a great idea—I'll send it to him. Where's my phone?"

"It's here!" Carmen bent and leaned forward, reaching her hand to the futon where her friend's phone lay. She wobbled as she lost her balance.

Stopping her fall, Beverly grabbed her arm. "It's time to get down before you hurt yourself."

She shook her friend's hand off. "I need more wine, anyway." She jumped high into the air, landing her ass with a thump several feet away, then got up and wandered to the entertainment stand where the wine bottles were.

The girls giggled and Mercy turned, bumped into Beverly, and thrusted her phone at her. "Send it!"

"Are you sure?" The older girl asked as she opened it and found the video online.

Mercy laughed. "Absolutely."

"This is it." Carmen lurched forward, her brimming red wine sloshed over the glass as she carried the bottle back to top off the other girls' drinks. "I *love, love, love,* this sonnnnggg." Then sang. *"Just give me the meat, a most awkward sound..."* she twirled.

"Those aren't the words–" Mercy turned and Carmen's hand flew past her face, hitting her wine. The force knocked it from her hand and it crashed onto the table, hitting the remote.

Instantly—a booming, male voice played through the speakers and the television came on. The girls each grabbed a handful of tissues and sopped up the spill. Beverly lifted the drenched remote, trying to dry it as she tested the buttons, trying to mute the noise.

"... Awarded the number one, non-committal

dating app of last year. Sugar Samples prides itself on providing discreet, enjoyable experiences for all of our members—male or female." A thirty-something clean-cut but, nerdy man wearing khakis and a polo shirt said.

With her ears nearly ringing, Carmen yelled as she wobbled to the kitchen. "Turn it down."

"... There's no better way to meet and mingle with men of wealth and fame than to be up front about what you're getting. Listen to these testimonials."

Beverly shouted. "I'm trying!"

Then a twenty-something woman in a conservative business suit started talking. "It was easy and only took me five minutes to sign up..."

"Sooo easy!" Beverly mimicked.

"... I'm a corporate woman and don't have time to meet men outside of work. After two days, I had requests and accepted three dinner dates. Now by night, I'm a social butterfly and attend stunning exclusive functions. And although it isn't the app's goal; I'm networking and making some great business contacts. The greatest part is it's free."

"O-M-G, it's free!" Mercy squealed, making fun of the commercial.

Carmen careened into the room, carrying three shot glasses and a bottle of whisky. "Shots!"

The girls adjusted to the loud volume as Mercy filled the shot glasses.

The video cut again. This time to a handsome midlife man in a tailored business suit. "It's convenient for me. My wife died three years ago, and I'm not interested in remarrying or becoming romantically involved, but my business dealings require a certain amount of socializing, and attending them alone is often uncomfortable..."

"Cheers, ladies." Mercy downed the shot, made an ugly face, and then poured each another.

"... Eight months ago, for a small fee, I signed up. I

dined with two other women before finding Alicia. She's smart, a skilled conversationalist, and welcomed as my companion by my social and business circle. People say time is money, and being in business, I know it. This isn't a romantic relationship. It's a business arrangement. I pay for her clothes, jewelry, and transportation. And I pay her well for her time—it's a job. And in return, she accompanies me when I require her. It suits us both..."

The three friends toasted and drank again.

On the television, a demonstration of the app played while a sultry voiceover whispered. "Ladies, what do you stand to lose? It only takes a few minutes to sign up, and it's free. Try it. What are you waiting for?"

Carmen gulped from her wineglass, then wiped her lip and giggled. "What are you waiting for, Mercy? You should totally do it."

Mercy laughed hysterically. "Me?"

"... It really is that simple to sample our sugar." The camera panned out to include the host. "Not quite convinced? Have questions? Visit us at www.-sugarsamples.com. For sugar samples dot com, I'm Jerome Peters. Next, stay tuned for Sally Murdock's wash-free dish set, here on info-mania network."

Beverly crawled to where Mercy's phone rested by the sound system. Once there, she punched the power button, ending the voices. "It's perfect."

Carmen dribbled more on the table than she poured into the glasses, then toasted. "They say, '*the quickest way to get over a man is to get under another*'."

Mercy drank. "Whose they?"

Carmen giggled and shrugged, "I don't know, but it sounds legit."

"Mercy," Beverly pawed her arm. "Mercy, Mercy. Give me your thumb." She pulled on the girl's hand and held her thumb to the phone. "I got this."

The three girls clambered closer to the phone and

Mercy giggled. "Let's do it. I could use some harmless fun."

The three girls took another shot.

Cotton-mouthed with a pounded headache, Mercy rolled over to silence the notifications on her cell. Her mouth watered with a sour taste as her stomach turned. The brilliant, harsh sunlight streamed through the window, punishing her.

Every muscle in her arm screamed as she drew the thick pillow over her head in denial.

An eighties chorus played from her phone, and knowing who it was, she blindly reached for it, then held it to her ear, still under the pillow. Her croaky voice answered. "Hello."

She was envious of the girl who was immune to hangovers. Beverly cheerfully greeted her. "Good morning, beautiful. Checking in. Are you all right?"

Ugh. "No."

"Anything broken?"

"What?" She was either confused or still intoxicated, she wasn't sure which. "No?"

"You're in better shape than Carmen then."

Mercy groaned and rolled over. "What?"

"We're at the hospital. Carmen–"

She sat up straight, tossing the pillow aside. "What?"

"She's fine. Broke her tailbone in three places when she dive-bombed off the coffee table."

Mercy searched her memory. Her brain protested, sending a sharp pain through her temple. She cradled it with her hand. "I don't remember."

"Not surprised." Beverly's loud laugh sounded.

She pulled the phone away. "Text me when you get home and I'll come over." She didn't wait to hear her friend's response. She hung up and laid back down—just a couple more hours of sleep and *maybe* she'd feel better.

But before she could fall asleep, a notification sounded on her phone. More awake, she realized it wasn't a sound she recognized. Curious, she lifted it— ten notifications from an app called Sugar Samples. She vaguely recalled the name, but couldn't place it. Apparently, she and her friends must have installed it the previous night. She'd have to ask them about it.

Two aspirin, five water bottles, and four hours later, sun-glassed Mercy wandered into her friends' living room and collapsed on the futon next to Beverly.

"How are you feeling?" Mercy examined the girl lying on the other couch.

Carmen smiled. "Lovely... Perfectly lovely."

Beverly whispered. "Prescription pain-killers. How are you doing?"

"I'll never drink wine again."

Her friend laughed. "It could have been the whisky. How's Roger?" Mercy's eyebrow lifted in question. "You texted him last night."

"No." Mercy fumbled to get her phone open and her mouth gaped. She shook her head in disbelief. "I didn't send him *that* video."

Beverly peered over the screen and pointed. "That *delivered* status says otherwise."

If she couldn't see it, it didn't happen. She deleted the conversation. A bar dropped down from the top. "Do you know anything about this?" She turned the phone to her friend.

Beverly smiled. "It's the dating app you signed up on last night."

Excited, Carmen sat up but winced. "She did?"

Beverly sighed. "Here's the short of it. You signed up on Sugar Samples."

Carmen let out an excited shriek and opened her own phone. "Did we sign me up too?"

The brown-haired girl shook her head. "No."

Furrowing her brows, Carmen frowned. "Why not?"

In exasperation, Beverly blew her hair upwards. "I don't know why not. Mercy signed up."

The injured girl pouted her bottom lip. "But I wanted to sign up."

Mercy remembered the conversation they had another time about the app. That's why it sounded familiar.

Beverly snapped her fingers in Carmen's face. "Come down from the clouds and focus." She turned to the other girl. "You're Mercy Richards—an orphan from Vancouver. Carmen's your cousin and you moved in with her because your field pays better here." She took the phone from her friend, opened the app, and pressed a few buttons, confirming some details, then turned it back to Mercy. "These are *dine-its*—dinner invitations. They'll include his picture, a message, and a link to view his profile. There are two buttons on the invitation. One *'kind of busy, maybe another time'*, and the other *'when and where'*. If you pass on five consecutively, they kick you off the app. We changed your voicemail to your first name. It's all set up. Look," she tapped the messages screen, "you already have an invitation."

"Why did I sign up?"

"Because you're terrible at choosing men?"

Carmen chimed as she rested her eyes. "Terrible."

Terrible at choosing—was an understatement. In high school, every girl wanted to be her and most boys wanted to date her. But she chose Robert Dancy. And their relationship was almost magical, as first loves went. The first touch brush of their skin, the intimate hand-holding, and the first kiss were new and exciting. She had complete, ignorant trust—believing this would be her happily ever after.

Her innocent delusion melted when she found him fondling another girl. Her world seemed to end, crashing down around her. She remembered days of crying, dry heaving, and gasping for air as a hard ball stayed pitted in her stomach and a near physical pain gripped her heart. She'd experienced so many firsts; hatred, betrayal, contempt, sorrow, and misery.

"... It gives you the opportunity to date without being recognized as Keith Haggins' daughter."

Carmen whispered as she dozed off. "Boo, Mercy Haggins."

Her name—reminded her of Jeff Conner. Short, with blue eyes and wavy brown hair, he seemed rather shy. They had shared the same classes for two months before he even spoke to her. She had been hesitant, but his persistence won, and eventually, she agreed.

The relationship blossomed, filled with flowers and inexpensive sweet tokens of affection. He never pushed for a physical relationship, and Mercy was grateful for it. They spent many celibate nights together. But she discovered that was his game—whatever made her happy. She found a scrapbook filled with publicity photos of herself taken by the press a few years ago, her class schedule, and articles about her father's financial worth. Flipping through the pages, she found other girls' names with dates and gifts. Each labeled; Louise Farnsworth - father filed bankruptcy. Stacey Evans - lesbian. Selena Thompson - wrong Thompson. Mercy Haggins - meal ticket.

She couldn't muster the same degree of pain, humiliation, and love over this relationship as she had for the first. These feelings were more of an '*I told you so, you stupid fool*' lesson. She deserved what he had done because she had trusted him.

"... You've reinvented yourself." Beverly finished.

"So tell us... How was Raymond?" Carmen smiled sweetly, wanting the juicy details as they ate their lunch a couple of weeks later.

"Remember his picture? I bet it was taken fifteen years ago. His profile claimed he's forty-four, but he's definitely closer to sixty."

Carmen giggled, and Beverly hid a grin.

"In the picture, he had gorgeous brown hair, but he's bald and wrinkly now." Her expression marred with disgust as she thought about the awkward hours she'd spent with him.

"Did you ask about his hair?" Beverly asked from her perch behind a desk.

"Yeah. He claims the app's administrators must have screwed up and sent someone else's photo. I didn't argue over the identical mole the two shared." She laughed. "Should I give up?"

"No." Carmen jumped from her seat to stand before her. "You can't give up after one date. One bad apple doesn't make a bad bunch. You've got to give it a little more time, a few more dates. Besides his looks, what was he like? Did you trip up your bio?"

"Tripping up my bio wasn't an issue. I wasn't given an opportunity to speak. He went on about how wealthy he was; his boat, his house, and his businesses. And the functions he would need me to attend and who his influential friends were." She shrugged. "He was very courteous. He stood when I stood, ordered for me, and held my coat when I put it on. He hailed my cab and paid the driver. When I rode away, I was thankful he didn't press for my number."

"So you got a free dinner and cab fare, and you didn't even have to entertain him? It doesn't sound half bad to me." Carmen giggled. "Who's next?"

She sighed and picked up her phone. "Thomas Dunfield, twenty-eight. I kind of know him already.

I've seen him in the tabloids and heard talk through my father's social grapevine. He's a true playboy—*he loves them then leaves them* guy. We meet next Wednesday at a scuzzy dive on 97th street, near Northgate Mall."

"I wonder why a dive?" Beverly asked.

"I don't know yet, but I bet I'll find out." She said, then took a bite of her sandwich.

The carpeted floor had passed its expiration date ten years before and the lighting above was dim through the neglected, filthy fixtures. The stench of cigarette smoke clung to the dusty drapes, and the walls were still yellowed by many years of tobacco use, even though smoking indoors had ended years prior. She rarely visited this part of the city, but when she did, her car doors were locked.

The restaurant was deserted except for one other couple sitting at the far end of the dining room. She located Thomas immediately.

As she approached, Thomas stood, his broad shoulders covered by an expensive black suit. His disheveled, curly blonde hair hung loosely past his ears and his emerald green eyes made an appreciative survey of her as well.

"I'm Thomas Dunfield, but please call me Tom." He held out his hand.

"Mercy." She stumbled. "Mercy Richards, pleased to meet you." She sat across from him as their handshake finished.

He lifted the menu. "You probably haven't eaten here before. I admit the décor leaves something to be desired, but the food here is delightful. May I order for you?"

"Please do." She responded as the lone waiter came to take their order.

In no time, their glasses were filled with wine, and food arrived. She enjoyed her meal, and he was an excellent listener. The conversation mainly centered on her. He asked her questions, and she responded, hopefully remembering all the right answers. Tom related few details about himself, and as the plates were removed, she admitted she was having a good time.

As the last of the dishes were cleared, Tom ordered coffee. Once they settled comfortably against their chairs, he spoke. "I've enjoyed your company this evening. I imagine you know who I am from the stories in the tabloids."

"I must say, I'm actually a bit surprised you need help to find dates?" She wondered out loud as she sipped the hot liquid.

"I admit, and don't take this as conceit, the women flock in droves." He chuckled. "Sorry, bad humor. I need someone who I can pay to be discreet and trust with my secrets. I will pay a tiny fortune for loyalty. It's time I *appear to be* in a committed relationship for publicity's sake. They've labeled me the *most eligible bachelor* of Edmonton and I need the press to back off." He swallowed his coffee, gauging her response.

"I'm flattered you chose me, but I must decline–" she started.

"Yes. I suppose you must. You're somewhat of a puzzle, Mercy. All during dinner, I listened as you told me about yourself, watched your perfectly manicured fingers, and studied your expensive clothing and jewelry. You don't need a tiny fortune, do you, Mercy Richards? Or should I call you Ms. Haggins?"

Shock choked her as she swallowed from her cup. "I beg your pardon?"

"You should. I knew who you were before tonight. Did you not think I would remember you from the few social events we've both attended?"

"Honestly, I didn't think you would." She recovered. "And if you knew who I was, then why orchestrate this dinner?"

"Because you're perfect for my purposes. And I know you have a secret. If your dating profile went public, it would embarrass your parents. You know how cruel the media can be." He told her.

"Of course, but I distance myself from them. I haven't received media attention since I was a young girl–"

"I'm desperate, and desperation can cause a man to consider dishonorable things. I have a secret and I need your help to protect it."

" H e's gay?" shocked, Carmen blurted. "Are you sure?"

"Some luck," Beverly interjected as she leaned against the wall in her apartment later that evening. "So now what?"

"After he told me, I convinced him I would rather my profile leak than participate in a very public, fake relationship. I explained my father's old-fashioned attitude and how I wouldn't risk fracturing our relationship further. However, I felt sorry for him and offered my help, anyway."

"If you won't date him, then how?" Beverly's eyebrow arched.

"Carmen's going to date him." Mercy stated, quite seriously.

Garnering Carmen's attention, she tossed her phone down and sat forward. "What?"

"I figure since this entire scheme was your idea, to begin with, you owe me. I may not be interested in Tom or in the way he approached the matter, but he's desperate. *You've* no ties here and no immediate family. So there's no reason why you can't do it. I told him you would be discreet, and I showed him your picture. He's willing to pay a lot of money, five hundred dollars a date—a few times a week, and if you give interviews a thousand. Tom needs a girlfriend to hang out with him and his boyfriend, which means some traveling and some very high-profile social events. He really seems like a great guy. I'd have helped him myself if I could."

"Can I meet him first? Maybe have a trial run at least?" Carmen sighed in dismay.

"Of course, I'll set it up. Will tomorrow night work?" Mercy picked up her phone as her friend nodded.

Beverly laughed. "Find me one too, please."

When the phone call ended, she returned to the girls. "Okay, it's all set, a double date for you both tomorrow night. It turns out he liked the idea of providing Beverly as accompaniment for his boyfriend, Gordon. At the same rate, of course, but no interviews." She giggled.

Beverly gawked. "I was kidding." She sighed, knowing full well she was committed, whether she liked it or not.

"No one goes unpunished from that disastrous night. I have another problem. Tom was right. I look rich. I can't continue to look this way. Even if he didn't know who I was, he could have deduced it by looking at me."

CHAPTER 4

I Want What You Paid For

JUNE

"Look at the time. You'll be late if you don't leave now. Relax and enjoy yourself." Carmen ushered her out the door. Not feeling the least bit guilty for sabotaging Mercy's final date.

Beverly glanced at Carmen's smug grin as she came back into the living room. "Okay, explain her appearance to me. I didn't want to make her nervous, but I don't get it."

"She's quitting the app and never gave it an honest chance." Carmen pouted, but her frown faded as she smiled. "Someone's going to be very surprised when she shows up looking like that tonight." She bubbled into uncontrollable laughter. "It's a harmless prank."

The next morning, the sun had barely appeared when Gwen entered the new corporate offices of Power Valley Holdings, her arms weighed down by her briefcase and the tray housing their morning coffees.

Her heels sounded as she leisurely walked along

the corridor. Before she entered the inside office, she heard Aurick loudly growl at Olivia, the office secretary. "If that's Gwen, tell her I want her now." Olivia looked up as she walked through the door.

"I heard him. Good morning." Gwen whispered. "How long has he been here?"

The secretary glanced at the door and whispered back. "He was already here when I got in, then started shouting immediately and hasn't stopped barking orders since. He wanted me to call you but I reminded him you had a personal appointment this morning."

Gwen handed her briefcase off, then quickly checked her short red hair in the wall of mirrors and swept into Aurick's office. "Good morning, sunshine." She hip-checked the door closed. "What's eating you?" Oblivious, she took a seat across from where he sat and placed his coffee down in front of him. Although for the past ten years, he'd been her employer, the two had been best friends since junior high—like brother and sister.

His mind continued to play tricks on him as he tried to block out thoughts of Mercy. He swore he still smelled her perfume and his body still burned where hers had pressed tightly against him. It'd been a sleepless night.

He swiveled his chair from the window toward her, his face angry as his hands slammed on the desk in frustration.

"The call-girl you set up to entertain me last night walked out." He sneered, running his fingers along his square jaw.

"The what?" Her mouth gaped.

"I want the number of the firm where you found her." He demanded as his coiled energy exploded and he walked to the opposite wall of windows, his broad back turned to her. "I want her fired, or I want what you paid for. Either way, it makes no difference to me."

"I paid for?" She muttered, gawking at him.

"I want it now." He yelled as he crossed the room, picked up the phone, and waited.

Gwen shook her head. "There must be some mistake. I didn't know she was a call-girl, Aurick. I swear." She rambled. "I wasn't told... I never paid her. Honestly? You believe I would get you a—" her words stumbled. "A prostitute?" Indignation boiled her temper as she rose.

Aurick's mind blanked as he put the phone down and sat on the edge of his desk. "She wasn't a hooker?" His mind slowly registered her comments. "Are you sure? She looked like a hooker. She said you got her from an app, Gwen. And you said I needed scheduled relaxation time. I just assumed–"

As her anger built, her voice raised. "You assumed I got you a hooker? Of all the disgusting things you've accused me of in the past twenty years... This takes the cake. You think I trolled the internet to find you a hooker?" She took a deep breath to calm down. "Your unwavering faith amazes me."

"If you'd have seen her..." It barely registered that Gwen was upset, as his mind replayed last night over, trying to figure out how he had come to the conclusion. "So she's a friend of yours, then? Or she works here? How did you meet her?" He mumbled his thoughts aloud.

She hesitated, then sighed with defeat. "I signed you up on a dating app to find you a companion while you're here. Her profile picture was gorgeous, she looked like your type and I read her profile. So I set it up. Was I right?"

"You did what?" He shouted.

"You heard me." Suddenly, a lightbulb flickered on in her mind. "Wait... What did you say to her? How come you assumed she was a prostitute?"

Embarrassed, he forgot his anger as he walked

around his desk. "Let's drop it. What's on my schedule for–"

"Oh-no, you don't! You don't get to yell at me, accuse me of things and then give me no explanation. Tell me what you did." She smirked and her eyes danced, waiting for an answer.

"Her dress was over the top, revealing—At least two sizes too small. It barely covered her, and her hair looked as if it had been tousled in someone's bed already. She wore cheap, trashy jewelry and thick over-done makeup." He breathed deeply, then shrugged as he admitted. "She told me you found her on an app. When she told me about herself, I questioned the details, and she asked if it mattered. She teased me by licking her lips and seductively running her fingers over her wineglass."

"And?" she prodded, enjoying his discomfort. "What else?"

He backpedaled. "You must understand. My blood boiled the instant I laid eyes on her. You were right. She was gorgeous and I could think of nothing else but getting her into bed. I've never had an urge quite like the one she stirred in me. Like animal instincts, it consumed me, like a moth to a flame. She looked like she was offering."

She gaped and as she giggled; she asked. "Oh my god, what did you say?"

"I told her I'm not accustomed to wining and dining hookers. Then I asked her how much, which I suppose isn't the worst part." He stammered to explain and quietly added. "I might have forced myself on her as well."

"Wait... I arrange for you to date a beautiful woman. Someone to keep you company and *you* accost her and insult her by calling her a hooker." She laughed hysterically. "Oh, I wish I would have been there."

"Gwen, please be serious." His fingers ran

through his hair. "How do I reach her? I need to apologize." He paused, then admitted in a whisper. "I want to see her again."

The interruption of a buzzer sounded. "Gwen, your ex-husband is on line two." The secretary announced over the interoffice system.

He answered. "He'll wait." He let the button go and returned his gaze to her. "What does he want?"

"Probably wants to argue. It didn't take him long to find out where you hid me this time." Her voice became vulnerable and her hands trembled.

"I should have knocked him out the first time I noticed a bruise and I should have killed him the day he put you in the hospital. You know how I feel about lying, there's nothing worse." He repeated his stance whenever they broached the subject of her ex.

"And as I have explained, who would take care of me while you were in prison? I knew what you would do... I saved you." Changing the subject, she continued. "If you didn't get her number last night, there's no way to reach her. It's a one-time communication app." She told him, retracing her steps to leave.

"*You* signed me up, and *you* got me into this mess. You will find me her number before noon." His growl demanded. "I don't care if we have to buy the fucking company to get it."

At lunch, Mercy and her two friends treated themselves to a restaurant. She barely ate as she replayed the previous night over in her head as she relayed it to her girlfriends. She stopped her story before he dragged her from the restaurant. There was no reason to shock or admit to her friends with how promiscuously she'd behaved.

"You make him sound like a character from an old romance novel." Carmen sighed.

"Then I'm explaining it wrong." She shook her head as she slowly replayed the elevator scene in her mind. Desire began melting her insides, and she had to force herself to stop.

"If only he hadn't mistaken you for a hooker. Huh?" Beverly sipped her tea.

"Oh, come on. I can't shoulder all the blame. It was an outfit. You must have given him the impression somehow." Carmen defended herself as she forked her salad.

Mercy laughed. "You're right, I threw myself on the table and told him all you can eat for under three hundred." Their laughter was loud and the other people gave them silencing looks. When they finished, she continued more seriously. "Anyway, that was it. Bev, when we get back to the office, I need you to take down my profile and take this application off my phone. I'm done."

"I can do it now, give it here." Beverly took the phone and started fidgeting with it.

"I'm really sorry. I shouldn't have dressed you like that. He sounds like the kind of guy you signed up to find." Carmen picked up her purse to pay the server.

"There'll be others. He was just a man." *And what a man.*

In her first relationship, Mercy had experienced passion, or so she thought, but last night proved it had been a young girl's inexperience. Her encounter with Aurick had left her yearning—for what, she didn't know. If he hadn't asked her how much again, she wondered how far it would have gone. Would she have slept with a total stranger? She was mortified she let him seduce her in the elevator, like a cheap whore —except wasn't that the role she agreed to play when she'd given in to his advance? "Tell me about Tom and Gordon."

"I pity them. They have to hide, even now, in this day and age. It's so sad. They're gentlemen and attentive when we're in public. Last night, we had drinks at a party for Tom's parents, then dined and went dancing at a club. When we were alone, just the four of us, they were easy to joke with, very affectionate towards each other and we weren't uncomfortable at all." Carmen shrugged.

"We're having fun." Beverly smiled. "We're free to date with discretion. I've never flaunted my relationships so it should work out just fine." She handed the phone back as it started ringing.

Mercy silenced it. "I don't recognize the number."

"So is there more to tell about Mr. Delicious?" Carmen giggled as they walked out of the restaurant.

From inside her desk drawer, Mercy's cell rang again. Opening it, she eyed the number. The caller was very persistent. The fourth call this afternoon.

"Answer that or shut your ringer off, I'm tired of listening to it," Connie called from her office.

She tapped the screen and rested it against her ear. "Hello?"

"Hello, Mercy." The deep flirtatious voice seemingly caressed his words. "Have I reached you at a bad time?"

"I'm at work. Who is this?" She scolded, trying to identify the voice.

"I'll tell you *if* you promise not to hang up until I'm done."

"All right, be quick. I hear my boss calling." She lied.

"It's Aurick."

Mercy's mind reeled. "Who?" She knew very well who, but she played it cool as if she hadn't given him a second thought.

"Aurick Spencer."

Her pulse quickened as her mind conjured his image. "I'm sorry, who?"

His seductive, easy tone pleased her as he explained. "Last night, from the hotel. I wanted to apologize for our misunderstanding. It seems—"

"Oh, yes... I remember. And, it was *your* misunderstanding. *How* did you get my number?"

Mercy heard him, but could not concentrate as her father approached her desk. She muffled the speaker.

"Where's the project file for Hotel Macdonald?" Keith demanded.

In 1915, the Grand Trunk Pacific Railway built the hotel on a site where a squatters' camp known as the "Galician Hotel" was located. The camp was named for the Ukrainian migrants from the Austro-Hungarian province of Galicia, who had settled there. In recent months, rumors had surfaced over a possible sale and everyone wanted it.

"I filed it." She whispered with her phone still pressed to her ear.

"Well, un-file it. It is your job. Or is this position a joke provided to keep the boss's daughter happy?" Without her mother present, he lashed out. Their relationship had yet to improve.

As she crossed to the filing cabinet, she heard Aurick. "Dinner tonight... seven pm... car service... Montel's..." But the words in between were lost as she searched with her father peering over her shoulder.

"I'm afraid I can't make it." She whispered and muffled the speaker again.

Aurick chuckled then questioned. "Is your boss there, Mercy? Agree or I'll continue to call until you do and—"

"Mercy!" her father snapped. "Get off the phone now!"

With her father's voice in one ear and Aurick's in the other, the phone on her desk began ringing. She continued searching for the file, and Connie came out of her office to see the commotion. The other staff in the nearby cubical area stared.

"All right." Mercy hissed. "Seven. No car service. I'll meet you there." Quickly, she hung up, found the file, handed it to her father, then answered the phone on her desk as she sat down.

When all quieted, it dawned on her. She had accepted Aurick's invitation, and she felt like an idiot. She was uncertain, as embarrassed as she was if she could face him.

CHAPTER 5

When You Beg for It

All afternoon, Mercy wrestled with the idea of standing him up. It wasn't until she was on her way home that she would attend. Telling herself it was only to prove she wasn't the woman from the night before.

Shortly before seven, she stood in the downstairs hall of her home, surveying herself in the full-length mirror. She had twisted her long blonde hair, pinned it on top of her head, and left wispy tendrils out to curl down the sides of her neck. She applied her make-up in shades of blue with accents of black to enhance the color of her eyes. Her long eyelashes were thickly coated in black, her high cheekbones lightly rouged, and her lips a coat of clear gloss.

She had chosen her favorite, long black halter evening gown, which exploited her swollen breast, hugged her curvaceous body, and flared openly from her knees down to the floor. A simple pair of diamond-studded earrings adorned her lobes and a gold chain with a single diamond pendant fell in the valley between her breasts.

Her reflection was captivating and elegant. She had surpassed her desired look.

She convinced herself the inkling of thrilled excitement she felt had nothing to do with seeing him again. No, it was because she'd make him regret the way he had spoken and treated her. And at the end of the evening, when she walked away, he'd still want her.

Her vanilla musk wafted in the air as she walked to the window to see if her cab had arrived. As she wrapped her black shawl around her shoulders and opened the door, her father emerged from his office.

His eyes surveyed her appearance. It was obvious she was meeting someone, and his tone was harsh. "Going somewhere?"

"Out. I won't be late." Her tone matched his as she stepped outside, wanting to escape before in anger either said too much.

At her dismissal, his face reddened. "Roger will be here for breakfast and I expect to talk to you both —together."

Her icy eyes met his. "There's nothing to discuss. It's over."

"You'll be at breakfast or face the consequences." He yelled, crossing the line, and the door vibrated from the force of her slamming the door.

Montel's was one of the city's most exclusive restaurants. Candelabras with white long-stemmed candles were mounted on the taupe walls. Heavy burgundy drapes covered the windows. The floor, a brilliant white, was littered with deep red rose petals. Lace cloth-covered every table with a simple, beautiful centerpiece of stemless roses and candles. The atmosphere was intimately elegant.

It was an odd choice for the last-minute business meeting, but in case it went longer than predicted, he didn't want to give Mercy an excuse to escape him. The restaurant was too crowded for what Aurick had in mind as he sipped his whisky. Getting lost in his thoughts, he continuously refocused his attention on the man seated across from him.

"This afternoon, when I received the offer on the apartment building, it surprised me. It sat for so long on the market. I began to wonder if I would ever retire." The gray-haired man chuckled, his eyes wrinkling from his aged skin.

"I appreciate your willingness to finalize the transaction today. What will you do now?" Aurick made disinterested small talk, wanting him gone before she arrived. His eyes scanned above the man's head, watching the door.

As the man explained, Aurick's eyes found her. Immediately, his heartbeat accelerated and his pulse quickened. She was stunningly beautiful in black, like a vision from a fantasy.

Disturbingly, her long slender body swayed and her breasts swelled against the dress as she walked to the reservation desk. She was breathtaking, and he swallowed his whisky to catch his breath. Time slowed as his mind and senses spun out of control. Abruptly he stood, then realized the man was still speaking. His behavior was rude, but he couldn't care.

"Excuse me, won't you?" Aurick didn't hear the response as he strode to her.

Her heart fluttered as he approached. He was animalistic, stalking his prey. His jaw muscle leaped in determination and his icy blue eyes were hungry, devouring her. His broad shoulder checked a waiter as his fingers ran through his disheveled black hair. No suit jacket obstructed his rippling, muscled chest as it strained against his shirt. *Delicious*, the reoccurring description came to her.

"Can I help you, miss?" Someone addressed from her peripheral, but she couldn't tear her gaze from the man striding forward.

"No, you can't." Aurick's deep voice answered for her. "I got this." He circled her, placed his hand on the small of her back, and guided her through the restaurant.

Discreetly, heads turned as the striking couple passed. The men couldn't help but notice the possessive hand the man held on her waist and the women envied the strong, handsome man holding her.

As they arrived at the table, the elderly gentleman stood. "My god, you're beautiful." He uttered as he took her hand. "I'm Rick Pearson, how do you do?" he placed a light kiss on her hand.

Before she spoke or reacted, Aurick lightly pulled her hand from Rick's, keeping it in his own. "I apologize for my rude departure. Though, you can appreciate the reason. This is Mercy Richards." He explained to her. "I had a last-minute business meeting, but we finished when you came in." He didn't let go as he turned to the man. "Care to join us for dinner?" Aurick cursed, having to extend a polite invitation. The last thing he wanted was a chaperon.

Rick chuckled, then winked at her. "I'm sure neither of you wants to spend time with an old man like me. Besides, the missus is expecting me. Enjoy your meal." He nodded and walked away.

Aurick's impeccably ingrained manners forced him to hold the vacated chair for her. As he pushed it into the table, his nose caught her vanilla fragrance and, without intention, his head dipped to enjoy the smell. His warm breath rushed over the side of her neck. Her toes curled in her heels and a wave of goosebumps traveled down the length of her body as her stomach fluttered.

"You're stunning, and you smell incredible." He whispered, then rounded the table to sit across from her.

Her bright eyes glowed with satisfaction. "Thank

you." She removed her black shawl, exposing her shoulders.

He studied her over his glass's rim as he downed the last of his whisky. Immediately, a waiter approached with another and she ordered a vodka tonic.

Aurick's body was having such an acute reaction to her, his heart was racing madly in his chest, his loins ached and he had barely touched her. *What the hell? I'm losing my mind. Get a grip. I'm not some forlorn teen with raging hormones.*

In irritation, he flexed his jaw and realized he was staring. Their mutual silence was edging closer to awkward. "Hi." He whispered with a devilish smile.

"Hi." Her heart skipped. Obviously, she had achieved the effect she wanted. *Eat your heart out, Mr. Spencer.*

She isn't going to make this easy. He cleared his throat. "May I start by apologizing for my behavior last night? It–"

"You could," she inserted.

The apology he had rehearsed all day, the one where she accepted half the blame, went completely out the window. "It was inappropriate, uncalled for, and extremely unkind. I assure you, I'm not in the habit of forcing myself on women."

"I feel *most* privileged." Her heart flipped.

"I can only blame a grueling, stressful week at work, jet lag, fine alcohol, and a combination of phrases." He paused. "How am I doing so far?"

"Keep talking." She ordered with a smile, enjoying his speech thus far.

His voice became huskier. "I was so overcome by your intense mesmerizing beauty–"

"Enough, I accept." She giggled and her cheeks flushed. "Now you're just groveling."

"Thank you." He chuckled as he watched her expression light with laughter. "Shall we order?"

She nodded.

. . .

The lamb, steamed beets, and cranberry salad were exquisitely plated in an intricate design that matched the wonderful flavors.

"I believe you mentioned you're an assistant?" Aurick thinly sliced the lamb and forked a piece into his mouth.

"Yes." She looked up and her breath caught as she watched his tongue dart the sauce from his lip. The delightfully skilled tongue that had trailed along her neck and played with her lobe.

He dipped his head, seeking her eyes' attention, and he grinned wickedly as if he knew what she was thinking. "I'm sorry if my phone call caused you trouble."

But he couldn't know, could he? She feigned concentration on her plate. "Are you? My boss was breathing down my neck."

His glance lingered on her collarbone, remembering how her skin bumped when his breath touched it and he was suddenly jealous of her boss. "But I'm not sorry for my tactics. They got you here."

His blunt response surprised her, and her eyes met his. "How could you be sure I would show up? I didn't even know if I would show up."

He relaxed back against the chair. "I couldn't be. If you hadn't, I'd have tried again tomorrow. I deserved the opportunity to make amends." He took a swallow from his glass. "Tell me about yourself."

"I'm an orphaned, only-child who grew up in Vancouver. Here, I live with my cousin, Carmen. What about yours?" She provided the emotionless detached account of her background again without a hint of victimization or self-pity. It intrigued him.

"My family is originally from Cuba but my parents and sister now live in Ontario. Have–"

Before he could ask another question, she steered the conversation. "What business are you in?"

Desirous, determined eyes raked her features, then met and held her gaze seriously. "I'm in the business of getting whatever I want."

The innuendo was there in his confident stare—he meant to have her. A pleasant, fiery heat ignited in her midsection. She didn't dare attempt to speak as she forked a beet cube into her mouth.

Aurick recalled the app's purpose—a place for very rich men to find accompaniment. Most likely, she had wanted to explore his wealth. "I'll tell you three things; there are many, they're successful and they're boring."

Her laughter brightened her eyes and wrinkled her nose. It wasn't a fake, pretentious laugh. It was beautiful, alive and the happiest sound he had ever heard, like a babbling brook in spring.

They finished their meal in friendly conversation and when the dishes were cleared; she sipped her coffee, silently admiring the charming man across from her while he told her a story. His face was strong, his jawline powerful, and his smile melted her insides. As he talked, his eyes animated, a clearer blue, reminding her of the ocean. His soft, deep voice sent shivers down her spine. Her mind wandered; imagining him behind her, whispering into her hair and his hands... She stopped herself and blushed.

After paying, he walked beside her along the sidewalk with a possessive hand on her spine. Her skin's warmth radiated through the shawl's sheer material, heating his palm. He was reluctant to send her off in a cab, ending their evening—with him alone in his hotel suite.

An idea sparked. "Would it be too forward of me

to suggest we take a drive? I want to show you something." Outward there was no change to his confident and nonchalant manner, but within he worried she would reject his suggestion.

They walked a few more paces. She was unaware of her tongue moistening her lips and her teeth biting into the flesh with indecision. For every reason she shouldn't, she came up with another why she could. She was tired of her regimented, mundane life. She wanted to go with him and explore whatever this was. Experience a world outside of her own. There was nothing to stop her but her fear and her ingrained role.

She lifted her brow. "That's ominous. *A drive... Show you something...*"

He turned to stand in front of her, his voice silky low as his hand's fingers kneaded her waist. "Point taken, but the app vetted me."

Today, he'd found out what the process had required. The app required five years of tax returns, a background check, an extensive criminal record check, and two letters of recommendation, which Gwen and his secretary Olivia had written. After a dozen phone calls and finding the app's legal counsel, Aurick had threatened to sue them for putting him on their app without his permission.

At the mention, she remembered how shocked she'd been when her first companion's complete history was sent to her—a total stranger.

She smiled. "Ah yes. You're a criminal bent on speeding who doesn't wear his seatbelt."

He was unhappy she knew so much about him, and yet he knew very little about her.

In defense, his eyes narrowed. "Those happened ten years ago." He shrugged. "I'll provide you the address and you can have your cousin track your phone. She can call every ten minutes to ensure you're safe."

She appreciated he understood her concern. "All right. Give me the address and I'll call home."

She made the call while he paid the valet for retrieving his car. When she was done, he helped her into the passenger seat of his luxury sedan.

When he slid behind the wheel, she expected him to initiate a tender kiss or for him to haul her against him in a lustful embrace. She was displeased when he didn't, and she berated herself. Weren't these the exact things men tried, and she hated? If she wanted it, why was she leaving it to him? One word—culpability.

They drove through the city's almost deserted downtown core, the brilliant colorful lights playing off the windshield, nearly made up for the lack of stars blocked by the tall buildings. His hands remained on the wheel and his attention stayed on the road. In no time, he pulled under the awning of an apartment structure.

Nervously, she eyed the building. "Tell me this isn't a repeat of last night." She laughed as he handed her from the car.

"I swear it's not, scout's honor." He held up two fingers.

Mercy grabbed them. "Were you even a scout?"

"I could have been." He laughed then with seriousness continued. "It's eight stories tall, with two apartments on each floor. The elevator opens directly into each apartment. The landscaping is beautifully highlighted by many trees here in the drive while the back flaunts a garden of flowers, shrubs, and a secluded pool. If you will follow me." He dragged her past the doorman, handing him the keys. "Keep it running." Then, entering the lobby, he draped his arm over her shoulder and steered them towards an elevator.

Her heart skipped excitedly, seeing it—anticipating the climb, the hunger, the fervent need.

When the doors closed, he punched in a code, then selected the eighth floor.

This was a bad idea—a torturous one, even. He forced his tempted hands behind his back, securing them to the banister. He wanted to pin her against the wall, feel her length against him, and hear her small moans as she gasped with pleasure. He watched the climbing numbers because he couldn't look at her. She'd recognize the lust in his eyes. He couldn't risk breathing too deeply or risk smelling her intoxicating scent. His muscles coiled and his throat dried, intensely reacting to her standing beside him. He'd prove to her, to himself, he could control his libido. He could give her what the app promised, a negotiated arrangement.

She glanced at him from the corner of her eye— waiting for him to touch her. Wanting him to seduce away her inhibitions and carry her back into the fantasy of the previous night. She fidgeted next to him, trying to remind him she was there. She ran her fingertips along her smooth hairstyle, then removed her shawl, draping it over her arm to entice him to make an advance. But he didn't. He ignored her presence, and it confused her.

The doors slid wide, admitting them into an unfurnished tan and emerald apartment.

He removed the shawl draped over her arm and took her clutch, placing them on an oak built-in next to the entrance.

On the left was a formal dining room lined with floor-to-ceiling glass-fronted oak cabinets. Its exterior wall was entirely windows overlooking the street where they had entered.

"Room for eight if needed." He walked backward, encouraging her forward.

On the right was a sunk-in living room, complete

with a fireplace and plush off-white carpets. This time, the wall of windows overlooked the river valley below. Skyward, the stars twinkled, and the moon filled the otherwise dark room with light.

"It needs furniture and blinds. Am I right?" He joked as he walked down the hall.

He was right, but what was her role here? Why was he showing her this place? He didn't seem the type to brag about his investments. This felt awkward and uncomfortable.

Beside the formal dining room, he showed her an expensive, elaborate kitchen with every modern convenience.

As they walked past it, an opening on the right led into a stunningly luxurious bathroom. Complete with plush white carpet, a stone-encrusted Jacuzzi tub, a fireplace, and a mirrored wall.

They passed an empty bedroom, and she tried to pull her hand free.

He sought to reassure her. "Almost done. One more room, I swear no hanky-panky." He walked into a huge master bedroom with dual walk-in closets and an ensuite bathroom which resembled the other.

She had little time to look as he pulled her out and they backtracked past a third bedroom to the living room. He spun her around to examine her expression. "What do you think?"

Her mouth was dry, and her uncertain voice betrayed her. "It's beautiful, I guess. What are we doing here?"

"Remember Rick?" He crossed to the stairs and sat, giving her space. "I bought it from him tonight."

"Oh." It seemed like days ago, not hours. She shrugged, not clear what her response should be. "It looks like a significant investment."

He patted the stair next to him and when she joined him; he pulled her down to sit. "I thought you could live here." He paused. "Like the app advertises, I want to be your sugar daddy."

Her mind reeled. *Live here?*

He put his finger to her gaped mouth and continued. "I'll pay you whatever you want. It's yours. I'll provide you with a full staff to look after the place. You can decorate it or I can hire someone. I'll give you an extensive wardrobe, jewelry, and car service."

Her mind lit and she understood. Live here as an employee, another possession he could buy. Not because of who she was as a person, but because of what she and her body could offer him. He was no better than any other man who had disappointed her.

"In return, you will attend all social and evening business functions with me and will accompany me with notice, on business trips. When I'm away, which is often, you may entertain within the apartment as you so choose. I can pay you enough so you can give up your day job." He finished, dropped his fingers, and searched her face.

He hadn't used the word prostitute, but Mercy's lip quivered and her stomach pitched. "How much?" She murmured.

He smiled, gifting her with an opportunity to better her financial future. "As much as you want. Name your price. I'll pay it." He watched a tear slip from her eye and mistook it for joy. She would sell herself to the highest bidder. It disgusted him, but he intended it to be him, no matter the cost.

"Five thousand a night." She wiped another tear as it rolled down her cheek. Embarrassed by her emotions' betrayal, she stood up, reached the elevator door, and pushed the button.

"A night?" His voice echoed through the empty apartment. "Are you serious?"

"You said to name my price, didn't you?" She goaded him as she heard the elevator arrive.

The greedy... He threw his hands in the air. "All right."

When she disappeared inside and pressed the main floor, he approached the opening. "Thank you..." He stopped in his tracks. "For turning me into the highest paid prostitute in the city. The answer is still no. I'm no man's possession."

The elevator closed. How could she have thought he was interested in anything more than a glorified trophy? It was what every man wanted her to be. Aurick wanted a prostitute, nothing more. *Why are you so upset? Forget him.*

He cursed under his breath. Once again, he made a fool of himself in her presence. At the time, outside the hotel, this had seemed like a good idea. He wanted her physically, and he knew he liked her intellectually, but he didn't want her seeing other men. He knew she needed money. Why else sign up on that disgusting app? Why hadn't she accepted? It made no sense to him. Damn her, he cursed, then kicked the stair. He only needed her long enough to get her out of his system. He knew he would think of nothing else until he had her.

The following morning, her mother didn't come down for breakfast, a sign her health continued to fade. Mercy thought about staying in her room and avoiding her father and Roger, but she knew her father would be angry then come up and demand her presence. She had spent the better part of an hour steeling herself for the argument she would have with her father while Roger was present.

"Good morning." She said coolly as she entered, more to announce herself than addressing the seated men. Her blue business jacket and skirt made a friction noise as she walked to the table.

"Mercy." Roger greeted with a sweet smile as both men stood.

While she seated herself on her father's left, the young housemaid offered to bring her something from the kitchen to eat. She refused politely and asked for coffee. As soon as the girl poured, she scurried out, feeling the tension between father and daughter.

She sipped the hot liquid. "What is it you wanted to speak to me about?" She eyed both men.

Her father cleared his throat. "This argument between you and Roger has gone on long enough. He has repeatedly attempted to apologize, and you have refused to accept any communication." He waved his hand as if she would speak. "Don't bother denying it. Our staff confirmed my suspicions. You need to work this out, so we can make wedding arrangements, buy a house in Los Angeles for you to live in, and announce his new position." Her complexion flushed with anger as he continued. "Our board requires reassurance of your commitment before the announcement."

Her reddening deepened with each sentence, and when he finished his lecture, it was her turn to be heard. "As sorry as you might be, Roger." Calmly, she glared at him. "I'm not interested in reconciling with you. My *father's* plans for you in *his* company have nothing to do with me. Whether or not I want you should have no bearing and I wish you luck."

Embarrassed by her dismissal, Roger's face twisted with rage. "You know it has *everything* to do with you. Without you as my wife, I won't be given the promotion. My education and experience don't support this promotion." He had nothing to lose if she refused him.

Keith Haggins waved his hand between the staring pair. "Enough, before you two have said too much to forgive." His angry gaze turned on Mercy. "You will accept his apology. You will be married within the month and then Roger will head the L.A. office. Now, accept–"

The force of her movements, when she stood, knocked over her chair and it crashed loudly against the floor. Indignation boiled in her veins, and her yell drowned her father's words. "I will do none of those things."

She walked out as her father bellowed, his voice echoing. "You will accept or I will not support you anymore. Do I make myself clear? Between your obvious disrespect for your position at the firm yesterday and your blatant disregard for my feelings today, you will leave me no choice."

Years of pent-up rage and hurt erupted. As she turned to her father, she seethed. "I'll make your choice easier. I'll leave *your* home tonight after work. That is if I still have a job? Good day to you both." Mercy strode out—leaving her life, the expectations, and all the people she had ever known.

S he fumed, waiting for her father or Connie to tell her, she no longer had a job but as lunch approached, she realized he had either decided to keep her or Connie had intervened on her behalf. At lunch, she replayed the story to her two friends, and they were shocked by the outcome.

As the afternoon progressed, Mercy's anger was edged out by distress. She had little savings, never needing it because of the allowance her father gave her. *What am I going to do?* She wondered as she studied the numbers on the spreadsheet.

Five hundred dollars was all she had. It wasn't enough for an apartment, even if she found one. She could stay at a hotel, but the money would only cover a couple of nights. She would have to buy food, switch her cell into her own name, and figure out transportation. The expenses were piling and weighing her shoulders.

Beverly and Carmen had offered her a futon, but the apartment was so small, and living on top of each other would end their privacy. It wouldn't work. Eventually, they would start fighting, picking, and grinding each other's nerves. Mercy shrugged off the idea. She could not jeopardize their friendship.

It wasn't until late afternoon when she had exhausted all other options that she finally accepted, she would have to take Aurick's offer. At this point, it made little difference what his opinion of her was. He was willing to pay for someone to be at his beck and call, and she desperately needed the money. No matter how degrading, she would accept his proposal for the time being.

Steeling herself, she picked up the phone.

Across the downtown core in the offices of Power Valley Holdings, Aurick's mind drifted as Gwen continued speaking. "Okay, so as far as housing our staff in the new apartment building, I have Ned and Brandt on the sixth floor. Their families will be here in a week. I gave them the day off to set up. I have Tony, the financial manager, on the seventh. He's going to be bunking with the structural engineer, Mike. I took the other apartment on seven. On the company dime, I hired movers to bring my things from Winnipeg. They will be here in two days. I hired an interior design company to furnish the apartments from the fifth floor up. I told them to have a skeletal decorating of your apartment completed by six tonight, so you can start staying there. I hired a contractor to revamp the other apartment on the eighth floor; leaving it one bedroom, a smaller bathroom, a secluded kitchen, and a large conference/dining hall. Is there anything I forgot to do?"

"No." His mind was elsewhere and Gwen was trying without success to draw him back.

"How long can we expect to be here?" She asked.

"Three years, maybe longer." He answered without thinking.

She walked around the desk and perched on its edge. "Want to tell me about it? What's the issue? You're distracted."

All-day he debated whether to tell her about the night before. "I don't know where to begin." He gauged her curious expression, threw his pen on the desk, and then sat back in his chair with his hands clasped behind his head. "It's that girl."

"You can't be serious?" She blurted, his admission throwing her for a loop.

When women were young, Aurick was what they fantasized about, but not Gwen. There was no romantic chemistry between them—like brother and sister. She couldn't figure this—this obsession. In all their years together, she'd never known him to be emotionally or romantically involved in relationships. He was habitual—cold and detached.

She circled back to her chair and sat. "Eesh! Tell me now, is this your midlife crisis? Make me understand. Or if this is male menopause, I deserve a warning. Your longest relationship was a year and only because you spent nine months of it in South Africa building that hospital."

"I'm thirty-two. Not midlife. I don't know what's happening." He rambled aloud, not really addressing her. "I can't explain it. She's beautiful. Her body invites my caresses and her eyes mesmerize me. When I'm with her, the building could be on fire and I wouldn't see or feel it. Her personality is electrifying yet so vulnerable and I have an overwhelming urge to protect her. She plays me perfectly. I'm jealous, angry, disgusted, and turned on all at the same time."

"Wow, you should crochet that on a pillow while you're delving into your feminine side." She needled him with sarcasm, then shook her head. "Christ, just sleep with her so you can get over this already and move on. I've never known you to give a second thought about a woman you've never slept with."

"I can't think when I'm near her." His eyes focused on his friend as if it only dawned on him now that she was listening. "I took her to the apartment last night and offered it to her."

Unable to believe what she was hearing, her tone scathed him. "Unreal. What were you thinking? You don't even know this girl."

He shrugged. "I know I want her and I was prepared to pay anything to have her. I kept thinking of her on that app, where other men could find her and be with her. How degrading and how ridiculous it was. Then as we left the restaurant, it dawned on me; I have the apartment and money to offer her and she's alone except for a cousin and an assistant's position. At times, a fleeting look, or expression exposes her vulnerability and, for reasons unknown to me, I want to save her. It's like it wasn't me at all. Before I knew it, we were sitting in the apartment and I asked her to name her price."

An uncomfortable laugh escaped her as she tried to douse his seriousness with humor. "Tell me this is fleeting and you'll get over it?"

"I got over it when she gave me a price tag of five grand a night."

Her eyes narrowed. "No vag is worth five grand."

"I accepted her terms."

Gwen stood, her body yearned for movement, and she hissed. "You did what?"

"After I agreed, she reneged her terms immediately. She thanked me but insisted she wasn't for sale.

How could I treat her like that? What's wrong with me?" With a blank expression, he asked.

"I reiterate, this may be a midlife crisis or perhaps you're spending too much time with me and my emotional side is rubbing off on you. In any case, you better get her out of your system before you develop breasts."

Olivia's voice announced over the office system. "Mr. Spencer, Ms. Richards is on line one."

Just her name constricted his throat and without a word, Aurick picked up the phone, punching the line as Gwen rushed out, closing the door behind her.

Mercy entered the apartment building's lobby at seven-fifteen. After picking up her things and dropping them off at a nearby hotel, she was running late. She pushed eight-oh-two on the elevator wall. A buzzer sounded, and it started to climb. When the doors slid open, she was surprised to find skeletal furniture had been brought in.

From the time of her call until she entered, his anticipation grew. Like riding a rollercoaster on an endless, steep incline, excitedly waiting for it to plunge. After seven, each passing minute felt as though the rickety track would collapse beneath him. And when the elevator's intercom had sounded, his pulse raced.

As she looked over the furniture, he studied her from the dimly lit kitchen. Between the cut of her evening gown last night and the blue, skirted business suit with white camisole she wore now, they revealed she spent her money on expensive clothing. Clothing meant to accentuate her vivacious curves when she moved while showcasing her delectable features. The urge to strip her curves naked, pull her hair free from the haphazard messy bun, and wash the pink gloss from her lips with his mouth was desperate. *Damn her, even after a day's work and fretting with worry, she looked good.*

He had to remind himself that he shouldn't—no, couldn't. Whatever their first encounter was, their second had been the opposite. He didn't know which version of her was real, but something told him, if he pushed her, she would run.

Silently, he lectured his semi-stiff arousal to behave, then picked up the mugs.

From the kitchen, Aurick appeared and handed her a coffee. He gestured for her to precede him into the living room.

Down boy, he chided as his gaze lingered on her rounded ass, his palms recalling the feel of its weight in his hands. Attempting to curb his enthusiasm, he ran his eyes to her heeled ankles. What could be sexy about—sculpted, delicate flesh he could bathe with his tongue before trailing up her muscled calf to... *Fuck.*

Unsure where to sit or how to begin, she perched on a rich brown chair and her nervous words tumbled out. "As I said on the phone; I'm forced to reconsider your offer." She bit her lip. "Carmen and I argued, and I felt it best to leave. But before I accept, I'd like to iron out a few things."

Even with tired bags, unkempt hair, and the wrinkled dress shirt with its sleeves rolled and collar gaped, he looked incredible.

He nodded as he sat on the matching couch. "What was your argument about?"

"Why should it matter?" She hadn't expected the question. He was hiring her as a convenient companion—not wanting a relationship. If he wanted one, she was certain there would be no shortage of women vying for his attention.

Though her tone was businesslike, her voice trembled. He leaned forward, placing his elbows on his wide knees, and arched his fingers together under his chin. "I know very little about you. The reality is you could be an addict, a murderess, or a thief and it would be foolish not to wonder what caused your separation from the only relative you have here."

"It's nothing so monstrous or interesting. Over the last several months, we've grown to nitpick each other and last night it came to a head. From moved or misplaced items, to bills, to food, we fought about it all. Though we made up, it's only a matter of time before it happens again and as you said, she is my only relative here and I wish to protect our relationship."

There were two sides to every story. He'd lived it with Gwen and the subject of her ex. Depending on mind-frame, experience, and vantage point, two people could never tell the same story. It wasn't dishonesty; it was perspective. He wondered how different Mercy's cousin's story would be.

He shrugged, letting it go. "What in our arrangement would you like to *iron out*?"

"I'd like to explain my presence on the app."

"There's no need. It's none—"

"You're right, there isn't a need but I would still appreciate the opportunity." She stood and paced as she continued. "My cousin dared me to sign up on the app. I never intended to date hordes of men. Prior to meeting you, I had two other dates which were ridiculous. I've never sold myself before."

She went to the wall of windows and looked down on the furiously rushing water of the North Saskatchewan River, feeling as if it mirrored her turmoil. Unconsciously, she dropped her shoulders and her arms wrapped around her waist. "I find myself alone and have little savings. In short—I'm between a rock and a hard place." She turned to him. "However, I can provide you with an escort, companionship, and be at your disposal, as long as it doesn't interfere with my daytime position. That is if you're still interested?" Mercy held her breath. He was her last resort. If he refused, she would be forced to crawl back to her father—his expectations and his anger. She needed to prove—to herself, to him—she didn't need his money or his name.

Her glassy eyes and her vulnerable stance affected him. He had an incessant desire to shield her from whatever caused it. And that desire angered him. He wasn't a heartless bastard by any stretch of the imagination, but this—her. How did she invoke these useless, intense emotions in him?

Steeling himself, he leaned back and draped his arm along the headrest, suddenly in complete control. "I'll give you..." Feeling less generous and more vindictive over the way she affected him. "Three thousand a month to stay here and five hundred per evening when you accompany me. I will supply you with a car, no driver, a wardrobe, and a credit card. You will send your clothing sizes to this number." He pulled a card from his breast pocket and placed it on the coffee table. "Do we have an understanding?"

She exhaled. "We do." A deep tiredness washed over her. "I was uncertain whether we would come to an arrangement so I booked a hotel."

It begins, his gaze narrowed. *How much will it cost before I sleep with her?* "If you give me the name, I'll take care of the charges."

His words reminded her of her father, who believed anything could be bought with enough money. She shook her head, dismissing the troubling thought, and picked up the card from the table. "There's no need. How soon can I move in?"

He walked with her to the elevator and pressed the button while she relaxed her back against the wall beside it. "Since your resources are small, I see no reason why you can't move in tomorrow. They have already moved a bed and linens into the bedroom."

She blurted. "And you can't pay me to sleep with you. There's no price for that."

Leaning in, their mouths separated by less than an inch, he whispered. "Trust me, the only way I'll sleep with you is *when you* beg for it." The doors opened, and she swept past him.

As the elevator sounded its descent, a mischievously handsome grin covered his mouth. *It may not happen tomorrow or the next day, but I'll have her, and she'll beg.* He congratulated himself as he stripped and headed for the shower.

CHAPTER 6

You Had to Know I'd Come

The next morning Mercy called her boss, claiming she was ill. She cringed with guilt as she hung up, having to lie again. She brushed her hair into a loose ponytail, forewent makeup, and put on an oversized sweatshirt with a pair of old blue jeans, knowing she would spend the day unpacking and cleaning.

As her taxi pulled into the apartment's drive, she was overwhelmed by the bustling activity. Men carried furniture inside, painters and carpenters worked on projects outside, and laborers unloaded boxes from trucks onto trollies.

The car squeezed past the many vehicles, stopping under the awning. Two women, one a short redhead, eyed her as she got out. Both women wore business suits, and Mercy felt underdressed and self-conscious. She overheard them as she supervised the driver, stacking her belongings on the curb.

"Understand Stephanie, we're on a tight schedule and cannot afford excuses. If you can't complete the job on time and professionally, I can replace you. I have a list of decorators willing to undertake this project. These trucks should have arrived and unloaded yesterday. You have an hour. Good day." The redhead dismissed her curtly before turning away, her anger apparent.

"I don't know who you think you're dealing with, Gwen. Perhaps I should call your boss?"

"And who do you think you're dealing with? I've already paid for the furniture and trucks, and these are *my* employees moving it in." Gwen's icy cold eyes stared the decorator down. "You're fired. Find yourself off my property or I'll have you removed."

Mercy's face reddened in embarrassed sympathy for the public reprimand the woman received, and she busied herself attempting to pick up her suitcases.

"You must be Ms. Richards?" the redhead called as she approached.

"Mercy." She stammered, wondering what welcome she should expect.

"Drop those and follow me," Gwen ordered. Her frustration was not quite under control when she turned to walk inside. "Frank." She called to a man, then motioned to the bags. "Add those to the trolley going to apartment eight-oh-two." She continued through the lobby to the elevator. She tapped her foot on the ground impatiently, waiting for it to open. "Things are hectic today, as you can see. I only have a couple of minutes."

As the elevator rose, Gwen examined the woman standing in front of her. She appeared typical, like any other woman, not some goddess or mesmerizing beauty. Regardless, she didn't like how this woman tied Aurick in knots. Her defensive instincts were in overdrive as the elevator door opened, admitting them into the apartment, now crowded with boxes and furniture. Her tone was cold and authoritative. "Your welcome package is on the kitchen counter. It includes keys to the blue sedan parked in stall eight-oh-two—downstairs, through the main entrance, and to the right. There are keycards and codes to the apartment and elevator. Inform Mr. Spencer, if you need to change the preset code. You'll also find your first month's salary and a credit card with a ten thousand dollar limit. At the month's end, you'll be compensated for any occasions you attend. I wasn't expecting you until this afternoon. Therefore, no one has unpacked or put away the furnishings yet."

Gwen strode across the living room and down the hall as Mercy followed. When she entered the master bedroom, the redhead threw open a closet door. "Your wardrobe arrived last night and I haven't had time to go through it. For anything you don't want because of size or taste, call the number posted on the refrigerator and they will come get it. You'll find other important numbers there as well. Questions?"

"Yes." Mercy clipped as she straightened her spine to her full height, towering over the shorter woman. "Are you finished addressing me like one of your employees?" The woman's demeaning tone had fueled Mercy's temper to the point of combustion. "You know very well I'm not *your* employee. You will treat me with respect and drop the attitude because I don't appreciate it. Now, allow me to explain myself to you." Her eyes narrowed on the redhead's blank expression. "Unless I otherwise request, *I'll* look after this apartment without help, which includes unpacking and deciding the layout. While you ordered and commanded me around, it must have slipped your mind to introduce yourself. I'll assume your name is Gwen since that's what the woman outside called you. *So that* is how I will refer to you." Her words were calculated as the speechless woman stared at her. "You're standing in *my* apartment, emphasis on *my*. I was raised to respect my elders. Therefore, I'll ask you to leave politely before I say anymore. Good day." She mimicked the girl's earlier statement, dismissing her, then ushered her through the bedroom door and closed it, listening for the elevator before she ventured out.

Aurick ended the call with his contractual lawyers, working through purchase negotiations for a drilling rig company. Talks between the companies stalled; for a reason, the other party's lawyers could not divulge. More often than not, sellers declined contracts over moral ambiguity and weren't willing to share them through lawyers.

He sighed and fingered the interoffice communication system. "Olivia, set up a meeting with Bryce Thompson tomorrow—whatever he agrees to is fine by me."

He waited a couple of minutes, then repeated his request. No confirmation came.

Swiveling his chair to rise, his gaze caught the windows. It was late, charcoal black blanketed the sky and a low cloud ceiling prevented a view of the stars. He'd lost track of time. Had anyone come to inform him they were leaving? Where was Gwen?

As he stretched his back, it dawned on him. Gwen wasn't in the office today. And it was she who usually came by to inform him the workday was over. He looked down at his wristwatch, the one accessory he refused to give up to advancing technology. It was after ten. He gathered the files on his desk, shoved them inside his briefcase, and grabbed his jacket.

When the elevator settled on the ground floor, Aurick smiled at Bruce, the old-timer night guard.

"Given your notice yet?" Aurick joked.

The gray-haired man crossed his arms. "You nag like my wife. She wants me to retire but I tell her it keeps me fit enough to chase her around the kitchen table and still catch her." His wrinkled, age-spotted hand lifted a basket from behind the desk, setting it on the counter. "She dropped off stew and biscuits for supper tonight. Ready to eat?"

"I think she plans to fatten you up so you'll stop chasing her." Aurick patted his flat, muscular stomach. "And, I'm gaining weight as a byproduct."

He grinned. "Nah, she likes when I catch her. You —you're her new stray—a lone man, working long hours to forget there isn't anyone waiting at home for him."

"I might have to steal her from you."

His eyes twinkled. "Phish, give it your best shot young'un." He dared, then laughed. "Are we eating?"

Aurick shook his head. "Not tonight."

Cool air rushed over his skin as he walked to his truck in the abandoned, dimly lit parking lot. At this time of night, the quiet, eerie downtown seemed sadly forgotten and lonely as the wind rustled the discarded coffee cups, newspapers, and debris. The destitute and addicts huddled inside bus shelters, doorways, and alleys to escape the cool night.

He turned the engine as he shut the door, then cranked the heat and stereo to block the sullen depression. He wasn't alone. He wasn't sad. And no one had forgotten him. Mercy waited for him. Escaping his melancholy, he gunned the gas.

As he drove the streets, his mind replayed Gwen's phone call early this morning, and he chuckled.

She was furious, typical of Gwen—easy to anger. Without breathing, she rambled over how Mercy had treated her.

"Did you provoke her?" Was all he asked, and her temper blew again.

"I have a list longer than my arm of things I need

to do, not one of them includes taking lip from her. I fired the design firm, which leaves me to supervise laborers, painters, electricians, carpenters, plumbers, and movers. It's too much Aurick. I'm not the domestic type. I belong in my office." She blew her hair upward out of her face. "Are you listening to me?"

"Yeah." Swiveling in his chair, he turned to stare outside and give her his full attention. "Wait. You fired the design firm?"

He thought he heard her stomp her foot. "Ooh! I knew you weren't listening..." Her voice pitched. "Yes, I fired the design firm. They hadn't completed three of the four tasks on time and then they asked for more money. We can't afford the delay. Did you hear me tell you about how Ms. Richards treated me?" Exhausted, her fervor waned.

His cheek dimpled as he teased. "Did *you* provoke her?"

Gwen closed her eyes and rested her head back against a wall. "I might have." She had but wasn't going to confess.

Sounding loudly through the phone, she heard his hysteric laugh, and she pulled it from her ear until he was done. It infuriated her further. He should be livid with the woman who had treated his best friend so poorly.

Gwen clicked her tongue, silencing him. "Just wait until you come up against her haughty temper. She isn't some airhead who's going to bend to your will. She'll fight, and you'll be sorry. I can't wait to see you, the authoritative tyrant, up against Ms. high and mighty."

"I've come up on the quick end of her temper already, remember?" He teased, his voice smiling as he continued. "Tell me, did you like her?"

For a moment, she contemplated her answer. "Not at the time. But I can respect a woman who holds her own. So I guess I do." She whispered. "Are you sure about this?"

"I know what I'm doing. I'm getting her out of my system. That's it." His last comment troubled him but couldn't finger why, as he hung up the phone.

Gwen—He loved her like a sister.

In junior high drama class, he was the uncaring jock, and she was the brain. They'd been paired to write and perform a two-person play. But he avoided her, leaving her to complete it, knowing she'd do it. And he thought he had ridden her coat tails to an A until it came time to act it out. From stage-fright, she froze, and he saved her by taking over and improvising. It cemented their relationship. If they weren't together, then they were texting on those old flip phones—one letter at a time. When their thumbs got tired, there were phone calls.

After financing his first company at twenty-one, he left her behind in Ontario to finish her degree in finance but promised her a job when she graduated.

Before she completed it, she met and married George Davis. Gradually, her attitude changed toward Aurick over the first couple of years, but he reasoned through it. She was married—grown-up, and finding time for him was difficult. Perhaps her new husband was jealous of their relationship and asked her to back it off. All sorts of reasons, except the actual.

In two years, he'd made two trips home. Unexpectedly, he showed up at her house. There was no answer, though vehicles were parked in the driveway. On his third trip, he literally bumped into her shopping cart at the grocery store. She had a bruise on her cheek. She laughed as she retold the story of opening a cupboard door too fast and hitting herself in the face with it.

Thinking about it reignited his guilt. How stupid he'd believed her.

One night, seven years into her marriage, Aurick's mother called to say Gwen was in a coma. He was on the next plane, rushing to her side. When he saw her beaten body and no one would explain what happened, the pieces fell together.

He still didn't remember leaving the hospital and driving to her house. When he arrived, he barged in uninvited and searched, looking for her husband. Luckily for Aurick, George wasn't there.

The house was tidy but destroyed—broken or unhinged cupboard doors, holes punched or kicked through walls, electrical cords cut or snapped, and doors and knobs missing. Her husband's belongings were everywhere, but he saw no sign of Gwen in the décor or contents. In a powerful rage, Aurick destroyed whatever wasn't already to ease his pain and guilt.

After physically exhausting his anger, he sat on a half-broken chair, buried his face in his hands, and cried for her. He made a pact with a higher power; if she lived, he would never leave her again. Bundling her clothes in a sheet, he left his attorney's card on the counter for George to find.

For two weeks, he stayed at her side until she awoke. And a month after her beating, they boarded his jet. Even now when he thought about it, guilt tightened his stomach and her lies angered him, momentarily renewing her betrayal.

Deep in thought, Aurick hadn't realized he had stopped under the apartment building's awning until there was a knock on the window. He glanced over to see the night man. Acknowledging him with a head tilt, he drove into the parking lot. As he stepped from the truck and wandered inside, fatigue weighed him down, caused by an early morning, a long day, and the unpleasant memories. He was glad it was over, wanting a hot shower and a good night's sleep as he punched in his code.

Habitually, physical activity relieved Mercy of stress, and today, she'd pushed her body's limits as she unpacked the apartment's contents. Paintings hung on the walls, throw pillows littered the furniture, books lined cases, and the kitchen cupboards were filled with appliances and dishes. She stacked the rest of the full boxes in the unused bedroom, intending to finish on the weekend. When she settled onto the couch, done for the evening, groceries arrived and as she organized them, she heard the elevator climbing.

It startled her when the doors opened into her suite and she spun around to see who it was. Aurick stood just inside as the doors closed and the elevator descended. His tall, broad frame dominated the entrance as he dropped his briefcase beside the side table and shrugged out of his jacket.

"I wasn't expecting you." She blurted, eyeing him.

"It's all right, I heard about today and it sounded hectic." He stretched his arms, first one, and then the other, over the back of his neck. As he pulled his aching muscles, he watched her flutter around the kitchen. Long lengths of immobility annoyed him, but some days he couldn't help it. Obviously, she hadn't been expecting anyone, dressed in an oversized sweatshirt and faded jeans—both dirty. Her face, void of makeup and smudged with dust, was soft and sexy. Haphazardly, her hair wound an elastic, and her bare feet pattered across the floor as she went to the refrigerator. Even now, quite domesticated and disheveled, he had to fight the urge to tangle his fingers in her hair.

She felt his eyes rake the length of her body. Goosebumps surfaced on her skin and her breath hitched. "See anything you like?"

"I'm contemplating it." He teased, then turned. Needing to remove the temptation, he descended into the living room. "How was your day?" He settled on the couch.

"Busy." She paused. The redhead would have called him. "But you *heard*." Carrying two glasses of lemonade, she joined him.

"I did." He sat forward, accepting the glass. "I've no comment. If you felt threatened and needed to defend yourself, then it is what it is. You two can work it out without me."

She placed her glass down and stretched to relieve the tension in her back. All-day, she had worried about this confrontation and now that she knew his attitude, her body relaxed, leaving her sore and tired. "Did you eat?"

"No, you?" He watched her sink into an armchair across from him and put her feet up on the ottoman, resting her head backward.

"They brought a supper cart in, so I grabbed a couple of sandwiches and a container of soup. There are leftovers in the fridge." She lifted her head to look at him. "I wasn't expecting you."

"I didn't hire you to attend to my daily needs. It's my fault I didn't call. Mind if I lay here for a while?" He asked, and she shook her head. "You could have a relaxing bath and clean yourself up." He settled his back into the couch, sprawling as he grabbed the remote, flicked the television on, and an economic news report covered the screen.

Disinterested, she mulled over her options. A bath sounded heavenly, but even though she was dirty, she felt uncomfortable bathing while he was here. *There's a lock on the bathroom door*. Tired muscles and frayed nerves won out as she excused herself. His attention didn't veer from the program when she disappeared.

From his horizontal position, he heard the squeal of the taps, then the heavy-pouring water splash and fill the tub. He silenced the television by shutting it off, then closed his eyes, straining to hear her movements in the water. Jealous of the inanimate liquid...

As he stepped out of his shoes and socks, he tugged the belt from his waist and tossed it into the chair. He freed his wrists from the tight cuffs and pulled his shirttails out of his black pants. Unbuttoning the front of his charcoal-colored dress shirt, he wandered to the bathroom door. He rested his palm on it as he listened.

The sound of her melodic humming and the water lapping against her naked body as she washed stirred his lust. There was only one way to find out if she wanted him. Slowly, his silent palm slid down the door. His fingers found the knob and twisted it easily. He pushed it open, then rested his shoulder against its frame, waiting for her to realize his presence.

Her eyes were closed as her slickly lathered digits trailed along her creamy, defined collarbone, then downward, capturing her breasts. Tight goosebumps surfaced as she kneaded the globes roughly in her palms. She stopped humming as she licked her lips and her fingers pinched her peaks, hardening them under his gaze. A tiny sigh escaped her as she lifted a breast to her mouth and suckled its point with her lips.

His hand freed the button and zipper at his waist,

allowing his erection the freedom to grow as the sight of her pleasuring herself thickened his cock.

Her other hand slid into the water, ran over her abdomen, and her palm brushed her nub as her fingers disappeared. He barely heard the muffled cry escape her as she turned her head, her eyes opened, and, embarrassed, she blushed prettily.

When her hand released her breast, he growled. "Don't stop." He peeled his shirt from his sinewy, bronzed shoulders and shrugged it off, allowing it to fall behind him as he stalked to the Jacuzzi's edge and sat.

Her eyes moved from his flat navel, up his sculpted ribs, over his chiseled pecs, and along his corded neck. Intense hunger animated her eyes when she met his penetrating stare. "I wasn't expecting you." Her coy, soft voice innocently invited.

His tone was thick with desire as he ran a finger along her shoulder, up her throat, and forced her chin upwards. "You had to know I'd come."

His mouth settled gently over hers, their warm breath mingling and the taste of lemonade on their tongues. He lifted her hand, pulling it to his face. His mouth left hers to caress the inside of her wrist and his hair tickled her arm.

As he moved her palm back to her breast, he pleaded. "Show me how you please yourself."

He shifted his body to lie on the edge so his face was level with hers as she relaxed against the side.

"Like this?" Her middle finger drew slow, deliberate circles around the swollen peak. Once... Twice... Three times, then her palm covered the round globe, and she pinched the hardened flesh between her digits.

He swallowed the lump building in his throat next to her ear. "Like that, but more."

Her head turned to him, and her lips moved closer. "When I'm touching myself, it's not my hands,

I imagine. I'm imagining yours." Her tongue ran over his lip. "I'm feeling your tongue bathing my nipple."

The blood pounding in his ears rushed southward. "Is that so?" His tongue stroked against hers.

Her small sigh and her warm wet hand gripping him through the fabric of his pants were the invitations he had waited for. He pressed a needy, forceful kiss to her mouth, then shoved away from her, standing tall above her.

His thumbs caught the material of his pants and briefs, pushing them down as they fell. His erection curled upward, reaching above his navel, and his scrotum tightened with anticipation between his legs.

He stepped into the steaming water where her legs laid wide. He extended his hand for her to take, and the one covering her mound took it. He pulled her to stand. He dipped his head to her breast as he hauled her against his length and lifted her. One of her hands gripped his hair and her other traveled between their water-slicked bodies. Her fingers wound around his stiffened shaft, guiding it to her opening as she attempted to impale her heat over it.

His strong hands palmed her ass, staying her folds against his silky tip and he lifted his smoky gaze to her lust drugged eyes. Her breath played over his chest as she struggled to drop and be filled by him.

Lightly, his lips brushed her as he whispered. "Do you want me?" He felt her head nod against his. "Do you need me?" She nodded again and rolled her head. His mouth now rested beside her ear. "Do you crave my entire thick length stroking inside you as my pelvis grinds against your button until you scream with release?" She whimpered in response, and he demanded. "Beg me."

An hour later, she emerged, wearing her fuzzy two-piece pajamas and flip-flop slippers, refreshed and quietly humming. She had braided her hair in two. The look was youthful, but she didn't care. Exhausted from the events of the last few days, she needed a good night's sleep.

Her footsteps padded soundlessly as she roamed the apartment, turning out lights. As she flipped the lamp off by the living room windows, she turned to find Aurick sound asleep on her couch. Contemplating, she chewed her bottom lip. *We're adults and technically, this is his apartment. There's a lock on the bedroom door and he didn't attack me in the bathroom. It's inappropriate, regardless of how innocent. It's late, and he's sleeping. Who will know if he stays here? Eventually, he'll wake up, realize where he is, and go back to his place.* When she draped a blanket over him, she couldn't help but notice the hand inside his pants, fondling his arousal. Embarrassed by her discovery, she hurried to her bedroom and locked the door.

The next morning, she woke to discover him gone; the blanket folded, coffee on, and a note. *Business function tonight, the Olive Garden, seven-forty-five. Meet there, Aurick.*

CHAPTER 7

Your Mouth Wasn't Begging Me to Stop, Sweetheart

Since her mother's illness, Mercy had attended many such functions with her father, an easy hostess for the wives, girlfriends, and mistresses. This was different. She didn't know Aurick's expectations were, and she would have to question every conversation. Would her alter ego have knowledge of the subjects? Nervousness butterflied her stomach as she drove into the restaurant's parking lot. The wind blew her cascading curled locks when she stepped from her vehicle. Scanning the building's front, she found Aurick lounging on a bench—completely comfortable and confident as if it had been placed there for his sole use.

As she approached, his eyes roamed over her body. *Jesus*! Last night's dream flooded back. He swallowed, pushing down the intense lust building within him. How would he concentrate on his meeting? Her business suit was sophisticated—and sexy, encouraging his sinful thoughts. Her white jacket V-lined the rise of her breasts and underneath, a black silk camisole clung to their swell.

On the pavement, her black flats clicked as she reached him. She ensured her appearance befit the occasion. *Why's he scowling? If anyone's dressed inappropriately, it's him.* No tie secured his dark blue collar and two buttons gaped, exposing his muscular neck. His black suit matched his black hair, which fell loose in untamed curls. The entire effect seethed with coiled power and meticulous control.

With a possessive hand on her back, he guided her inside. The smell of his masculine musk heightened her senses as he bent his mouth to her ear. "We're meeting Bryce and Emma Thompson, owners of a drilling rig manufacturing complex. I need to acquire it. You'll entertain his wife while Bryce and I deal with the particulars. There's our table." His demeanor changed from professional to inviting with a smile as he gestured to a table in the back.

The older couple stood and Aurick as host made the introductions.

He clasped the old man's hand. "It's good to see you again." Then palmed the wife's hand for a moment. "And you must be Emma."

Returning his hand to her spine, he drew Mercy forward. He glanced at her as she shifted her hair over her shoulder. "This is Mercy Richards. My..." Her gold chain caught on her finger and a cylindrical, long pendant hidden in her breasts' valley pulled upwards. His throat dried as she slid it back inside. With the dream so fresh in his mind, his imagination went there.

In one fluid and discreet motion, Mercy elbowed him, then sailed her hand across the space, locking it first with each person. "... Companion." She smiled, knowing the maneuver went unnoticed.

Get your shit together. Aurick took a long breath and shook off the torturing image as the three others spoke and sat. Not wanting his behavior showcased, he hurried to join them. He never lost control like this.

He angled his chair to face Bryce, who sat on his left and completely eliminated Mercy's presence from his vision on the right.

"My legal team suggested we meet," Aurick said as Mercy poured a glass of white wine from the decanter in the table's center.

Bryce shrugged. "I–"

Emma placed her hand on her husband's wrist. "You know, I hate business topics while we eat."

He smiled at his wife. "Of course." His expression was apologetic as he addressed the younger man. "Let's table this for an hour."

As their waiter approached, Aurick nodded and invited them to order before him. He acknowledged both older people as they ordered, but when Mercy's turn came, he studied his menu.

Since his blunder, he hadn't looked at Mercy and it set her in an uncomfortable, insignificant spotlight. As if everyone spotted his ignorance. Her father and his associates had unwittingly groomed her for any situation. Though her light-hearted, friendly demeanor didn't change, her annoyance was quickly elevated to anger. What *am I doing here?* Entertain the wife. It was her job and his current attitude meant to keep her in her place.

Aurick was certain everyone in the room was staring at him and speculating over his flushed face. His semi-stiff arousal twitched each time he attempted to look at her, threatening to harden. *What'd Bryce say? Hockey?* He raked his mind and cleared his throat. "I hear the Elks are doing well this year." *Phew, nailed it.* He smiled as he motioned for the waiter to bring him another drink. He could handle this, *focus on sports, and the old guy —ignore her.*

Mercy's laugh trilled. *Jesus, fuck!* It twitched.

Bryce grinned. "It's the Oilers. Not a sports fan?"

He finished chewing the bite of food he'd taken. "I'm sorry. You're right—*the Oilers.* I like sports, but my loyalties are with whoever has the strongest team in a season. Can't say it's been them since Wayne left."

Bryce nodded his agreement, and the two started an animated debate over when each pro team's downfall happened.

Perhaps he isn't feeling well. Mercy chided herself for laughing when he named the wrong team. For a man who seemed completely perfect and intelligent beyond those around him, it had been a gigantic mistake. One she wouldn't have expected, and it took her off guard.

Emma attempted to draw her into conversations about society; the theater, the boutique clothiers, and the upscale eateries. Ms. Richards wouldn't frequent these places and, therefore, couldn't converse on the topics. Instead, she asked about the woman's family and the other took to the change.

Before long, the remnants of their meal were removed, and the couples relocated to the dimly lit lounge, where soft music played and people swayed on the dance floor. The men walked together, leaving the women to follow. Aurick led them to a table where Gwen waited.

Aurick grabbed a chair from a neighboring table as the older couple sat on one side, leaving Mercy to sit next to Gwen and across from Emma. Immediately, the business conversation started with the redhead furiously scribbling notes.

She couldn't see Aurick—his body turned to Bryce and was blocked by Gwen's presence. The two women, left at the table's end, continued their conversation. The older woman was very skilled in small talk, inviting the younger into a chat about books and authors.

Emma excused herself to call home and Mercy listened to the men as she fingered the rim of her glass.

"... I'm wary of selling my company to anyone. When you contacted us, it wasn't on the market and I really have no interest in selling. I grew this business from a dream with my own hands and I know every employee by name. I won't threaten their livelihoods for the sake of money. It would be challenging for some to find other employment because of their age and I'm loyal to those who have been with the company since the day I opened it twenty years ago. It thrives and as you can see from all accounts, it still prospers." Bryce explained. "I appreciate the terms you've outlined. They are tempting and flattering."

"The stance you're taking suggests you're more interested in the welfare of your employees than in your own, which is an honorable trait. However, it doesn't diminish the fact I need your factory. I understand your apprehension and reluctance to sell to a conglomerate. Most would break it apart and sell it off. That's not my intention." He said matter-of-factly. "For your peace of mind, I offer a solution. I'm prepared to add into the contract all employees who've worked six months or longer would be protected for a term of ten years. Also, we could add a provision to the sale. If I choose to sell the company, I would pay the employees five years of wages outright."

A pregnant pause electrified the atmosphere around them. "From a corporate position, it doesn't sound particularly lucrative for you. It would essentially tie your hands. It's risky." Bryce spoke what Mercy silently wondered.

"No risk." Aurick offered. "I've no intention of selling or letting your employees go. I'm prepared to concede these allowances to demonstrate their welfare will be handled according to your wishes."

"Then on those terms, I would accept. However, those terms would have to be outlined in detail before I endorse anything." Bryce rose, taking his wife's hand as she returned. He pulled her to his side. "If you'll excuse us for a few minutes."

The couple weaved a path to the small dance floor as Aurick addressed Gwen. "It went well."

"I think you eased his mind. You think you convinced him?" Gwen asked.

"It's one thing to say and another thing to establish it on paper. It's detrimental when you care more for your employees than the interest of your business, but I respect it. I'm pleased we got it before someone realized what our intentions for it are."

Gwen offered her congratulations as the couple returned. When they seated themselves, Aurick pardoned himself and clasped Gwen's hand. Bryce's eyebrow rose, and he met Emma's puzzled gaze. Mercy was dumbfounded as the pair stepped away.

Aurick turned Gwen into his arms, seemingly a familiar gesture as she smiled up at him, then rested her head on his chest while the two slowly moved in perfect unison. Aurick dipped his head, whispering to her, and she nodded.

Mercy couldn't take her eyes off them as a tide of emotions passed over her. Embarrassed by the affectionate display, she seethed. She noticed his hand resting on the girl's waist. His face held a content grin as he dropped his chin, settling it on the top of her head.

Mercy heard Emma whisper to her husband, glad he didn't treat his secretary like that, and hot jealousy flashed through her. When the song finished, she turned and caught Emma's sympathetic glance. The couple returned; Aurick sat next to Mercy as Gwen bid good evening to the Thompsons and took her leave.

Escaping the sudden tension, the married pair excused themselves again.

Aurick sipped his whisky as he studied Mercy's trained, bland expression. "Jealousy is unbecoming on you. It distorts your face..." he tsked, "... frown lines everywhere." He goaded her, then winked.

"I'm *not* jealous." She hissed defensively. The last thing she wanted was to feel this way, but to have him hit so close to the truth angered her. She angled away from him as he chuckled.

His hand gripped hers, pulling her to her feet. "Come, let me fix it for you."

He ushered her into the open space and spun her into his arms before she could struggle. His arms tightened on her back like a vise and her trapped hands laid flat against his solid chest. He pressed his leg between hers as he gently swayed her to the melody. Her anger smoldered just below the surface as he took his liberties with her. He was either unaware or ignoring it.

"You look beautiful tonight." He whispered, rubbing the small of her back with his fingers. "I'm impressed by how you managed Emma at supper and Gwen's presence. I know you don't like her, but regardless of what you think, she respects you."

Had his heartbeat increased under her palm? She ignored it. "Respects me? Is that why she was clinging to you?" Her eyes glowered. "You looked like you enjoyed it."

"So you *were* watching?" His chin dimpled and his eyes leaped with amusement. "I'm enjoying you more." When he dipped his head forward, she swung her face to evade his lips and his hair tickled her cheek. She felt his chest heave with laughter under her hand. His left arm tightened on her spine, leaving his right to cup the back of her neck. She started to struggle, then ceased when he whispered. "Emma and Bryce are staring." Not wishing to make a scene, she surrendered.

After a few minutes, the combination of alcohol, the romantic lighting, and the smooth melodic music relaxed her against him. He was an excellent dancer, and her apprehension evaporated. He lifted her hand, brushed his lips to her wrist, and drew it up to lie in the hair at his collar. Repeating the motion with her other hand left her entire length exposed to him. He dragged her closer as his hips and leg rocked her body to the rhythm. The music ended, and she attempted to draw away.

His hold tightened as his cheek caressed hers. "Not yet."

She didn't protest.

When the next song started, Aurick's arm continued to hold her while his deliberate fingers trailed down her ribcage and side, creating goosebumps in their wake. Her heart hammered in her ears as butterflies flitted in her stomach. She was finding it difficult to swallow. Under her palm, she could feel his increased reaction to her with every passing second, almost catching her own. She closed her eyes, savoring the pleasant burn in her midriff. She inhaled his tantalizing scent—a combination of wood and musk—affecting her like a drug. Intentionally, she massaged the chords in his neck, needing an outlet for her desire.

His clothed body absorbed her fiery heat. When he felt her encouraging fingers stroke his neck, his mind clouded. Every thought and propriety fled, leaving only her. Their friction thickened him as he rocked her thighs against his muscled leg. He wanted her now. He danced them into a darkened corner, away from the dim lights and the eyes of others.

She was powerless when his fingers softly lifted her delicate chin and his lips lightly brushed hers. Ravenous, her hands tugged his neck, wanting him to intensify their kiss. His mouth greedily answered her demand as his whisky-laced tongue massaged hers. A rough, needy growl escaped his throat, and she swallowed it. She was drunk with passion as his forceful hands slid down her back, arching her length into his solid, taut frame. His hardened erection pushed against her stomach and it excited and strengthened the yearning heat building inside her. He inhaled, then locked her mouth again, desperate to drink from her. Her fingers sank into his collar as she sighed into his mouth. He hoisted the back of her jacket up her hips and ran each palm down her pants, cupping and kneading her ass in his hands.

He savored her alluring natural scent, blended with vanilla and the taste of wine on her breath as he melded her to him. Without restraint, his hands traveled over her quivering body. His intimate touch was everywhere—reeling her heightened senses—uniting them in purpose. Her responses were innocent and primitive as she met every action with one of her own.

A full second passed before she realized the music no longer played and another to realize his bare, calloused hands kneaded her backside unobstructed. Sometime during their embrace, the hindrance of her zipper was removed. Her passion-dazed eyes opened, meeting his partially cloaked as she shoved out of his arms. His chest labored for air and her lipstick smudged his lips. Humiliated by her behavior, her gaze bounced around the room as she zippered her pants and righted jacket. Only two other couples remained, and neither seemed to have observed them.

With urgency, she sought to slow her breathing and furious heartbeat as she walked back to the table. Her fingers combed her hair as she sat, uncertain what her attitude should be. *Should I be angry, embarrassed, or nonchalant?* The short-lived time for decision passed when he settled next to her, his breath still a little erratic as he took a sip of his watered-down whisky.

Once again, he'd crossed her invisible boundary, and he wondered how much damage he had done. Dammit, she wanted him. It was evident in her reactions, but something stopped her. *Undoing her slacks in public—what was I thinking?* That was the issue. He couldn't think when he was around her, touching her, holding her. And why should he apologize for wanting her? *You undid her pants.* He berated himself, astonished by his actions.

She darted him a quick glance, wondering what he was thinking. "When Emma and Bryce return, I wish to leave." Still heated by lust and their scandalous display, her face reddened. The last thing she needed was to be recognized by anyone, behaving in a manner less desirable than expected. Especially in any establishment where the wealthy frequented and press could camp.

While he downed the remaining whisky, he stared at her. "They left after the first song. We can leave now. Give me your keys." He rose and extended his hand as she dug them from her purse.

"You needn't accompany me to my vehicle. I can find my way." She replied more sharply than intended and then stood to step past him.

Instantly, he turned, and his hand snaked out, gripping her elbow. "Your desire to stew in self-disgust alone will have to wait. I gave Gwen my truck so she could leave. Which means I'll be traveling with you." He maneuvered her through the lounge and into the open air. Pulling the keys from her hand, he opened the passenger door and ushered her in before striding around and sliding behind the wheel.

As he predicted, her weighted conscience wrestled with the unfamiliar feelings he forced from her. *Are you crazy, making love in public? You don't even know him. So what, you didn't harm anyone? Being attracted to someone isn't a crime. Many people have sex with acquaintances.* Before she knew it, they were pulling into the apartment's parking lot.

Wanting to escape him and her humiliating behavior, she rushed from the vehicle into the building and waited for the elevator. It arrived as he appeared at her side. She entered and punched her code into the pin pad. To her surprise, he reached past her, entered his code, and punched number seven-oh-one.

"I get it," she mumbled deliberately, wanting to provoke an argument that would assuage her other emotions.

"Don't embarrass yourself by assuming you know what my relation to Gwen is." He warned. He clutched her wrist and backed her against the wall, using his body to pin her there.

"Infusing business with pleasure..." She searched for something cutting to say. "... it's what you do." She accused. The tension built as the elevator climbed. Irritated, his jaw muscle twitched as his eyes narrowed on her.

The elevator door opened, but he held her there with one hand as he straightened, holding the door open with his other. Gwen turned, speechlessly stunned and rooted in place by his angry expression and the sight of Mercy pinned against the wall.

"My keys." His barked order sent Gwen rushing to the counter and back, handing them off. "See you in the morning." He said as the elevator closed.

Finally, the door opened into Mercy's apartment. When he let her go, she rushed past him.

"You've seen me here... good night and get lost." She dismissed as she traveled down the hall to her bedroom.

His eyebrow lifted in challenge as he pursued her. "*Your* apartment? Are the men's clothes in the closet your size and style? It's *my* apartment too. And—I'm not going *anywhere* except to bed."

She swiveled around, confronting him as the significance of the information hit her. She hadn't required the other closet and hadn't opened it. "You're not living here! That was never part of our deal."

"No, it was part of the fine print you never asked about." Aurick sneered with delight at his devious intelligence when he had neglected to disclose it earlier. He stepped past her into the bedroom, leaving her in the hall. He opened the closet door and withdrew a dark green suit.

"You're *disgusting*." She hurled the words at him. "I hate you!"

He retraced his steps to her, where she stood in the doorway and she backed into the wooden doorframe.

Frustrated, he glared. "I'm sorry I unzipped your pants..." When his hand went to his hair, she flinched as if expecting his touch and it angered him. "It seems I'm constantly apologizing for *our* behavior. However, I won't apologize for wanting you. We're the same—hormones in overdrive and demanding a workout."

"No, I'm nothing like you." She hissed between her teeth, scowling at him.

Only a breath separated their lips as he leaned in and his eyes accused. "No? Contrary to what you might believe, your mouth wasn't begging me to stop, sweetheart." He swept past her, leaving the room.

"Oooh!" she shrieked as she slammed the door and locked it.

As she laid in bed, she contemplated. Why did he disturb her so much? Why did she lose herself to him every time he touched her? Was she wrong to refuse him? Could this be her body telling her it was time to give in to its physical desires? Was he right? Did she just need to do it? Could she sleep with a man—one she wasn't sure she liked but lusted over? Dizzily, the questions swirled until she closed her eyes and fell into an exhausted sleep.

Aurick didn't sleep soundly either, as his mind plagued him with dreams. Dreams of her gone or embraced by another. During each waking period, he ached to touch her but didn't dare seek her out after their earlier quarrel. He didn't understand her hesitancy. *She desires me. Why won't she give in? Everyone's having casual sex, why shouldn't we?* He knew it wouldn't have taken much to persuade her once they were alone. Why hadn't he tried? He needed her out of his system.

Ever since their first meeting, when he closed his eyes, he saw her in his erotic fantasies. He would daydream and Gwen would snap him out of it. He flopped over, punched the pillow, then glared at the clock, five-fifteen. He buried his face, trying to salvage some rest.

CHAPTER 8

How Do You Want Me?

Tired, Mercy rested her cheek in her palm as she reviewed the numbers on the spreadsheet again. In the days following their close encounter, her relationship with Aurick became amicable. Neither spoke of the incident nor attempted to rekindle the fire. But she was powerless to stop her dreams from revisiting it, and she woke many times each night with a profound yearning. It was much more than physical; it left her feeling cold and alone.

Her father's voice sounded down the hall as he and Connie approached her location. She kept her head low, hoping to go unnoticed.

"... It's time the young buck from Power Valley Holdings kisses the ring. I'll teach him what power is." His voice seethed with anger.

"Which conference room?" Connie asked as she jotted notes down notes.

"The Strong Hold." He said. They paused at the offices' other exit.

Mercy hated the appropriately named room. It was a massive, intimidating room on the top floor where a bulky, medieval table for twenty dominated the space, and rows of theater seating backdropped her father when he sat. Behind those and along the height of the wall were west-facing windows. Used in the afternoon to blind anyone sitting on the opposite side.

"Insignificant with undertones of affluence?"

"Exactly." He grinned, pleased the woman understood. "Have every manager and our legal team attend. I want every seat filled on our side."

"I'll have the arrangements made immediately."

Keith left, and Connie went to her office.

It wasn't a conversation. It was a ruler strategizing a war. The room was reserved for only the most masterful adversaries. Whoever the company was, they were a threat. But they had yet to face the force of the Haggins' Hotel Group, and it was undeniable. They would crumble under the weight of her father's authority.

Mercy scrutinized the long table set with the custom-made Waterford Irish Lace tumblers engraved with the HHG logo. The crystal exuded money, each costing a few hundred dollars. On her father's side of the table, the glasses were filled with water, but on the other they were left empty, ensuring his foes recognized their insignificance and leaving them to fill their own from the five equally expensive pitchers set between the ten chairs.

As the mandated attendees filed inside and took their seats, Connie shielded her face with her hand as she strode to Mercy's side.

She squinted, the sunlight hurting her eyes. "Looks fantastic. Nice touch out-facing our logo. I'll need you to warm Paterson's chair. He isn't going to make it." Connie pushed a notebook into the younger woman's hands. "He's third row, fifth chair." Indicating where she should sit in the theater seating, then quickly took her own seat at the end of the table, glad to be out of the sun's punishing light.

. . .

Mercy climbed the stairs and walked past those already seated. She sat down, only to realize too late, Roger was seated next to her.

His face distorted with a sneer as his eyes met her gaze. "Daddy's princess sat amongst the commoners? Your tiara's slipping."

She trained her expression with disinterest, her tone was icy. "Careful Roger, *daddy* won't be in charge forever."

She wouldn't stay. Damn her father, damn his need for superiority, and damn his meeting. Later, she'd take a tongue lashing, but now she rose to leave.

The black, sleek limousine waited at the curb as Aurick, Gwen, and two other Power Valley Holdings executives were flanked by four security guards who accompanied them to the eleventh floor. The guards' presence was meant to be intimidating and uncomfortable—a tactic Aurick had used many times—none of them were intimidated.

His head swung back to ensure one of his men carried the small oak box, then his excited eyes caught Gwen's as he winked and grinned at her. This was what he lived and breathed. The dance. A formidable opponent who would underestimate his business prowess and then suffer the consequences. It happened in every city and every country. He was the despised and feared unknown. However, he wouldn't stay that way. More Albertans would know him than the Lougheed family when he finished devouring what businesses he wanted and moved on.

When the doors slid open, they followed two of the guards. Aurick didn't need to follow them. He'd bet his entire fortune they were headed down the long, wide antique-filled hallway to the sole door on the left. The west-facing door. *Well played*, he acknowledged his rival's skill.

He dipped his head and murmured to Gwen. "Prepare yourself, there'll be windows." He didn't have to tell the two accompanying them. They would mimic her.

As expected, one guard entered, and the other stayed out, directing the Power Valley Holdings entourage inside.

Before he entered, he heard people fidgeting in their seats and flipping through whatever they held. Otherwise, it was silent, so his team could not estimate how many they would face.

The brilliant afternoon sunlight struck his easy, charming expression, but he focused on the table. He showed no sign the tactic bothered him as his hand traveled over the chair backs, making his way to the center where he knew Keith Haggins would be standing.

What sounded like a muffled gasp sounded from somewhere above, but he covered it with his greeting.

Mercy had only stood when the security guard entered. Undeterred, she meant to leave anyway, but as she moved past the person next to her, she caught sight of the black, shoulder-length curls and the handsome features bathed in brightness. Her hand covered her mouth as she gasped and swiftly took her chair again, sinking down in hopes he wouldn't recognize her. She shook her head. This couldn't be happening. Her father's enemy couldn't be *her Aurick*. No, she had to be dreaming. Their worlds could not collide. She wouldn't allow it.

But it was his sexy, deep voice that spoke too happily. "Keith," he extended his hand across the table. "Such a pleasure." He used the name with familiarity, and she knew it would instantly irritate her father.

But there was no evidence of it when her father matched Aurick's manner. "I thought it was time we meet since our business dealings are so closely aligned."

Aurick's hand went to redhead's waist, inviting her forward. "This is Power Valley Holdings' Vice-President, Gwen Davis."

When she darted a glance her way, Gwen blinked, reminding Mercy those below were nearly blinded. She took a deep breath and straightened in her chair, curious how the two men would stack up against each other.

"Please sit." Her father sat. "I hope the presence of my immediate staff doesn't bother you. I could hardly deny them the opportunity to meet you."

She recognized the deviousness of his half-grin before he spoke, unapologetic. "It's unfortunate we can't stay. As we arrived, I received word that my River Valley apartment building is undergoing a sudden city code inspection." He lifted the pitcher and filled one of the glasses, then raised it, examining the HHG logo. As if it interested him more than the conversation or the man who had summoned him here.

He swore, on the expensive glass, lingered the scent of musky vanilla—Mercy's vanilla. His mind was playing tricks on him as he swallowed, then returned and pushed the glass aside to make room on the table.

As Aurick spoke, he motioned, and a man came forward. "I'm glad you appreciate Waterford crystal. This morning, I had these flown in for you." He opened then spun a wooden case around to face her father.

Mercy couldn't see what the significance was, but she could hear the anger-filled undertone in her father's voice as he thanked him.

Aurick lifted his head as if he were surveying those above. As if he could see each one of them. "Another time." He spun and guided Gwen out, sauntering without a care.

Several minutes passed before the watching security guard signaled the elevator's descent. Her reddening father marched out, followed by those who had sat at the table. She heard his raised voice muffle as his office door closed. Then a mass exodus occurred, leaving Mercy to orchestrate the janitorial staff in righting the room.

Curiously, she wandered to the table where she found the two handmade Irish crystal tumblers etched with Waterford city's lion and sturgeon crest. They matched a pair she had bought her father for his birthday once. The pair cost more than all the HHG logoed glasses combined. She waved the staff forward as she returned them to the box and secured the lid.

She smiled, pleased to learn Aurick played this corporate game well and had bested her father.

L ater the same night, Mercy was curled in an armchair reading when the elevator doors opened. She glanced at the large decorative clock on the wall. It was after ten. As usual, without a word, Aurick walked into the living room and opened his briefcase on the coffee table, and silently withdrew his files, then stood the briefcase on the floor. He never interrupted her, but respectfully waited for her to finish. She knew he wouldn't speak until she spoke or fidgeted.

She marked the end of her paragraph, closed the

book, then stretched. "There's roast chicken with mashed potatoes and green beans in the fridge."

"Thanks. How was your day?" He piled the folders and pushed them aside, giving her his full attention.

She rested her head against the back of the chair. "Good. How was your inspection?"

In question, he lifted his eyebrow. "My inspection?"

Nice slip Mercy. What inspection? What are you talking about? She furrowed her eyebrows right back at him. "Your vehicle inspection?"

He shook his head. "My truck went in for servicing yesterday, not an inspection."

"My mistake." With nonchalance, she shrugged and walked to the kitchen. "What about your day? How was it?"

When she withdrew the leftovers from the fridge and turned, she collided with his solid, warm chest.

In the process of following her into the kitchen, he had discarded his suit jacket, loosened his tie, and unbuttoned his cuffs and neck. His hands grabbed her waist, steadying her, then just as quickly, took the containers from her. The momentary contact of his hands on her sent a thrill down her spine and she felt a flush redden her face.

Without looking, he pushed the containers onto the counter as his eyes noted her rising color. He stepped into her. Only an inch separated their lengths.

When he dipped his head, her eyes closed, and her tongue moistened her lips in anticipation. She felt his breath wash over her sensitive skin as he whispered. "Are you ready?"

Her hooded eyes slid open. "Ready?"

"To beg?" He replied, then grinned, and she shook her head, backing away from him. "Too bad." Not the least bit affected. He shouldered past her as he finished unbuttoning and pulling his shirt free. "I got to shower. Good night."

Frustrated and vindictive, she put the food back in the fridge. He could get it himself later if he wanted it. She wiped the counters and table again, then wandered into the living room. She straightened the blanket on the chair where she had sat earlier and turned to the table.

He had pushed aside the centerpiece and her need to tidy, urged her to fix it. Afterward, his stack of paperwork wasn't sitting straight. She shuffled them into a pile, and one folder's label caught her eye.

HAGGINS—in bold red letters.

She heard the shower's spray as she stared at her family name. Sinking onto the edge of the couch, she contemplated whether or not she should open it. She had a right to know what he knew about her, about her family, and she wanted to know how Aurick's and her father's plans intersected.

Carefully, she noted where in the pile she withdrew it from, then laid it flat on the table and flipped open the cover. She turned the early newspaper images of her parents over, then found more recent ones of her father. The next were several embarrassing images of her as a teenager taken outside her home when she'd gone through a phase of wearing wigs and large, dark sunglasses to avoid the press.

After leafing through the images, she skimmed a report dated this morning:

For three days, we've had an investigator watching his residence and tasked another with tailing Keith Haggins. We're certain with time, we will uncover more. Below is the information we discovered before your deadline.

The document outlined her father's movements over the past few days, a list of his powerful associates which Mercy knew to be his golf buddies, and several other thorough facts.

... Martha, Keith's wife, has terminal cancer... A doctor who attended her regularly...

... A rebellious daughter who evaded the press by using disguises... No recent images... Uncertain whether she resides in the family home, elsewhere, or is traveling... Several failed relationships... Rumors in the business community claim her current engagement may be in jeopardy...

The taps squealed, signaling Aurick would emerge shortly. She righted the folder and placed it back into the pile, then headed for the sanctuary of her bedroom to think about what she had read.

JULY

"This is insanity!" Mercy blurted during lunch with her girlfriends several Thursdays later.

"I'd have to agree," Beverly said as she covered her smile, taking a bite of her sandwich. Laughing at Mercy wouldn't help the situation at all.

But Carmen burst into uncontrolled laughter, unable to contain herself.

Mercy silenced her with a scowl. "Of course you would find this hilarious."

"How isn't it? You're domesticated. Who's cooking?"

Mercy cringed. "I tried for a couple of weeks, but I couldn't stomach what I cooked. How could *so many* recipes be *so bad*?"

"I'm sure it was the recipes." Beverly had to look away from Carmen's grin, which threatened to advance into laughter again. "So you're ordering in then?"

"Sort of... I've been stopping to pick up ready-made meals. I transfer them into my dishes, then drop the containers into the garbage shoot before Aurick arrives. I can't keep this up, I'm having to use my salary from here to hide it and I'm running low." Mercy reddened over her guilty admission.

"I get why you can't use the credit card, but what about the cash he pays you? Where's that going?"

"I can't bring myself to spend it. It feels dirty. This was about my ability to make it. Jumping from my father's bank account to another proves nothing." She basked in her newfound liberation—coming and going without questioning or supervision. However, part of it was learning to budget her salary from her father's company, and she gained an appreciation for the effort it took to earn her money, concentrating it on her bills and fuel. "Besides the cooking, I'm enjoying the cleaning, the responsibility, the–"

"Delicious man, you get to cuddle up with every night?" With a smile, Carmen finished.

Mercy shook her head. "Not what I was going to say. And, since the night at the Olive Garden, Aurick's made no advance towards me. In the evenings, when we're in the apartment, Aurick works or watches television from the couch and I curl into an armchair or stretch out on the loveseat and read. If we speak it's trivial; about our day, current events, or safe topics like the weather. On the rare occasions I accompany him, Aurick touches me only when absolutely necessary. It's like—at least for him—whatever was there is gone. Who knows, maybe he'll be giving me an eviction notice before long."

This was how Mercy talked now; Aurick this, Aurick that.

Beverly tried to count the number of times her friend said his name but lost track. She gave Mercy a pointed look. "When is a touch absolutely necessary?"

Mercy narrowed her gaze. "You know when a man guides you as you walk, pushes in your chair, helps you with your coat, or introduces you."

"Cause you couldn't follow him, couldn't pull

your own chair or put on your jacket? And how does introducing *you* require *him* to touch you? I call bullshit."

Carmen smiled. "Well, whatever he does or doesn't do, it looks good on you. You seem light-hearted, softened, and content. I've never seen you laugh or smile so easily before."

"Only with you guys. When Aurick and I are together, it's business."

"Of course." Beverly agreed too readily for Mercy's liking.

"What's that supposed to mean?"

Beverly shrugged. "It's how you treated Roger and your father—keeping them at arm's length. Why should this guy be any different?"

"Aurick isn't and I don't do that." *Do I?*

Roger—their relationship had been much colder and much longer. It was logical, and she'd guarded herself in the first year. But with passing time and his patience, her affections grew. And that's why she'd accepted his marriage proposal. Because he would allow her to use her mother's illness as an excuse to postpone it. And she hoped the time would provide her with deepened feelings. But was it arm's length or self-preservation?

Well, at least she knew she didn't hold her father at arm's length. No, she shielded him from her stupidity, her shame, and humiliation her previous relationships had left her with. The only reason he knew anything about her and Roger was because her ex-fiancée had formed an alliance with him afterward.

Right now, if she was keeping Aurick at an arm's length, she was doing a piss-poor job of it. Because she couldn't stop him in her dreams, where he would destroy her carefully constructed behavior. He'd seduce her and love her, then leave her feeling empty with an insatiable craving for him.

For nearly two months—every night, he fought for the mental and physical strength not to touch her. And the few times he had found an excuse to do so had been torturous.

When Aurick pretended to study his reports in the evening, he'd catch her lost—in the words, in the worlds—and her expression would run a gamut between brightened enjoyment and darkened fear as she read. It was incredible, and he wanted that. He wanted her to react so easily, so emotionally with him, but she still maintained the invisible barrier between them and he didn't know when or how it would be removed.

Fridays were the worst. The one night when she left him to spend the evening with her cousin. He wondered if she really was with her cousin, or on a date. Then he would pace, unable to concentrate on the television or find relief in sleep until he heard the whirl of the elevator climbing. Then, he'd shut himself inside his room, not allowing her to know he waited up for her. Today was Friday.

"... The architect tonight at seven." Olivia finished relaying his schedule.

He continued to study the file in front of him. "Cancel it."

"You shouldn't. We've rescheduled six times in two months."

Her words warranted his attention, and he growled. "I'm well aware of how many times I've canceled. Cancel again."

She stammered forward, not wanting his anger but needing him to know. "Ummm. He's starting to question–"

Gwen strode in. "Whether or not we're serious

business." She waved her hand, dismissing his secretary. "Are we serious business, Aurick?"

"What in the fuck do you mean by that?"

She clicked her tongue as sat on the desk's edge, crossing her legs as she faced him. "We *were* serious business. Now, all we do is reschedule, make excuses, and leave our employees to fend for themselves. I don't even know who Olivia was talking about, but everyone's asking the same thing. *Does he care?*" She shrugged. "I don't even know anymore."

"Of course I do. So what if I've stopped micromanaging and rescheduled a few meetings? Nothing's suffering. If it were, I would see to it."

"Would you?"

"Absolutely."

She hopped off his desk and walked backward away from him. "I'm extremely happy to hear it. I was just informed the labor challenges in South Africa have broken into protests and there are riots. I'll have Olivia call our pilot and arrange accommodations for a couple of weeks. We'll leave at seven."

His smile quirked when he realized. "You played me."

Her bubbly laugh sounded as she opened the door. "You are my piano. And I... I'm Mozart, *darling*."

He teasingly growled as she stepped out. "Hey, Mozart? Remember the last time you played me?"

She peered back inside. "Indeed, I believe you got yourself a nice-looking wife."

Disgusted by the term, he shook his head. "She's not my wife."

"Isn't she though?" Gwen whistled a tune as she pulled the door closed.

She left him alone to call Mercy. To make his apologies. To explain. Sure it was *something* men did with their wives. But another thing they did with their wives was strip them naked, bathe their bodies in kisses, and fill their eyes with ecstasy. Nope, she wasn't his wife.

But God, how he wanted to pretend.

The three girls ate their lunch with excited chatter. Carmen and Beverly were animated, telling her of their previous weekend in Miami with Tom and Gordon.

"So this alligator leaps out of the water—" Carmen stopped, interrupted by Mercy's buzzing phone.

When she checked the caller ID, her eyes filled with excitement, and she smiled. "It's Aurick. Give me a couple."

The two girls knowingly grinned at each other as Mercy answered and wandered several feet to the window for privacy.

"Hello?"

"Mercy?" His deep, melodic tone played in her ear.

"Yes." Her pulse quickened. "Is something wrong?"

"Labor challenges in South Africa." He said, then sighed as he ran his fingers through his hair. "There's no alternative. I'm needed there."

"I'm sorry. I can't take any time off work right now. It's unthinkable on such short notice." Though she silently wished there was.

"You couldn't come, anyway. It's too unstable. We're one of the few major employers in the region and it's volatile. I should have gone weeks ago to avert this."

He doesn't even want me with him. The blow to her pride and her assumption embarrassed her and sharpened her tone. "How long will you be away?"

Aurick mistook her reason for asking, and in a detached manner, he answered. "Don't worry, I'll have Gwen leave next month's salary on the kitchen counter, in case I don't return on time. I'll be back sometime around the twenty-eighth, two weeks, perhaps longer."

He muzzled the receiver while he addressed someone in his office.

"I wasn't asking for that reason." She mumbled, a bit stung by the reference to their arrangement.

The muffling ended, and he spoke into the handset. "I've got to go. I'll call you."

From the window, she shifted to see the girls collecting their things. Lunch was over and Carmen's story was forgotten as they headed back to work.

"He's traveling." Mercy said as they strolled down the hallway. "The four of you should join me sometime next week for supper. It'd give you the opportunity to see the apartment and we could catch up."

"Maybe? Are you cooking?" Carmen coughed, spying Beverly's grin.

Mercy smiled. "I can't screw up spaghetti sauce from a can?"

Carmen flipped her hair. "You'd be surprised, but let's plan it. I'll talk to Tom and let you know what day works."

"Are we getting together tonight?" Mercy asked.

"Sorry." Beverly shrugged. "There's a new restaurant opening in Calgary and we're leaving right after work with Tom and Gordon."

"It's all right." Mercy lied, covering her disappointment. "I'll call you tomorrow."

The girls separated, heading for their respective workstations.

Mercy lingered at work, dreading the empty apartment. When she did go home, she scooped the money from the counter and took it to her bedroom, uncomfortable by its significance. She heated a bowl of soup, then went directly to bed. She didn't sleep well as she tossed and turned, knowing she was alone and not liking the feeling.

On Saturday, she phoned the country club to ensure her father had booked his normal tee-time. Once confirmed, she grabbed the oversized bag from her closet and drove to Kingsway Mall. She used a bathroom stall to change into the jogging suit, a long brown wig, and dark, large sunglasses, then hopped on a bus and traveled to her parent's home to visit her mother.

When she knocked on the door, an aging Polly, once Mercy's nanny, now her mother's nursemaid, answered with a warm smile. "Dear girl, come in." She pulled her inside, hugging her. "Your mother is expecting you."

She hung the bag on the coat tree, removed her wig and glasses, stuffed them inside, and followed the woman. "How are things?"

"She's getting weaker and hasn't left her room this week. Your father has stayed by her side. But, she insists he continues his weekly game. I think she knows you won't visit if he's here."

"She's right."

"Nonsense, the two of you. You can't imagine the strain your mother's health has placed on him. He loves her and is scared. He believes the weight of your happiness and future rests squarely on his shoulders. He only wants to do right by you. Perhaps his harsh words and condescending actions don't appeal to you as a modern woman, but these are ingrained traits passed down through generations. Even though you still may be angry, I'm certain he's sorry.

"His ingrained beliefs are barbaric! I'm not the half-witted, dependent, incapable woman he believes *we all* are. Sorry? He knows where I work if he feels the need to apologize."

"No, you're his little girl—who he must protect at all cost. The pair of you are pig-headed!" Exasperated, Polly threw up her hands, then opened the bedroom door and smiled brightly. "You have a visitor. I'll go to the kitchen and have the cook prepare lunch." She walked away as Mercy entered.

The room was filled with vases of brilliantly colored flowers, and the French doors stood open, allowing the warm summer breeze to heighten their floral scent. Her mother turned down the television and reached for Mercy's hand as she slid a chair next to the bed.

"You look lovely." She kissed her mother's forehead. "How are you feeling?"

"Really, your lies grow more outrageous each week." She laughed, but her expression flashed with pain.

"They're not lies."

"I see right through you. I know you aren't living with your girlfriends and you've changed. Either you're treating me like a frail, sick woman who can't handle the truth, or you're hiding it because you don't want to face it. Which is it?"

"Can it be a little bit of both?" Innocently, Mercy smiled, then kissed her mother's hand.

Polly entered with refreshments and her mother's sedatives, then their lunch. As they finished eating, her mother's eyes drooped. The pills were working and soon she would be sound asleep while Mercy spent a couple of hours reading by her side.

The grandfather clock in the foyer chimed, striking two. She wanted to leave before her father returned at three. Silently, Mercy tiptoed from the room, placed one hand on the doorframe and the other on the handle. She pulled the door slowly closed, fearing the sound would wake her mother.

From the security system muted bells rang, alerting the household someone had opened the front entrance. As she strolled down the long hall, she couldn't help but wonder who it was. Her mother's friends had stopped visiting, and it was common knowledge her father golfed on Saturdays. It would have to be a delivery of some sort.

When she entered the wide foyer, the door was closed. No packages littered the large round table, and no one waited inside. She turned to pull her belongings from the coat tree and was startled when she found him.

Her father stood motionless as his lonely, yearning eyes swept her appearance. If she didn't know him, she would have thought he wanted her in his arms—but she did know him. He wasn't one for grand gestures of affection or doing things outside of propriety's sake. Other than his eyes, he was business cool.

"May I have a word?" He swung his arm for her to precede him into the living room.

"Of course." She whispered, swept past him, and sat in one of the red-leathered, button-puckered highback armchairs.

She hated this room. The oversized walnut-stained accents, the uncomfortable formal furniture, and the intricately patterned rugs. Its décor screamed domineering masculinity, and it ensured women knew they were insignificant.

He pulled the pocket doors shut, ensuring their

privacy. She barely heard him when he spoke. "You look well. Independence suits you."

The weakness in his voice surprised her. "Thank you."

She watched him move to the sideboard table. His hand shook when he lifted the crystal decanter of bourbon and it clinked against the rim of his glass.

With his back to her, he cleared his throat. "Do you need money?"

Defensively, she hissed. "I didn't come here for a handout. I came to visit—"

Her answer turned him to face her. "I wasn't insinuating..." He shrugged, his tone defeated. "I'm forever saying the wrong things to you. I'm aware you visit your mother on Saturdays while I'm golfing. I'm *offering* you money because it cannot be easy living in a two-bedroom apartment with your friends. Perhaps if you accept, you three could move into a bigger, less rundown apartment."

"How do you know our apartment is rundown?"

"I... There have been times..." He huffed out a long breath and threaded his fingers through his hair. "Cowardly, I've parked outside trying to muster the courage to apologize, but couldn't."

Her mind reeled. What if he had knocked? How would her friends have handled that? She couldn't believe the admission from her heartless, never-admit-fault father. "We're fine. Getting by. I appreciate your concern."

"Of course, I'm concerned. You've never been so angry with me. You left, giving me no opportunity to atone for my stupid old-fashioned... You're capable and smart. But, I worry when I die, you'll be alone. And, although it's not a good reason for heavy-handedly attempting to force you into a marriage, it is the only reason I have. I'm human and make mistakes."

These were the most emotional words he'd ever used in her presence. She had worshipped him much like a god—an unbreakable, dependable, unwavering force. Nothing touched him, especially mere mortal emotions. This man was different. Defeated, like his world was on tilt and he was free-falling.

Overcome by his words, his expression, and his slumped shoulders—she rushed into his arms, sharing a moment made of her childhood dreams. "I love you, daddy."

"I love you." He smiled down at her, but his features still looked uncertain. "Won't you come home? I'll grant you your every freedom and won't interfere."

"I can't." Leery, she wondered if his change was a calculated manipulation. "I need my own life."

He planted a light kiss on the top of her head. "Know you can always come home with no conditions."

Her cheek rested on his shoulder. His sheltering arms held her against him. For the first time, she felt loved, accepted, and understood by him. "Thank you." She whispered.

On Sunday, she kept active, cleaning. The hours sped by and finally exhausted; she dropped to the couch, laid down, and turned on the television. She shifted to her side and a whiff of Aurick's cologne from the couch's arm assailed her. A warm soothing sensation enveloped her body, and she closed her eyes to enjoy it while she listened to the news.

After ten minutes, the mention of South Africa made her sit up to focus. "A turn of events in the region today as Aurick Spencer, CEO of Power Valley Holdings, held talks with local dignitaries and the union delegates. When we spoke to him and I'm paraphrasing; he suggested that although they had achieved gains in the labor dispute, there is still work ahead over the next few days. He also told us that by this evening, the union representatives should have their employees under control and the protests will end. Power and telephone to this region should be back up and running by tomorrow night." The reporter stated. "Reporting for Universal News, I'm Brad Simon."

She was pleased to learn his efforts were progressing with success and understood why he hadn't called yet. But she was disappointed they hadn't interviewed him on camera. She muted the broadcast and turned into the couch, burying her face in his scent, then fell asleep.

M ercy heard the shower's spray end as she arranged the cutlery on the heavy oak table in their dining room. The late evening sun streamed warm light through the windows, casting a glow over the furniture in front of her.

Aurick's footsteps sounded in the carpeted hall, and with his every step, her anticipation grew.

His fleshy arm snaked around her waist and his fingers bunched the front of her black silky-laced slip as he hauled her backward against his naked, solid chest, resting her ass in the cradle of his thickening arousal.

He pushed her hair aside and dropped his warm lips to her shoulder, trailing a path with his wet tongue to her neck.

God, he smelled good—his soap, his shampoo, his natural scent—emanating as his avidity intensified.

She lolled her head to the side, exposing the sensitive spot behind her ear. At her midsection, her hand held his.

He flexed his muscled hips into her and hoarsely whispered. "I love the feel of your incredible body against mine." To prove his point, his other hand ran down the silky material, then pushed it upwards as his palm kneaded her thigh.

She sighed as she reached over them. Her fingers tangled in his unruly locks, inviting him to continue. Her skin prickled as excitement balled beneath his hand.

"You taste like honey and vanilla." His sensual mouth dragged back over her shoulder, and she felt his nose nudge the narrow strap of her slip, sending it down her arm.

Through his thin jogging pants, the hot, curled length of his shaft twitched against her back. Enticing him, she pressed backward as his fingers dropped her other strap. His hand tugged the soft material, and it slithered down her length, pooling at her black-heeled feet. His rough palm grazed over her flesh as she turned to face him.

He prodded her chin higher, smearing the deep red lipstick as he devoured her tempting mouth with his eager tongue. He tasted like mint and whisky—intoxicatingly masculine. His hand cupped her shapely leg and hauled her smooth thigh upward to his waist as his other drove the table settings aside, crashing them to the floor. In a single motion, he knocked the chair away and pushed her into the table. His long fingers kneaded the soft flesh of her ass as he lifted her onto the cool surface. The contrast sent shivers down her spine.

"I need you." His voice nearly pleaded as his lips traveled along her jaw, and hers roamed over the taut flesh of his pecs. Mindless desperation fueled the cravings of their interplay. His hands, his mouth—her limbs, her tongue—sought to fulfill the other.

He lathered his fingers and thumb with his mouth, then slid his hand southward and slowly rotated his lubricated thumb over her button, hardening it under his assault. His digits massaged her snug opening, enticing its muscles to relax.

A delighted breath hitched in her throat as she felt two fingers slip inside, then angled and retracted. His palm pushed forward, this time embedding the long digits to their hilt. They curled against her soft, heated walls, then withdrew. The clock's perpetual sound set the heave of his hand.

Tick... In, out. Afire, she fixated on his hooded, smoky stare.

Tick... Deep, shallow. Against the table, she strained her palms and arched her back.

Tick... Straight, curl. Her hips writhed, intensifying the heavenly sensations.

Warm sunlight kissed her naked spine as her tongue darted over her dried lips and she moaned to the rhythm of his slickened fingers.

His head bent over her and his hair tickled her ribs as he tongued the budded peaks of her breast. "Take it from me, Mercy. Find your release."

When she cried out, her muscles narrowed, and a rush of fluid bathed his digits.

He stood tall, locked her eyes with his, and watched her tremble as the cresting waves of her climax crashed—soaring, rippling, washing,—over her mind and body.

His fingers twined with hers, and as his eager tongue ran along her small wrist, his other coarse hand hauled her liquefied body against his heated skin. His gentle palms moved to massage her defined back, melding her rounded breasts against his chiseled chest.

His mouth fluttered over her cheek, trailing a path to her lobe. "Honey, I want to be inside you."

Her fingers trailed lightly down his bronzed torso as he bathed her throat with kisses. Against her breasts, his heart hammered as his quick expecting breaths raised bumps along her skin. She hooked her thumbs in his waistband, pushing the material downwards over his firm buttocks.

His breath caught, then swooshed heavily against her ear as he puttied her ass in his kneading hands and pulled her warm center against his hard shaft. Her damp, soft folds tortured him as she tongued his nipple. Her long blonde hair fluttered over his chest, pushing his barely held control to its limit.

He wound her hair in his strong hand, forcing her mouth upwards, and as his mouth drank from her lips, his eyebrow arched. "How do you want me?"

Her leg lifted and bent, rubbing the inside of her thigh down his sculpted leg as her foot pushed at the material. He stepped one way, then the other, freeing himself. His hand traveled down her smooth side and over her abdomen. His finger slid back inside her and her nectar coated his digit, ready for him.

His arms flexed as his hands spanned her ribcage, and he raised her above him. Her hands pressed against his shoulders and her hair cloaked over them as he captured her breast in his teeth, then swirled his tongue over it. Instinctively, he knew where he was going when he turned and walked several steps. He lowered her enough so her legs could wrap his ribcage then pinned her spine against the wall. His hand reached away from her but instantly came back.

She knew she would know satisfaction if only she could slip lower and impale her swollen folds over his thickened length. One of his hands held her ass as his other swept light caresses over her back. She felt his indecisive mouth bounce from her rounded breasts, to the definition of her collarbone, along her neck, then with uncontrollable hunger, he feasted on her lips. The curls of his hair skimmed her flesh, triggering red-hot tingles to fire through her. So when a bell sounded in the recesses of her mind, it didn't register.

Their naked bodies ricocheted from one wall to another until he was satisfied with their location.

Seven... She cradled his defined jaws in her palms and pulled his forehead to hers. Their ragged breath mingled, their eyes only knowing each other as his hands left her and she slid southward. As her velvety passage stretched and glided down onto his veiny, hard manhood, she watched his pupils dilate and heard his sharp intake of breath. "God, you feel wonderful."

Six... Every first entry exhilarated her—her muscles' initial protest, her sheath concaving, her nub meeting his pelvis as he forced her to accept him. A beat passed, then his hands curved over her supple hips, poising her a few inches higher. Agonizingly slow, he stroked inward, causing her body to slide up the wall. As if she were falling, butterflies fluttered in her stomach. His greedy mouth covered her bruised lips, and his rough tongue softly manipulated hers as she whimpered.

Five... In opposition, she scraped her long nails over the taut, golden skin of his shoulders. And in response to her demand, he drove his hips upward into her—entering, then withdrawing in quick succession.

Four... She flexed her pelvis into his hurried rhythm, intensifying the knotted need in her midsection. Their motivations were animalistic, independent of thought, enslaved by primitive lust.

Three... Unable to breathe, he tore his mouth from hers and his breath labored over the skin along her neck as her rapid, aching cries harmonized with his pleasurable husky groans. "Find it. I'm waiting for you."

Two... She felt swirling heat build in her abdomen. Her body's flesh stiffened, and she fixated on the blackness behind her eyes.

One... His hand left her, opened the panel on the wall, and overrode the system, preventing the door from opening, then punched their floor.

Two... Her sleek cavern and smooth walls compressed around his engorged member. He fought his climax, wanting to wait until she was ready.

Three... His hands pulled aside her hair, and he buried his thirsty mouth in her neck. Her fingernails raked down over his sinewy back, then climbed to his shoulders, repeating the motion to his rhythm.

Four... His pelvis rocked perpetually against her swollen nub and the harder he ground, the more her muscles clamped around him.

Five... Her mind soared and whirled. There were no thoughts, no images. Complete blackness fueled her lascivious desires.

Six.... Tiny lights fired behind her closed eyes. She felt her grip tighten and heard his satisfied grunt as she urged his release. In an instant there was nothing. Then she felt like she was free-falling over the edge of a cliff. Pleasant, thrilling sensations spasmed over her, forcing her quivering body to relax.

Seven... His mouth clamped over hers, stifling her climatic moans as he pitched his hips upward, rolled onto his toes, and strained to reach her deepest recesses. The tip of his soft cap jerked and delivered jolts of his hot, satiny fluid inside her. She felt it punch her cervix as he growled with ecstasy into her throat.

Eight... His skilled hands maneuvered her pliable body into the cradle of his arms. She rested her head against his sculpted chest as the doors slid open and he carried her inside.

Under his breath, Aurick cursed as he set the phone back in its cradle. Three hours ago, the lines were restored, and he'd repeatedly attempted to reach Mercy with no answer. Gwen glanced up from her work.

"Mercy?" Instinctively, Gwen knew.

"Yeah." His fingers ran through his hair. In the previous four days, he had slept a total of six hours.

Tired lines and bags circled his eyes. He picked up the phone and dialed again.

T uesday, as Mercy entered the apartment, the phone rang. With her arms full, she scrambled to the dining room table, dropped her things, and rushed to the landline before it stopped.

"Hello?" She held her breath, hoping it would be Aurick.

When she answered, his unnecessary concern was replaced with relief. "Mercy? I've called a dozen times. Are you all right?"

His deep, velvety tone was sexy, causing a tingle along her spine. "Yes, I'm fine. After work, I went shopping. Is something wrong?"

Until now, he hadn't realized how much he missed her. "No, I thought I would check in and see if you're surviving without me," he flirted. "I tried your cell, but it went straight to voicemail."

"It died this afternoon, and I didn't have a charger with me." She shrugged out of her sweater, draping it over a chair, then kicked her shoes at the entrance.

"One second." He covered the phone and asked someone to leave.

His command thrilled her, eliciting an instant warm smile from her. He wanted to continue their conversation, and he required privacy to do so.

Then to her, he said. "Are you keeping busy?"

Caught off guard by their sudden contact, she neglected to erect the invisible barrier between them. At his question, she giggled. "How can I when seventy-five percent of my daily cleaning has disappeared?"

Relaxing his back against his chair, he chuckled. "Seventy-five percent? That's a big number."

His playful tone caused her to blush as she visualized his expression—his glimmering eyes, the curve of his mouth, the furrow of his brow. "You're a big man."

Her melodic voice soothed him and he yearned for more. "How are you filling the endless hours without me?"

"Sleeping, organizing, and working long hours. Catching up on things I've had to sideline because you're so demanding." She said with a small laugh.

Innocently, he pictured her putting the groceries away, walking back and forth. Her long, blonde hair would be loose, brushing over her shoulders as she moved.

He sexily smirked. "Sweetheart, I've yet to show you demanding."

Sweetheart, another shiver traveled down her back. And the promise of his latter words liquefied her abdomen. Physically, a million miles separated them and no harm would come from matching his banter. "Tell me more about these demands."

Until now, their conversations had been businesslike in nature and her sudden boldness ignited, then fanned heat through his veins. Briefly, the serious circumstances of his trip washed away, and he allowed himself to be in the moment.

His desire deepened his voice as he whispered. "What are you wearing?"

Her hand midway to the cupboard froze. She wanted this—the game; it had been too long since he'd touched her and too soon after her delightful fantasy. Could she risk this changing their relationship? Could she risk opening herself to him without being hurt when it ended?

Had the line disconnected? His throat cleared. "Mercy?"

Her tongue wet her lips. "A black, mid-thigh, silk slip with spaghetti straps." She bit her bottom lip, waiting for his response.

Blood rushed from his head southward, deliciously dizzying him. "Describe it."

She went into the living room and laid on the couch as she answered. "The back sharply vees to my waist and the front vees..." She didn't know how to finish it.

"... along the inside swell of your breasts?"

She stole a deep breath of his cologne from the fabric by her head. Her toes curled in response. "Yes." She sighed then embarrassed. She covered her mouth with her hand as her cheeks flamed.

"You sound tired. I'm sorry, let's save this discussion for another time." He offered her an excuse, and although disappointed, she accepted it.

She changed the subject. "I suppose I am. Have you finished the job or what?"

"Not yet, but I'm working on it. I would have called sooner, but the phone and power lines have been out." He admitted.

"Do you know when you'll be home?" She asked, continuing to inhale his tantalizing scent.

"Uncertain yet, soon I hope." He didn't want the conversation to end but knew it must. "I'll let you go so you can sleep. Good night, Mercy."

"Good night, Aurick." She twisted into the couch and closed her eyes, looking forward to her dreams.

He held the phone to his ear until the frantic, loud beeping alerted him he still gripped it. He hung up and thought of her words. *Do you know when you'll be home?* Home—a simple slip of her tongue, but it conjured emotions he didn't know he had. His mind drifted, and he nodded off.

Friday, Mercy reached home shortly after work, changed into a pair of designer jeans and a tan-colored top, then began preparing for tonight. Her efforts paid off. The atmosphere was inviting and informal. The dining room was dimly lit by the glow of candlesticks with the table decorated and set for five. She could hear the water boiling in the kitchen, and her stomach groaned as the smell of garlic bread and pasta sauce lingered. A log burned in the fireplace, further adding to the coziness while the air conditioner purred, keeping the room cool as heat emanated through the bay of windows.

The elevator sounded, and Mercy entered her code. It took only moments for first, Carmen, and Beverly, then Tom and Gordon, to step inside. The girls chattered as they explored the apartment while the men sat in the living room. When the tour ended, Mercy excused herself to finish preparing the meal.

She heard their conversation and every once in a while, one would yell a comment to her and she would respond. The overall feel was contagiously fun. She called them to the table as she sat with her back to the windows in the dining room, facing into the apartment. Leisurely, they ate while talking, teasing, and telling outrageous stories.

As time passed, the wine flowed and after opening a third bottle; the effects caused the group to talk louder with animation. She was enjoying the reprieve from her solitude and thoughts of Aurick.

Aurick glanced at Gwen in the passenger seat. The long hours and the uncomfortable flight back had drained her. In the span of seven days, he pressed his staff to the verge of exhaustion and passed it. He reveled in the challenge of a good contract negotiation and had fixed the labor issues, toured the facility, and talked to the dignitaries. They performed two weeks' worth of work in just over a week. He'd refused to accept any delays while he demanded a solution and manipulated the labor union to his will.

Aurick was tired, but the second he stepped from the jet, he felt invigorated. He ushered Gwen into his truck, impatient to see Mercy. Since their phone call, he had thought of little else. Often he replayed it, delighting in her openness and cheery demeanor. It sounded like she wanted to talk to him and maybe even missed him. He knew he missed her—her company, her voice, and admiring her whenever he wanted.

"Why are we stopping?" Gwen straightened and peered out the window as he put the truck in park.

"Flowers." He gestured as he exited, trotted to the street vendor, plucked a bunch, and returned.

"Oh, lord." Gwen rolled her eyes as he pulled back into traffic. "What's the occasion?"

"When we get back to the apartment, I'm going to tell her I'm in love with her." He revealed to his long-time friend. It had occurred to him a few days ago, after he talked to her, but had kept it to himself, mulling it over. Even if he had wanted to share it with Gwen, there had been scant opportunity to have a personal conversation in their cramped working conditions. "Opinions?"

"Pleased. If I wanted for anyone in my life to be happy, it would be you. You know that, but you're just going to blurt it out? Are you confident she'll respond well? From all our discussions, I'm under the impression that she's closed off to intimate relationships. What if you scare her?"

She worried about his approach. It didn't seem like a good idea. Evidently, someone or something had damaged the young woman, and even if Aurick didn't want to accept it, she could turn tail and run faster than he could blink.

She tried again. "If this was a company you were trying to obtain, you wouldn't go off half-cocked without learning all there was to know. Even if you think you know her, does she know you?" She put the questions for him to contemplate, then settled back in her seat.

"After I tell her, I'll persuade her." He winked at her with a devilish grin and it dimpled his chin, now uncertain in his decision.

"Cute. Use that dimple too. You're gonna need all the help you can get." She chuckled, then closed her eyes.

In silence, they traveled the remainder of the drive as Aurick thought about what he would say to Mercy. As he pulled under the awning, he envisioned her enthusiastic reaction, and he could already feel her warmth in his arms. He handed the keys to security and helped Gwen to the elevator. Tonight was going to be special, a night he would never forget. He was confident in her reaction. When the elevator stopped at Gwen's, she brushed his cheek goodnight and wished him luck.

Before the elevator door opened, Aurick's heart dropped. He heard laughter and voices, realizing she wasn't alone and his plans were thwarted. He hesitated a second with the flowers in hand and straightened his tie as the doors opened, then stepped into the entrance. Unnoticed, Aurick took in the scene as four others besides Mercy sat at the table exchanging loud laughter. A radiant glow emanated from her face as it twisted in giggles, and she fought to regain control. The sound was exquisite, and he wanted it to continue.

Mercy's eyes watered and she tried to blink away the tears of laughter. Her gaze swung to Aurick standing beyond the room. She blinked again, wondering if her mind was playing tricks. He wasn't expected back until the beginning of next week. She tried to erase his form from her imagination as her oblivious guests continued their conversation. Her heart stalled, then leaped into a ragingly furious noise as she realized she wasn't fantasizing. The voices around her faded as she fixated on him. It took everyone a few moments to realize she was staring off into the darkness and they turned curiously. All quieted as Mercy rounded the table.

"Don't let me interrupt," Aurick commanded as she reached him. Jealousy flowed through him as his jaw jumped and he grasped Mercy's hand. "Excuse us for a minute." He pulled her behind him into the living room, away from the others, as Tom attempted to cover the awkwardness by telling another story.

Speechlessly, Mercy followed. For days, she had wished him here and now he was. His unexpected arrival caused a warm giddiness. After leaving their audience behind, Aurick abruptly turned, propelling her body forward into his solid length as he wrapped his arms around her and bent his head to savor her lips.

The touch of his muscular arms and the pressure of his mouth were more intoxicating than the wine she had consumed. His masculine scent and cologne consumed her. She joined her tongue to his, but he ended the embrace almost as soon as it began, leaving her disappointed and needing more.

After he let her go, he combed his hand through his hair in frustration and stepped back to look at her. "You look gorgeous." He uttered, lifting the flowers between them.

"I wasn't expecting you so soon. I hadn't heard from you." She rambled as she accepted the flowers and sniffed, inhaling their fragrance, hoping they would help regulate her quickening heart.

Irritated, his evening was spoiled, his voice was sharper than he meant. "I can see you weren't expecting me." Hoping to lighten his first remark, he added. "You have company." Restlessly, he fidgeted, wanting more than anything to take her in his arms and seduce her.

"It's just my cousin Carmen and my friend Beverly with their boyfriends. We're finishing dinner and I'm certain they will understand if I ask them to leave." The alcohol shed her inhibitions as she reached her hand out to caress his arm, craving the physical contact he could offer her.

"No," he shook his head. "Don't bother. I'm tired." He lied. "I was planning an early night, anyway. I only interrupted to give you the flowers and to say hi." He lifted the hand resting on his arm, kissed its palm, and dropped it to her side.

"Are you sure?" Her eyes watered, and she swallowed her sudden disappointment. She wanted him to demand her attention after their lengthy separation. "It really isn't any trouble."

"It's fine." He turned, removed his jacket, loosened his tie, and started to unbutton his shirt as he strode toward the hallway. His heart sank. He preferred his original plan, but it would be impolite and overbearing to make her company leave.

"Aurick." Her voice broke as she softly called, and he angled his body to glance over his shoulder. "I missed you." She stammered, uncertain how he would receive her admission.

"I know." A boyish grin lightened his expression, and he winked. His self-control waned, seeing her vulnerability. Before it snapped, he left her there. It would only postpone the unavoidable—her return to the dinner party. He didn't know if he would have the strength to let her go a second time.

She ran her fingertips under her eyes and plied a bright smile as she re-joined her guests. Though they attempted to restore the light-hearted nature of earlier, Mercy's withdrawn gaze and quietness made it impossible. An hour later, they left, declaring the late hour.

Leaving the cleaning for the morning, Mercy turned out the lights and wandered down the hallway to her room. Outside Aurick's bedroom door, she stopped to listen for any sound indicating he was still awake. After a few moments of silence, she shut herself inside her own room and got ready for bed.

During the long week of separation, she accepted the fact her feelings were building. She hadn't pinpointed what they were exactly, but while he was gone, she had felt lost. When he appeared tonight abruptly, her emotional reaction had taken her aback, and she regretted the shortness of their embrace. She needed time to consider both.

Turning out the bedside lamp, Aurick stripped and climbed into bed. Intently, he listened to the group, trying hard to catch the sound of Mercy's voice, but she seldom spoke. When he heard them leave, he contemplated getting dressed and re-joining her but decided against it. She had revealed she missed him, and he felt like a jerk for not responding in kind. He realized the courage it took for her to admit it, and repeatedly, he replayed her sweet words over in his mind.

When she moved down the hallway, he saw her feet shadow under the door as she stood outside. Silently, he pleaded for her to turn the knob or knock. He held his breath in anticipation, but she moved into her room, closed the door, and literally shut him out. He fell into a dreamless sleep, soothed by his love and her words, he slept soundly.

CHAPTER 9

You Said Nothing

Aurick woke with a start—remembering where he was and eager to see her. First things first; he needed a shower. He lathered his hands, running them over his length as water cascaded down his bronzed body. He thought about the previous night, whether it was sleep deprivation or exhaustion, he realized Gwen was right. His plan had been terrible. He needed to devote more time to Mercy, making her more comfortable, before he disclosed his feelings and she hightailed it out of his life.

He dressed in blue jeans and a white t-shirt, then plagued by his thoughts and needing physical activity; he cleaned the kitchen. With the task completed, he cooked breakfast. Bacon sizzled, potatoes fried, and he was stirring the scrambled eggs when Mercy emerged, rubbing her eyes innocently like a child. Her hair was a tangled mess and her nightgown rumpled from a good night's sleep. His lips tingled, wanting to kiss her into submission.

"Coffee's ready." He grinned down at her as he removed a cup from the cupboard and handed it to her. "Breakfast is almost done. Sit and talk to me while I finish up?"

"Smells delicious." She leaned her head against his upper arm as she poured the strong coffee. His muscles jumped under her face and she straightened. "Did you sleep well?" She asked as she seated herself at the table, watching him at the stove. Freely, she admired every contour—his toned thighs, his firm, tight ass, and his athletic back. The view was extremely satisfying.

"Better than I have in days." He shrugged as he approached, placing the two plates down. He smiled and settled into the seat beside her. "What are your plans for today?"

"Housework I suppose." The apartment needed no cleaning, but there was little else to occupy her day. They ate the rest of their meal in relaxed silence.

She walked her plate to the sink and poured herself another coffee. "What time are you going to work?" Her eyes turned as he stood.

"I'm not." He stepped to where she was, brushing his shoulder against hers as he held out his cup for her to refill. "I thought we could spend the day together, take in some sights and relax a bit. It's been a long week." Lightly, he ran his palm down her arm as he sipped from the mug she handed back.

"I like your plan better." She smiled, stepping backward to end the contact. His size dwarfed the kitchen and his closeness overwhelmed her good sense. Her movement didn't go unnoticed, but he didn't comment.

Playfully, he shoved her out of the kitchen with a laugh. "Get ready while I tidy up this mess, again."

She went to her room and called her parents' home, informing her mother's nurse she wouldn't be stopping by today.

On this particular morning, traffic was heavy as Aurick maneuvered her sedan through the crowded streets. The sun, exceptionally intense and hot, heated the buildings and vehicles, causing near-invisible waves to radiate from them. The radio's quiet melodic tune played in the background and the air conditioning cooled their skin as they shared the events of the previous week. When they pulled into the parking lot of West Edmonton Mall, she righted her denim shorts and smoothed out her pink tank top as he circled and gripped her hand.

"I don't want to lose you in the horde of people." He winked. "Have you ventured here since you moved to Edmonton?" She shook her head, and he continued. "It boasts being one of the largest malls in North America. It employs some twenty-three thousand, includes more than eight hundred stores, and is visited by over one-hundred-thousand people daily. Let's go see." He rattled off the few facts he'd looked up earlier to impress her.

Entering the mall through the ground-level entrance, several stores lined the hallway, but he paid them little attention as he admired the huge ship jutting out in front of them. It was a model of Christopher Columbus' Santa Maria. The largest ship from his first voyage was intricately detailed with carved railings, stained dark sides, and painted to appear centuries old. He lifted his hand to her waist, steering her to a security railing for a closer view. Upon closer inspection, it was more juvenile than he had first thought, but nevertheless, a sight to see in the middle of a mall.

He threaded her fingers with his and strolled past the stores and booths. The striking differences between the shops impressed him. Almost anything a consumer wanted to purchase was housed somewhere in the miniature, independent city-like structure.

When she lived with her parents, Mercy had haunted the mall and knew the layout well. Opposite from where they entered, better than a mile away, the posh and chic stores were located and she needed to ensure they didn't get that far in their tour, in case someone was to recognize her. The flow of bodies made it virtually impossible to get anywhere with any speed, but she didn't mind as she listened to his observations and enjoyed the possessive touch of his warm palm.

As they passed the underwater sea life caverns—housing more than one-hundred species of amphibians, fish, and reptiles—music played to announce an upcoming show. At one point, it had been a dolphin show, but now it was California Sea Lions. He purchased tickets, and the two weaved their way down to sit in the bleachers.

Periodically, he would brush her leg with his as he watched the seals perform their tricks. Since she had seen the performance before, she focused inwardly. She was a little disappointed that the intimate embrace from last night hadn't amounted to anything further this morning. She'd been pleased when he suggested they spend the day together but was further disheartened when he brought her to the crowded mall. *He's acting the perfect gentleman when all I want is for him to manipulate me.* She thought as they exited the stands.

Further, into the mall, they wandered, stopping to admire the booths displaying an array of products. Eventually, they arrived at the Ice Palace, a small ice rink in the center of the building. Many stood staring through the glass as two professional skaters mastered their routine. To the wonder of the crowd, the male threw his female partner in the air and caught her, showing off their precision. Unequivocal trust between them was obvious as he maneuvered her into spins and tricks. Mercy faked a shiver as she stood beside Aurick, then eyed him, waiting for a response.

"Cold?" He took the bait she set out for him.

She applauded herself while she smiled up at him and lied sweetly. "A little. I didn't plan for this chill in the summer heat. Maybe it's because it looks cold." Her laugh trilled as she rested her head on his shoulder.

"I didn't bring a coat. Want to leave?" He eyed her skeptically. It was the flimsiest excuse he had ever heard. *Cold in July? Indoors?* He wanted to laugh. He preferred to hold her but was enjoying her coy little scheme too much to give in.

"No." She turned back to the window to gaze at the skaters. "I love watching them, skimming over the ice. It's magical." She sighed. *Well, come on, take the hint. What are you thinking?* She darted him a glance as he moved away, shifting himself to stare at her.

He was smirking and his chin dimple was showing as he crossed his arms over his chest.

"Seriously." Embarrassed, Mercy pouted with a nervous smile, knowing he had caught her. "You're going to let me freeze?"

"Pretty much." He laughed. "Let's go."

He seized her hand, urging her to follow as he re-traced their steps. They left the cool confines of the crowded building for the heat-ravished parking lot and it was a relief when they climbed inside the car. As they drove away, the music from the radio was louder, covering the awkward silence between them. Each left wondering what the other was thinking.

The blistering sun beat down on the streets, the temperature peaking at the height of the day. It was almost two in the afternoon and there wasn't a cloud in the sky to be seen. It wasn't long before Aurick parked and led her down the sidewalk towards Churchill Square. It didn't dawn on Mercy until she saw the immense crowds milling around that the Street Performer's Festival was taking place. Acrobats, mimes, musicians, clowns, and dancers were performing all over the grounds while children with balloons and animals almost ran freely as excitement filled the air. They sauntered through the crowds while they gazed at the various performances, but they scarcely registered, as both were absorbed in their thoughts. *What had happened?* She wondered at this abrupt change in his attitude.

They strolled with no destination in mind as he silently debated broaching the subject of their feelings. When they came to several deserted trees, he let go of her hand, walked a few paces, and turned to meet her. His intense eyes examined her. "We need to talk." He feared this discussion would scare her back behind her wall, but he couldn't hold it off any longer, tired of playing games. *I'm too old for this,* he muttered to himself.

"About?" Puzzled, she asked. She felt her internal barrier rising, and he saw it as her cheerful expression shifted to one of reservation.

"About that, that right there!" He pointed at her. "One minute you're giddy and bantering with me, but the second anything happens between us you close off, like a faucet." He accused, running his hands through his hair to draw it back from his face in irritation, then dropped them to his sides. "I want to talk about what's going on. I want to know where you stand and I want you to know where I stand."

"I don't know what you're talking about." She crossed her arms, gripping her sides with her fingers, her face blank as she glanced away, feigning interest in her surroundings to escape his searching stare. She wasn't ready to voice her feelings.

"Don't!" He ordered her, his harsh tone forced her head to snap back to him. "Stop hiding behind that wall of pretended self-pity and righteousness. You told me you missed me last night. Did you forget or are you going to blame the liquor?" His voice raised, commanding her to answer. When she didn't respond right away, he grasped her upper arm.

"No, I remember." She quietly started, then cleared her throat and hissed accusingly. "I remember I said it and you said nothing." She jerked her arm out of his hold and took a couple of steps backward. "You want to talk about walls! The only emotion you've offered me is lust. Do you want to hear me admit it? I want you? Is that it? Okay, I do. You want me to spread my legs in the grass so you can go at it? Get it out of our system? No feelings, no emotion, just sex? Tell me, is that it?" Her voice shook as she finished, and he could see her struggling with her emotions, but his anger was stronger than his desire to comfort her.

"No!" He barked at her, his temper and frustration almost out of control, as a neighboring musician began playing noisily. "I want you to admit that somewhere inside, you indeed have feelings. And *maybe*— after the time we've spent apart, you might have some for me. Dammit! Is that so hard for you? Do you prefer to play games? Like the act at the ice rink, work me into your plans, then condemn me afterward, like I caused the entire situation? I will not be your marionette. Tell me or show me what you want! I'm tired of pretending there is nothing between us. I'm tired of playing make-believe–" He was interrupted as a little hand tugged on his and he glanced down to discover a small child with long red unruly curls openly staring at him, an enormous smile of welcome on her face.

The child's huge blue eyes inspected his expression as innocently, she asked. "Why you tired of playing? Your mind isn't good to think of new games? I'm good, I can show you."

Struck by the child's innocence, he stooped down, forgetting his anger and the conversation he was having with Mercy. No older than four, the girl wore filthy, torn white stockings with no shoes and a red dress uncomfortably too small for her. Aurick's eyes scanned the surrounding crowd, searching for anyone who might be frantically looking for her but saw no one.

As he surveyed the vicinity, Mercy stepped closer and kneeled down beside her. "I'm Mercy." The child pivoted her focus. "What's your name?" She noticed how skinny and dirty the young girl was.

Her youthful eyes twinkled with friendliness. "Bethany. Want to get a balloon?" Her smiling face became serious. "But you got to pay, I got no money." She stated matter-of-factly.

"Bethany," Aurick said to draw her attention. "Do you have a last name? Your parents are probably searching for you." He raised his eyebrow.

"Bethany Harper." Then she snickered. "No silly, my dad don't walk so he won't find me. Want to get some cotton candy?"

"Okay." He scooped the girl into his arms and put out his hand for Mercy to accept. "Watch for the police or anyone who looks like they are hunting for her. Which way for food?"

He bought her a hot dog, a juice box, and a bag of cotton candy, then promised with a smile. "After you eat your hot dog, can you show me where your father is? And I'll give you the cotton candy as a prize." Patiently, he reasoned.

"Okay." The girl flopped down on the ground with the hot dog in one hand and juice in the other, while they continued to scan the neighboring crowd. After a few moments, Aurick spotted a mounted police officer, and after signaling his plan to Mercy, he strode away.

The officer sat on his horse, observing the throngs from a distance while Aurick approached him. "Beautiful day." The official spoke. "What can I do for you?"

"That girl there." He pointed to where Mercy sat chatting with the girl as she danced around in front of her. "She says her name is Bethany Harper and–"

"That's Bethany Harper all right." The officer nodded.

Aurick was surprised when the man confirmed the child's identity. "Is she missing? Is that how you know her name?"

"No, she belongs to a homeless family who keeps illegally camping over on the other side of the park. This is my usual beat so I've had a few run-ins with them." He wavered, then continued. "Sad story... Her father lost his legs when a drunk driver struck him and because of it, he lost his job. His wife works to support them, but you know how it goes—she doesn't make nearly enough. After the accident, they lost their home to a fire and had no insurance. Now they live out of the back of their van and a tent." He shrugged his shoulders. "They seem like good enough people, not addicts or criminals, just down on their luck. Bethany is constantly wandering around bothering folks." He pointedly questioned. "Want me to get rid of her for you?"

"No, I don't. Point me in the camp's direction." He demanded the information. The officer gestured and Aurick stalked off to get the girls aggravated by the man's question. When he reached them, the girl dropped to the ground, giggling. He put his hand out and Bethany entwined her fingers with his. He pulled her up to stand, and she reached her other for Mercy's hand, smiling as she accepted. The girl chattered as she walked and Mercy listened to her stories, injecting commentary when required. Aurick didn't interrupt as his eyes searched for the van and once he located it, he altered their general direction.

When they came around the back of the van, a man was sitting on the ground and was desperately struggling—without the benefit of his lower legs—to get into a battered old wheelchair. Without help, he was having a very tough time performing his task. Aurick noted his clothes were much like Bethany's, while she scrambled to his side.

"Let me help papa." The young girl clutched his arm and, with all her strength, sought to hoist him into his chair without success.

The man's expression was stern as he looked at her. "I don't need help getting into my wheelchair if you're here. I was going to search for you. You can't just run off by yourself. Your sister is sleeping, and it isn't easy for me to come find you. Someone could take you and I would never see you again. You need to be careful."

"No one taked me, papa, they did." She pointed to the couple, drawing her father's attention to them. "They got me hot dog, juice, and my prize cotton candy." She ran to Aurick, snatching the bag from his grip. "You promised." Her eyes grew big as she looked up at Aurick and backed away to show her father. "See, I'm back!" She chimed musically.

Bethany's father eyed Aurick with his fancy hair and his clean, expensive clothes, then shifted his gaze to the beautiful woman at his side. His pride drove him to sit a little taller on the ground as he spoke. "Thanks for returning her. Eventually, I would have found her. It would have taken me some time."

Aurick recognized the man's pride and admired him for having any at all under these conditions. "Mind if I relax with you while my..." he considered an explanation. "My girlfriend takes your girls for a walk. I'm tired of watching these performers and could use a peaceful break." He worded it so it would seem the man was doing him a favor.

"It's a free world, but she doesn't have to take them." He stated as he wearily watched Mercy.

"If she doesn't, she and the girls will stick around and there will be no peace. It would be a waste of a decent quiet spot." Aurick offered.

"I can't roam around the festival alone. I'll have no one to appreciate it with." Mercy threw her sentiment in with his as she grabbed Bethany's hand and reached for the sleeping child. "It's really no trouble, and I'll be back in thirty minutes. You can keep him as collateral." She grinned and winked at the man, then turned, taking his silence for approval.

After the girls disappeared, Aurick studied the battered vehicle. It was rusted through with holes. He doubted it ran well, judging from the puddle underneath it. As a family of four, it'd be cramped quarters. He sat on the sidewalk next to the man and darted a quick glance at him, then away. "Are you going to lie in the street all day, or are you going to let me help you get into your chair?"

"Whatever satisfies you," the man leaned back on his elbows. He maintained eye contact as Aurick stood and lifted him into the chair. "Name's Ben Harper, you?"

He sat on the curb. "Aurick Spencer. Pleased to meet you." He extended his hand.

Ben chuckled as he gripped it. "Because it's every day you want to interact with a homeless cripple?"

"Now that you mention it, it does seem like an odd hobby to have." He pretended to ponder. "It's more her hobby than mine." He smiled.

The men idly conversed until Aurick was satisfied. "Can I ask about your situation?"

The man crossed his arms over his chest. "A drunk

driver ended my career and put me in this chair." He shrugged, seemingly unaffected by it. "My wife got a job, but the pay wasn't enough to cover two children and a household. We sold what we could and let a few things lapse, including our insurance. At the time, it didn't seem like such a huge deal until one night our house burned down." He smiled with a distant expression, absorbed in the memory. "We're grateful we all survived and still have this van."

"There must be government programs you can apply for?"

He nodded. "Sure, but there are people worse off than we are. Leave it for those who truly need it."

Aurick didn't understand his positive manner and generosity. He wasn't certain he'd have the same attitude if their roles were reversed. "What type of work does your wife do?"

"Right now she works at a Timmy's," Ben said.

Aurick told the man about his apartment building, Gwen's relentless desire to have someone oversee it, and ended by confessing reliable staff were tough to find.

Ben recognized the man's intention and rejected it, but it only took Aurick a few minutes to persuade him.

"If my wife found out I refused your help, she would probably leave me. This has taken a toll on our children and it's hard to see my family go without."

"Don't consider it charity because it isn't. It's a matter of the right place at the right time." Aurick shrugged as he scribbled the address. "I require someone to look after the building and haven't had time to fill the position. I can be an excessively demanding employer. The hours could be very long and sporadic as situations arise. In a few months, you and your family could grow to despise me. This position would come with accommodations so she could be accessible whenever she's needed." He handed the note to Ben and excused himself to make a phone call.

Mercy waddled through the crowds back to the van, the toddler in her arms becoming increasingly heavy with every step. Bethany gave up holding her hand and hopped merrily ahead, singing all the way. As they came into sight, Aurick noticed Mercy struggling to hold the girl. He lifted the child from her arms and gently laid her back down in the van. When he finished, he kneeled to talk to Bethany.

"It was nice meeting you." He stuck his hand out to her, and she quizzically studied at it. "You're expected to shake it." He gripped hers, then jiggled her arm furiously, and she giggled happily. The couple said their goodbyes and started back towards their vehicle with their fingers interlaced.

After a few minutes, Mercy asked. "Did you give him money?"

"No." He provided no explanation.

"No! What do you mean, no? I assumed that was the reason I took the girls away?" She couldn't believe his words. *How heartless do you have to be not to give them money?*

He stopped and shifted so she could look at him, his face serious. "He wouldn't have accepted it, anyway. The man still has pride, as ridiculous as it sounds."

She thought about it. "I suppose you're right. His pride is all he has left. But..." She pulled his hand to walk again. "I put forty dollars in Bethany's pocket, so at least she'll find that."

"I wouldn't have expected less from you." He grinned down at her as they reached the vehicle. "Dinner?"

"Starving." She waited until he started the motor. "Home?"

"You bet." Still grinning, he winked, then pulled into traffic. She leaned back in her seat, exhausted from their day, both emotionally and physically.

Later that evening, while Aurick laid on the couch watching television and Mercy read a book, the intercom buzzed. Gwen informed him there was an issue in the lobby which required his attention. He knew it meant the Harpers had arrived, and he intended to surprise Mercy with the news.

"Join me?" He eyed her from the elevator door as he pressed the button.

"Why?" Tired from their excursion, the thought of moving from her comfortable, relaxed position didn't appeal to her.

"Because you want to come with me?" Sending her a knowing look, he teased her into accepting.

"Yeah." She stretched and approached him as he held the elevator. "Because the lobby is *so* interesting." She answered with a smirk and stepped inside, then rested her back against his chest.

When the doors opened, Mercy was pleasantly shocked to discover the family standing by the elevator, waiting with Gwen. Aurick held her against him as he backed against the far wall. The family shuffled inside as Gwen entered a code and pushed the numbers for apartment two-oh-one.

"Did you find it okay?" Aurick addressed Ben, the younger of the two girls sleeping soundly on his lap.

"Yeah, it was easy enough. This is my wife, Thelma." He presented his wife, who was carrying a sleeping Bethany, as the elevator opened and they exited.

"This is your apartment. If not before—see you Monday morning." Gwen pushed the button for Aurick's apartment before she followed the Harpers out. The doors closed, and the couple was alone again.

"Why didn't you tell me this afternoon?" Mercy shifted in his arms to look at him.

He loosely held her. "Give a man a fish... I could have offered him money, further depleting his dignity and merely helping them in the short term." The doors opened. He pushed her into the apartment and down the hall towards the bedroom. "Instead, I offered his wife a job here and told him it came with an apartment. Hopefully, they can save up enough someday to purchase another home." He pushed her through the door of her bedroom, then turned and opened his own. "Good night Mercy."

She came into the hallway and watched as his door shadowed the hall as he started to close it. "Thank you." Her words stopped him and he peered out.

"I didn't do it for you." He shrugged. "They needed help, and I was able. End of story, good night."

For a second time, his door moved, and she called. "Aurick?" He stuck his head out again.

"Yeah?" He waited for her excuse for the delay, a grin still fixed on his face. "Did you need something?"

"Well." Suddenly uncertain, she looked at her feet and hunted for the appropriate words to use as she moved towards his door. "Earlier today, you suggested all I had to do was tell you..." He opened it wide, and she shuffled into the doorway with her eyes still averted. She whispered, "... what I want."

"And." His tone invited her as he placed his fingertips on her chin, raising her eyes to meet his. "What is it?" He rested his other palm on the side of her neck and her pulse leaped under his thumb.

"Could you kiss me good night?" She stepped closer, and she splayed her fingers across his chest.

"Try again." He mumbled into her mouth as her lips settled on his. "Tell me, don't ask."

She groaned, then asserted. "Kiss me now dammit."

His lips fluttered over hers for a few seconds, their lips meeting and retracting several times. But before the kiss consumed them and he lost control, he backed her away from him, disentangling her arms from his nape. He kissed her forehead and deliberately backed her out of his room.

"Good night, Mercy." He pecked her mouth, then closed and locked the door. He knew if she approached him again tonight, it wouldn't end with kissing, and he realized it could ruin everything.

"Good night, Aurick." She whispered as she closed her own door and locked it behind her. She couldn't trust her hunger if he came to her in the night and she knew she wouldn't turn him away. Mercy wondered if it happened. Would she regret it?

CHAPTER 10

Did You Appreciate My Performance?

SEPTEMBER

The powder blue empire-waisted, floor-length dress swished around her bare feet when she left her bedroom in search of Aurick. The morning's warm sun played through the windows as she walked down the two stairs into the living room.

At the same time, he rounded the other corner and came down into the room, carrying two mugs of coffee. His easy smile fluttered her heart when he stopped at the coffee table and waited for her. His eyes raked her figure as she appreciated his taut muscles pushed against the well-tailored business suit.

While still holding the cups, he opened his arms. "Come here."

She needed no more invitation, gliding across the floor. She pressed her body against his as she lifted onto her toes and settled her lips over his mouth.

He pulled back before passion could heat either of them and whispered. "Lipstick?"

"On you?" She laughed as she took the coffee from his hand, then sidestepped him. She shifted her black kimono cardigan as she settled down onto the couch.

"Yeah. I'd appreciate it if you would warn me when I'm smeared with it. Gwen's been having a field day with her teasing." He pulled up his pant leg as he sat next to her, their shoulders and thighs brushing against each other.

Her laughing eyes met his. "I'm not wearing any yet."

His brow arched as he placed his mug on the table. "Really?" One of his hands took her cup as the other pushed her hair over her shoulder.

After he set it down, both of his hands cupped her face and his lips dipped to taste hers again.

Playfully, her brows furrowed. "What are you doing?"

"Taking advantage of your nakedness." His thumb pulled her chin down, opening her mouth, and his tongue swept inside. For several seconds, he drank from her, drugging her with his devastating kiss.

When his hands fell and slid inside her cardigan—wrapping her waist and pulling her closer—her hands pushed at his chest. His mouth trailed over her cheek to her throat.

Her toes curled into the carpet, as delicious shivers ran down her spine. "We don't have time for this."

His breath rushed over her ear as he whispered. "I can make time."

Unwillingly, her hands curled into his jacket. "As much as I want to, I can't."

"Quit and I'll pay you more. We'd have all the time we need."

The mention of their arrangement punched her gut, dousing the building heat in her body instantly. She wouldn't let him see how much the reference affected her. "Tempting." She pushed him away, picked up her coffee and turned on the television. "Plans this evening?"

"None." He settled his back against the couch and planted his hand on her thigh as they watched the news.

Fifteen minutes later, the intercom buzzed and hand-in-hand; they took the elevator down. He guided Mercy to her vehicle, kissed her, then went to his own, where Gwen waited in the passenger seat.

Blushing, Mercy smiled at her cell and typed a flirtatious reply.

"Earth to Mercy?" Carmen snapped her fingers.

"Huh?" Her eyes darted from her device to her girlfriends, where they lounged in the makeshift lunch room. Her expression flashed with guilt as she laid it face down on the table. "I'm sorry. What were you saying?"

Her two friends shared a concerned look. Then Beverly shrugged. "Nothing of great importance. How's Aurick?"

She answered the question literally, hoping to avoid a franker discussion. "He's running late and wondered if I preferred he ride home with Gwen instead of waiting to pick him up."

The straight-shooter, in their friendship, would not be sidestepped so easily. "Not what I meant. We need to talk." Carmen nodded, showing her solidarity as Beverly took a deep breath, and then continued. "I feel like this is all my fault. I pointed out how you keep people at arm's length. And from where I'm sitting, it seems you've decided to prove me wrong. You're completely invested in this relationship built on lies. We don't want to see you hurt. What happens when he finds out?"

Defensive, her tone was sharp. "I'm not *completely invested*. We aren't sleeping together." Both had taken many a cold shower to douse the passion they created in each other. Aurick hadn't pressured her, and she was too afraid of her emotions to give in.

The concern in their expressions weakened Mercy's voice. She wrapped her arms around herself and leaned back in her chair for support. "I've tried to tell him—several times. When we're alone, cuddled on the couch, and he's telling me outrageous, personal stories about his life, his friends, and his family. I try, but the courage evades me. I've rehearsed every word and contemplated his every possible reaction."

Carmen moved to her side and rested a hand on her shoulder. "The longer you wait, the harder it will get."

"What if, after telling him, he ends this?" She shook her head, dismissing the dreadful thought, then admitted. "I think I'm in love with him."

Beverly reasoned. "What if he falls in love with you? Or what if he finds out the truth before you tell him? What if the next time he enters this building, he finds you?"

"I don't know." What could she say? Her friends were right. Every scenario she ran through in her head ended badly. How could she tell him who she was and confess without him ending their relationship? She needed more time to figure this out.

"Hey there." His deep voice answered the phone as he sent Gwen scurrying out of the office with a flip of his hand.

"Hey yourself." Mercy leaned back in her chair as she took a much-needed rest from the figures laying on the desk in front of her. "I saw your text. What's up?"

"Travel with me?" His tone sent a wave of anticipation through her as she envisioned his mouth just below her ear. Her toes curled of their own volition.

"Sounds tantalizing." She playfully responded with a light laugh. "Keep talking."

"I need to be away for a few days, and it would please me if you would come. It would require you to take a day off from work." His voice pleaded with her to agree.

She twisted in her chair to see Connie entering the offices. She held her finger up to halt her. "Which day?" She grinned into the phone. "I would need to take the ninth off?" She repeated his words. Her boss spun the calendar, considered the date, and nodded her approval as she continued through to her own office.

Mercy sighed. "I don't know. I think I need to hear more before I make such an enormous request. Convince me?"

In a hoarse whisper, he obliged. "It would be easier in person. Then I could run my tongue along your silky shoulder and suckle the spot below your ear. Let me take you somewhere romantic, where you'll beg me to worship you for hours."

She giggled, her voice astonished. "Hours?" She giggled, her voice astonished. "Could you even?"

"With the right motivation, absolutely."

"Okay, I'll go." Then she listened to something he said. "No, Connie walked through the office as you asked me and she gave me the go-ahead to take it off. See you tonight." She laughed as she ended the call. She returned her focus to work. The fundraiser was on the twenty-third and numerous tasks still needed finishing before the event.

s their journey ended, Aurick, Mercy, and Gwen drove under a thick canopy of woven branches heavily laden with leaves along the driveway. Luscious green hills surrounded the massive colonial dwelling like a warm emerald blanket, and forest green vines of ivy cascaded down the residence's four pillars. Elaborate flowerbeds and shrubs made beautiful displays on either side of the veranda in every color. The effect was breathtaking as Mercy emerged from the car to appreciate the surroundings.

"You two go on in and I'll grab the suitcases." Aurick popped the trunk and began removing their belongings.

"Okay, I'll meet you in the study in about an hour, Aurick. I want to freshen up a bit before you put me to work." Gwen started up the stairs as an older man opened the door and descended them, passing her without a word.

"Let me bring those suitcases, sir." He reached for the first bag as Aurick left them to join Mercy.

"Let me give you a tour. It's an incredible house." Grasping her hand, he noted the excitement in her eyes as he pulled her up the stairs.

They entered through French doors into a magnificent foyer with a vaulted ceiling, a crystal chandelier, and a grandfather clock. An expensive Spanish carpet covered the hardwood floor leading to an enormous curved staircase carpeted in burgundy and railed with dark walnut in the room's center.

Aurick turned right into an extensive library where books adorned two walls, ceiling to floor. Another wall had a few small windows showcasing the manicured lawns and the other a stone gray fireplace. Without design, various green loveseats, and armchairs were placed. Animal furs, turned rugs, littered the hardwood floor. The mood was rather cozy and

Mercy could visualize herself, blanket-wrapped, in an oversized armchair reading.

"That door." He pointed to the back of the room. "Is the office and that door beside it is a small washroom, but I'll show you those later." He turned them around, retracing their steps.

Back in the foyer, they continued straight through into an elegantly set dining room. A grand table for twelve laden with white china and large candle sticks dominated the space. Another set of doors opened outside and Mercy peered through to view the beautiful veranda surrounded by one of the flower beds she had noted when they arrived.

"That door," he gestured at the far left side of the room, "is the kitchen, if you need anything. Another small bathroom is inside. If you choose to go riding or muck around in the garden, it's where you wash up."

He whisked her back to the foyer and up a winding staircase. "Come on. Let me show you where you'll be staying." Once above, they crossed a door on the left, Aurick explained. "Gwen's." Then another. "The main bath."

He went through an opening and pulled her in behind him. A giant four-poster bed, shrouded in mint green and rich brown pillows, stood centered under three open windows as a gentle breeze blew the curtains. Fresh-cut flowers adorned a small table encompassed by two chairs. A massive oak bureau spanned one wall, and a delicate vanity in a corner completed the room.

"This is it. Do you like it?" He smiled as his gaze gauged her reaction.

Her eyes shimmered with awe. "It's perfect."

"There's a small bathroom through there." He

pointed. "You can freshen up. There are matters I must attend to. I'll be in the office. Do you remember where it is?"

She nodded as he planted his hands on either side of her face and dropped a kiss on her forehead. When he stepped into the hallway, Mercy called after him. "Aurick? What kind of business do you have here?"

"Family business. It's my parents' home. My father's in sugar." His mouth lifted into the chin dimpling grin, and his tone was cheerful and innocent. "Did I neglect to mention that?"

"Your parents? Do you mean your parent's own *Spencer Sugar*? They're sugar barons? You're a billionaire? You know damn well you failed to mention it." Her eyes leaped in irritation. "I wouldn't have come." Her mind reeled. She was standing in his parents' home. It was apparent he trusted her, felt something for her. But—he had no idea he was living with a stranger, and at this point, a liar. What initially had started as a way to distinguish herself from society was becoming more complicated by the second. *How can I stay and not tell him? How do you tell him here, in his parents' home?*

Aurick returned to stand in front of her. "My parents are billionaires, not me. I'm making a name for myself without them. I know you wouldn't have come, but what does it matter? You're here to be my companion, as agreed upon. Can you try to enjoy yourself?" His hands trapped her arms and trailed upwards to her shoulders, where he ran his fingers through her hair and dropped his mouth on hers to smother her annoyance with his lips. He had known she wouldn't have come if she had found out beforehand. That's why he hadn't told her. He needed more time for them to get to know one another and being far away in a place she didn't know without distractions would allow them it.

Mercy enjoyed his slow drugging kiss, and she forgot her displeasure over the span of the few seconds. Her heart pounded in her ears and her body drifted closer, pressing against his while her hands circled his neck. His lips responded to her invitation as he ran his palms down her back and settled them tenderly on her backside. Neither heard Gwen enter.

"Aurick, your parents are here. They're pulling in now." Gwen interrupted, and the couple dragged themselves apart.

His eyes stayed on Mercy. "Okay, thanks. I better go greet them." He planted a demanding kiss on her lips before leaving.

When the two girls were alone, Mercy demanded. "Did you know we were coming here?"

"Of course." Gwen regarded the girl's accusing expression for a second, then realized. "But you didn't? Oh, my..." Her exasperated voice filled the room. Of all the hare-brained schemes Aurick had contrived, this one took the cake. "He didn't tell you? What an underhanded thing to do."

Believing the other woman innocent, she sighed. "I believe you didn't know that I didn't know. If that makes any sense." She giggled with a light smile.

"Let's be frank?" When Mercy didn't respond, Gwen continued. "I wasn't sure how I felt about you when we first met. Then you gave me attitude in the apartment..." The girl looked like she would interrupt. "Then you gave me attitude which I deserved. I discovered you were headstrong, smart, and charming. Now Aurick. I love him like a brother and I didn't like what meeting you did to him. He became obsessed, single-minded, and I worried about his behavior. I, myself, have been there and before a person realizes it, they can be lost. I don't dislike you. In fact, quite the opposite is true. I respect you and if I had known he hadn't told you about our destination, I would have.

We are two women sharing one man's life and I'd like us to be friends."

"At first, I assumed you were his glorified assistant, but soon realized you were more. I appreciate your commitment to your career and to him. I become defensive when I feel inadequate. It's a matter of getting off on the wrong foot."

"I'd like to make amends?" A mischievous smirk overtook Gwen's expression, and she sat on the bed and patted it. "Let's have some fun, shall we?"

When the girls entered the library, Mercy noted they had rearranged some of the furniture to form a circle around a low table. Aurick's parents, Mick and Amanda, sat curled together on a loveseat opposite him, where he relaxed, facing into the room. Sabria, his sister, lazed in a recliner with one leg over the arm and her other underneath her, listening to her brother.

"I'm home," Gwen announced, and the family rose to greet her, exchanging hugs and sentiments.

Immediately, sudden doom pitted Aurick's stomach—recognizing his best friend's devious grin. Needing reassurance, he reached for Mercy's hand and pulled her around his loveseat for a quiet word. She smiled up at him—too brightly, too happy. What the hell happened after he left them?

Gwen was primed to enjoy this. When everyone returned to their seats, she sat in a vacant armchair to Mercy's right. Their eyes met in silent understanding.

When Aurick sat, Mercy followed him down.

He draped his arm over the back and to his astonishment, Mercy curled into his side. He peered down, studying her expression. Unexpectedly, her palm reached up and settled on his neck, dragging his lips to her own.

He presumed it would be a platonic greeting. But it wasn't. His pulse quickened when she disturbingly intensified the intimate kiss. One beat... Two beats... Three... Somewhat flustered, he raised his head, ending it when he remembered his parents were present. Then, using his fingers, he pried her palm from his neck and settled it in her lap.

"So adorable, aren't they?" Gwen gushed to fill the room's silence. "Aren't you going to introduce your guest, Aurick?"

He could tell by Gwen's sugary sweet grin, she was enjoying Mercy's display. Mercy ran her fingers up his chest, releasing his buttons as she went, and the hair on his neck stood up in reaction to her intimate touch.

He grabbed for Mercy's hand and his startled gaze looked down on her upturned face, noting her sickly pleased smile. He held his gaping shirt closed as Mercy's hand delved inside, spreading heat over his toned ribs.

His glance at Gwen screamed *rescue me,* but she shook her head.

Sabria gawked and Aurick's parents sat in silence, waiting for him to introduce the young woman.

"Apparently," Gwen said, shifting everyone's attention to her, "he's forgotten his manners. Mick, Amanda, Sabria meet Mercy Richards."

Aurick didn't think Mercy could get any closer to him, however, she proved him wrong when her right thigh overlapped his—practically sitting on his lap.

His eyebrows puckered at her.

Her voice was nearly a purr. "So formal, Gw—"

Aurick covered her mouth with his palm.

Sabria's jaw fell as she watched the newcomer grope her brother. Their mother looked uneasy and

Mercy, to some extent, wished she hadn't started this —only marginally. Their father planted a kiss on his wife's cheek, trying to soothe her while pride filled his chin-dimpled grin.

"Too much alcohol on the jet," Aurick explained. "She'll be fine in a few hours."

He was doing a miserable job of checking her wet kisses on his neck, traveling to his ear, and silently he thanked Gwen when she drew everyone's attention again.

Intending to pull Mercy away, his hand snaked into her hair. Warm, electrified lust built and traveled from his loins. His fingers betrayed him and, with encouragement, they caressed the base of her collar.

"It's been a long time since we were home and I noticed not much has changed. I admit this will be a splendid break from the big city. Don't you agree Mercy?"

All eyes swung to her as her lips tugged on his ear.

At the sound of her name, he slanted his head, breaking the contact, trying to escape her. Suddenly, he was aware that at some point his pants had tightened. He lifted his arm from behind them, then gently shifted her aside, moving his hands to cover his lap.

"So splendid." Mercy bit down hard on her lip, causing her eyes to pool with tears. "I've been upgraded to a sugar princess." The bite had been a smidge heavier than she meant, and she only managed a half-smile.

Rolling his eyes in exasperation, Aurick brushed his palm up over his face and into his hair, not quite grasping the game here. Though not religious, his eyes raised, and he begged for whatever this was to work in his favor.

"Finally, after all our time together, Aurick sprung this trip on me. I was so eager to meet my new in-laws."

His head whipped down to glare at her. His pale brown expression was now white from her revelation.

Complete silence and immobility gripped the family.

Gwen pretended to glow at the news as she reveled in Aurick's reaction.

Sabria's long black hair tumbled over her shoulders when she stood. "What?"

"They're getting married, silly." Gwen blurted to cover the shock.

Excusing themselves, the two girls went to get ready for supper. They laughed hysterically as they made their way to Mercy's room.

It didn't take long before Aurick followed them, closing the door as he entered.

The girls took one look at him, then made eye contact and disintegrated into giggles.

"Married?" His voice commanded them to stop. "Cute. I can't determine which one of you to take over my knee first."

"Ah, duh." Gwen exaggerated the speech antics of a teenage girl. "You're missing the silver lining here." She draped her arm over Mercy's shoulder.

"Oh? Enlighten me." He half sat on the dresser, his stern face glancing between them.

Following the other girl's lead, Mercy finished. "We're getting along. Hall-a!" She put her palm up to signal a high five, and the other girl's hand connected instantly.

"I can't believe you didn't tell her we were coming here." Gwen blamed him, justifying their actions. "You played her. So we thought it only fair that she play you back."

"Right." Sarcastically, he nodded and shrugged. "So it's my fault we're engaged?" He admitted. "I forgot, of course."

Mercy walked to where he perched on the dresser's edge. She rounded her hand up his thigh as she pressed her body against him. Her breasts brushed his chest as she raised her head to his neck and planted a kiss just below his ear. "Did you appreciate my performance?" She whispered loudly with a giggle, then backed away, evading his reaching hands.

"It was all right. A little over the top if you're wanting an honest opinion." He critiqued. "As the weekend continues, your performance will improve."

Mercy's eyes startled. "You didn't explain to your parents it was a joke?"

"And watch my mother's dreams of grandchildren vanish? Ah... No. I'd rather call her and tell her of our breakup when we get back." His eyes smiled at Mercy's discomfort. "We're going through this charade for the entire trip. Remember? I'm your boss and we do what I want. There is one slight complication though..." Mercy raised her eyebrow, and he continued. "After you left, my parents gave us permission to share one bedroom and, struggling to perform my part as the devout fiancé, I accepted." He paused. "Graciously, of course."

Mercy was stunned. "You better go downstairs and graciously un-accept!"

"No." He studied his fingernails. "No, I don't believe I will." He chuckled with his chin dimpling grin. "An unwanted perk of your scheming little prank, and I mean to enjoy your discomfort. Don't attempt to play the player, Mercy."

"You expect to deceive them this entire weekend?" She searched for another reason to remove his presence from the sleeping arrangement but came up empty.

"Oh, ask Gwen about that. I'm a tremendous actor. As a matter of fact, I'll probably receive an Oscar for this performance." He winked as her mouth gaped.

Gwen withdrew, closing the door behind her. She'd caused enough trouble already.

The casualness of the dinner surprised Mercy. So unlike her childhood home, where meals were formal no matter who was present. The family spent the time catching Aurick and Gwen up on the gossip since their last visit. Everyone chattered over top of each other and it was very relaxing. The natural, loving relationship they shared made her yearn for a similar connection with her own parents.

"I can't believe Betty finally married." Gwen laughed, her red hair fell forward. "And to all people, Doug."

The other women laughed, except Mercy and the men.

Aurick's eyebrow arched. "Why not Doug?"

"Can you imagine..." Gwen's voice turned into a sultry whisper. *"Oh, Dooouuug."* Then she moaned and this time even Mercy laughed. It was the most unromantic name ever.

Sabria nudged Gwen, sitting beside her. "How is it any different from, *oh Geeeooorge?*" Sabria laughed, but no one else did and Amanda placed her hand on her daughter's wrist, stopping her laughter.

A sudden awkward silence descended. Gwen's face turned downward and Aurick attempted to cover it. "Mother, have you added any new plants to your gardens this year?"

Thankfully, his mother easily grasped the subject and elaborated until the previous conversation would be forgotten. It wasn't his sister's fault. She had been so young when Gwen's marriage ended. No one saw fit to explain the circumstances to her. Perhaps now they should consider it.

After eating, the group moved to the library, where this time Gwen and Sabria sprawled out on the floor in front of the television, whispering, and giggling, more like siblings than friends. Aurick's parents relaxed in armchairs side by side, holding hands and reading. Claiming a headache and exhaustion, Mercy excused herself, hurrying up the stairs to her room.

The bedside lamp illuminated the room in mellow light when she emerged from the small bathroom in a silk floor-length mint-colored nightgown. Unaware she was being scrutinized, she wandered to the vanity and brushed her long blonde hair, considering her reflection in the mirror. A movement in the mirror's corner revealed an intruder, and as she pivoted, she lifted her housecoat from the chair's back and dragged it to hide her chest.

"I was wondering when you were going to notice me." Aurick relaxed in a chair at the small table, watching her. "Don't let me interrupt." His eyes admired her body through the clinging, flimsy material.

"I didn't see you." She caught his eyes traveling over her length, and feeling exposed, she swung away to shrug into the robe.

"Are you ready for bed?" He unbuttoned his shirt as he crossed to the bed and dragged the covers back. Tantalizing visions played through his mind of her stretched naked against him on the soft mattress.

Mercy knotted her housecoat and turned to discover him by the bed. "You're not sleeping with me." She watched as he discarded his shirt, noting the smooth skin over his contoured muscles. Her heart galloped and her breath caught at the unobstructed view.

"There's only one bed. What would you have me do?" He asked, his voice hoarse from his thoughts. "And before you create an argument, I'm not sleeping downstairs or on the floor." He waited for her reply, but she said nothing as she stared at him. "If it makes you feel more comfortable, I'll sleep above the blankets. Get in so I can cover you." He presented the solution to end the conversation. *Lying in bed with her will be enough for now.*

Leaving her housecoat on, she clambered into the bed and he chuckled as he covered her, then laid on top, switching out the lamp. He twisted to face her. "Comfortable?" Only a few inches separated their mouths.

"I guess." Her heart hadn't settled. "You?"

"I'm all right." He murmured. "Come here and kiss me goodnight." His hand caressed her cheek, then tangled in her hair, pulling her mouth onto his. His pulse erratically jumped.

She let his hand guide her. She settled her mouth on his and her tongue invited him to intensify the kiss. Passion built, then blazed through her. Her midriff ached as he withdrew.

He ended the embrace before she did something she would regret. He shielded her from herself, and she was glad he was strong enough for them both.

He turned onto his back, urging her to come closer as he extended his arm above her on the pillow. As he folded his muscular arm around her shoulder, she snuggled into the crevice of his collarbone, resting her head on his chest.

His body heat emanated against her skin. She closed her eyes, feeling comfortable and protected as she floated into a dreamless sleep.

He angled his face into her hair, inhaling her scent. While his frustrated libido made him ache, he listened as her rhythmic breaths became shallow, and he cursed her for being able to sleep.

Mercy came down as Aurick and his father strolled out of the dining room. Aurick's hair appeared damp from a shower and he wore a pair of faded jeans and a black t-shirt. Similarly, Mercy wore a tan-colored top with her hair in a ponytail.

"I'll be right in." Aurick shifted to watch her as his father continued into the library. "Good morning." He extended his hand for her to take. When she did, he drew her to him and brushed his lips against hers. "Sleep well?" Adding, "sweetheart" when his mother and sister entered the foyer.

In the unfamiliar bed, she had slept amazingly well, wrapped in his arms. But disappointed, she woke up alone. A depressed loneliness plagued her and only ceased when she encountered him a few moments before. Sabria and Amanda halted their steps to observe the young lovebirds.

"Good morning, darling." Mercy's glance darted to them, and she pulled herself free of his hands as her cheeks reddened.

"Aww, so delightful, you're blushing. They witnessed your wanton actions yesterday, honey." He smirked, savoring her discomfort as he grasped her waist and hauled her back into his arms. Dipping his head to her neck, he nibbled, and she felt her heart flutter as she attempted to twist her head away. He whispered. "They're staring, perform your part." She didn't have to pretend as she turned her neck into his enticing exploration, allowing him to continue.

He released her, glanced over at the others, then holding Mercy's hand, he caught and held her eyes. "As much as I'd like to carry you back upstairs and do wicked things to you, business calls. Acquaint yourself with my family. I imagine my mother will gladly accept your help in her garden." When his mother nodded, he grinned down at her. "Kiss me so I may bear the long lonely hours without you."

Irritated by his effortless performance, she pursed her lips, rolled onto the balls of her feet, and pecked his lips.

Foreseeing her actions, his hands captured her face, holding it while his mouth opened onto hers, massaging her mouth with his tongue until submissive. She reacted and heightened the kiss.

He lifted his head to gaze into her half-closed eyes, then louder than necessary mentioned. "We'll finish this tonight, sweetheart." He hurried out of her reach, planted a kiss on his mother's forehead, and rumpled his sister's hair as he strode out of the room.

Mercy and Sabria spent hours helping Amanda, their mother, with her flower beds. The elaborate floral pattern gave the woman great pleasure.

Again, Mercy wished her relationship with her own family was closer. The affection between mother and daughter was apparent as they bantered back and forth. Sabria challenged her mother's desire to change something but willingly moved it, anyway. They would touch often; a squeeze on the shoulder, a pat on the back, or a kiss on the forehead or cheek.

Meanwhile, they included her and although Sabria was a bit stand-offish; she tried to make her comfortable and invited her to contribute to the conversation. When she couldn't, she would ask her a question about her life or tease her about her brother.

Amanda's eyes turned prideful as she relayed some childhood memory of her children. Over the afternoon, the aging woman touched Mercy a few times in an affectionate gesture of approval.

In the afternoon heat, the entire family joined together in the garden. Everyone laughed when Gwen playfully grabbed Sabria, tugging her onto her lap. Mick helped his wife up from her knees and led her to a wicker loveseat. Aurick draped his arm over Mercy's shoulder, and after roaming around the garden for a few minutes, they returned.

Aurick slipped into a chair and pushed Mercy forward. "Bring me a drink, woman," jokingly, his voice growled.

Sabria smiled her agreement. Delighted to know the woman hadn't wholly overpowered her brother.

"That'd a boy." Mick encouraged his son, laughing.

Amanda scolded, moving her eyes between the pair. "Barbaric! It would serve you right if she left you to get your own."

Gwen giggled and Mercy's mouth gaped as the housekeeper rolled out a cart with a pitcher of iced tea and another of water.

"What's the point of taking a wife if she doesn't do my bidding, mother?" He asked with a laugh as Mercy moved to fulfill his request.

His mother clicked her tongue and admonished. "You're lucky she puts up with you."

With both hands, Mercy lifted the pitcher, brimmed with water, and turned. Everyone saw it coming except him, who was focused on teasing his mother. Mercy hauled her arms back and heaved the water with all her strength into his face.

"Luck–" Water splashed into his open mouth and he sputtered as it went up his nose. Everyone laughed hysterically. His hair was drenched, his clothes were soaked and Mercy's actions warranted satisfaction as he wiped his face and stalked towards her with a playful, angry scowl.

She shrieked with giggles. "I'm sorry..." she stepped backward behind the table, "it was an accident?"

"I'm going to show you an accident." He picked up the pitcher of sweet tea and raised it into the air.

Her hands lifted in front of her in anticipation as she breathlessly laughed. "No... Please... Really... I'm so sorry."

"Not sorry enough." As he rounded the table, she raced away.

With a backward yell, she screamed. "Don't you dare!"

He plunked the pitcher onto the table and chased her through the garden and out onto the expansive lawn. He let her outpace him. He heard her laughter as she looked back and darted up the side of a hill.

However, once out of sight from the others, he easily snaked his arm around her waist and fell with her into the soft grass. Their breaths pitched from the exertion of the run.

Out of breath and spooning each other, he hoarsely whispered. "I've caught you, now you will pay."

"Never." In lighthearted fun, her small hands fought his hold, trying to break free, but the vise of his arm easily held her.

He laughed as his hands grabbed her wrists, then forced them above her as he rolled her onto her back. His strength outmatched hers, but spirited she still wrestled against him, her foot kicking his shin.

"Careful or you'll dash my mother's dreams of grandchildren." His leg trapped hers as he climbed over and settled his waist between her legs.

"Unless you can tuck it into your sock, my aim was much too low." Her eyes were bright with fight as she bucked her hips, causing friction against his groin. Instantly, their contest of strength turned into seduction.

His warm breath washed over her skin as his mouth dipped to her ear. "It seems you're sprawled in the grass." The echo of her previous words delighted her. He heard her swallow as his rough tongue ran over the sensitive spot behind her earlobe.

"Aurick," she pleaded as he let go of her hands, but they didn't push him away. Her palms pressed his ribs, urging his weight down to cover her torso, and her fingers lightly ran over the tight cotton, stretched across his back.

Her firm, demanding touch whirled the embers of his tortured prolonged lust, igniting an urgency within him that rose and burned adoration into his heart. He loved her—the single word wasn't enough —indescribable. She writhed beneath him as his parted lips found her moistened mouth.

Her tongue laced his, devouring his every stroke. It was as if, during her entire life, she had starved and only something he could offer would satiate her. Her hands dragged the fabric up his back, exposing her fingers to his heated, bronzed flesh. His muscles rippled in response as he shifted upward onto his haunches and fisted the material, discarding the barrier over his head.

Her yearning, vivid eyes met his radiant stare as her eager hands fondled his forearms, guiding his fingers to her waist. Then, she lifted to her elbows as he pulled her tan-colored top over her silky long hair. His gaze raked her naked abdomen, her navel, up her rib cage, and settled on the blue seductive lace of her bra which hid the round, full breasts he'd once pleasured.

He couldn't move his eyes from it—the promise beneath it.

In this moment, there were no lies and no one else existed. Only what she felt, what she saw in his eyes, and what they each needed mattered. As the bright afternoon sun bathed the fragrant grass, creating a warm, natural bed to envelop their bodies, her fingers disappeared under her back, snapping the clasp apart.

At the sound and the motion of the slackened material, his questioning eyes found her reassuring ones. His hurried fingers dragged the straps down, tossing the blue lace away as her fingers trailed down his chest, raked his ribs, and discovered his buckle, pulling it loose.

He needed a beat—they needed a beat. Their labored breaths, his thwacking heart, and the deliriously happy birds and insects chirping, nearly deafened him. His palm wrapped over her fingers at his waist. He lifted her hand to his mouth, caressing her wrist with his tongue. Her blue eyes coerced him as he laid his naked, chiseled chest over her soft, satiny torso. When her breasts brushed against the flesh of his ribs, it nearly undid his chivalrous intentions.

She couldn't let this end like this, not now. She ran her tongue along his neck, pushing his head to the side with her jaw as she fastened her warm mouth on his skin. Trailing a wet path of love bites down his chest, she rounded his nipple with her tongue.

He savored every second of her exploration as he half-heartedly tried to evade her advances. Never had he thought he'd be the one to stop this. Her hands, her fingers, her palms were everywhere at once as her fluid body churned beneath his hard frame. It was as if her need was causing her agony.

His fingers twisted in her hair, and he tugged, bringing her ear to his mouth. There was a tortured undercurrent in his raspy tone when he whispered. "Mercy please, beg me to love you." As difficult as it was, he gifted her an instant to stop what was happening.

The breathless air from her parted lips washed over the skin of his neck. "Love me."

Christ, the things the short phrase did to his body, to his essence, were unimaginable. He'd expected her to retreat, to push him away, to fight against their passion. Not this, her effortless surrender and her absolute confidence in her decision.

His lips nipped her throat, provoking tiny needful moans from her. One of his rough hands squeezed her breast and tightened her fleshy peak on its path downward. His other palm flattened against the grass, bracing his upper body higher.

In a flurry of activity, her delicate fingers outran his hand, yanking his leather belt free and working his jean's button open, then glided the slider down, scraping it against the vertical teeth. When she exposed his firm, naked buttocks to the beating sun, the material slumped around his contoured thighs.

She heard his sharp intake of air, then felt his thickened shaft land against the dampening vee between her legs. Its feel was heavenly and exhilarating. Of their own volition, his hips flexed forward, causing a warm rush of goosebumps to tighten over her body as his taut, veiny member rubbed against her cloth-covered tightening button.

He was losing the battle between his want and her need. His cock twitched with anticipation, enticing Aurick to hurry by moving against her. Sinking his molded chest onto her exposed breasts, her heartbeat hammered nearly as fast as his own. He tongued the warm flesh of her shoulder as her fingers ran through his unruly locks.

He had no desire to rush their first coupling, but he learned her want was greater than his when she begged. "Pleeeaaase, I need you."

His fingers cupped her jaw, forcing her glazed eyes to meet his. For a second, they communicated without words before his ravenous mouth drank from her welcoming lips, stroking her glistening tongue with his own. The urgency in her response was wielded like a weapon, driving him to satiate her.

His mouth left hers before her body's demand forced his to rashness.

"Soon." His tender lips kissed a path down her chest as his hand fondled the round globe of her breast. His skilled fingers massaged her rosy peak, stiffening it further before his wet mouth clung to it, eliciting a wanton cry from her. His hands snaked to her waist, curving along the soft skin and splaying his fingers on her back, holding her midsection still beneath him.

"Now." She scraped her fingernails over his back in protest.

His fumbling, shaking hands gaped her jeans open and her bottom wiggled upward, aiding him in removing the obstruction.

His rough tongue bathed her navel as he guided the material and her blue lacy underwear downward.

The warm summer breeze and the foretaste of his prowess tickled and tensed her budding clit. Her smooth hips gyrated upwards, imploring him to touch her there. Thrilling waves of anticipation prickled her skin when his hair dragged downward, brushing over her mound. His breath settled between her legs. The musky scent of her lust tempted him and his top lip grazed her fleshy nub as he plunged his tongue inside her warm folds, extorting a satisfied gasp from her throat.

His dense arms laid over her ribs, their weight forcing her to lie still as his needy palms squeezed her breasts. His rough tongue played between her folds, coaxing and stretching her coiled tissue, readying her for the entry of his hard, thick shaft.

Between her sweet moans, he heard her almost inaudible words. "Nooowww, pleeeaaase."

Those words were all he could take of torture he had inflicted upon himself. His labored breath washed over her body as he inched upward, positioning the crown of his penis against her slickened opening.

His eyes locked with hers, watching the rapturous want consume her. He flexed his unfamiliar tip forward, dipping his cap inside her hot entrance. Her tightening pleasure exulted in knowing his foreign member. She felt their mixture cling to him as he withdrew.

"Oh my–" followed by a loud gasp, alerted him instantly to their surroundings. Aurick covered her, crushing her beneath him as his head snapped upward, determining who had seen what. Gwen had her arm around Sabria's shoulder. It was obvious she'd turned them both away from the very intimate display.

Aurick cursed under his breath as his passion evaporated and his cock went flaccid. The two intruders stood at the top of the rolling green hill, unable to see anything but his naked back and his sheltering arms.

Disappointed and embarrassed, his sharp tone accosted them. "What?"

Without turning around, Gwen answered. "Your mother sent us to collect Mercy. It's almost time for dinner."

He looked down at her pale face, where her eyes were tightly closed. He lifted his head to be heard. "She'll be in immediately."

He watched the pair rush away, as uncomfortable as he and Mercy were. He rolled off onto his side and whispered. "They're gone."

Her eyes remained closed as he planted a light kiss on her cheek. "Mercy," his voice coaxed, "are you all right?" His hand settled on the flesh of her midsection. "I'm sorry."

Snapping open, her eyes bore into his. "Don't, don't apologize. I wanted what happened."

He chuckled as he pulled her into the cradle of his

arms. "You mean what almost happened. I barely started."

Playfully, she pushed him as she reached for her jeans. "We should dress before someone else comes looking for us."

His hand pulled her nude back against his hip as she struggled to pull the legs of her jeans upward. "I'd rather continue, but their appearance caused the most disastrous side-effect."

She rolled away from him, then her eyes followed his gaze to his shriveled cock. "Want me to kiss him better?"

It twitched at her words. "You teasing temptress." He sat up and gathered his clothes, shielding his manhood from her eyes, which were slowly awakening it again.

He watched her ease as she fastened the bra behind her, then popped her top over her frame. Already he missed the sight of her intimate flesh.

With her nakedness covered, she stood, smiling down at him. "Are you going to dress?"

He fell backward into the grass, giving up, and stopped fighting the new erection springing between his legs. He shook his head, ensuring his clothes still covered the growing beast. "No, I'm going to lie right here for a while." His grin dimpled his chin. "You should go though before my mother sends out another search party or Gwen and Sabria have time to wonder why your absence continues."

She dropped on her knees beside him and ran her finger upward over his bronzed chest before dipping her swollen mouth to his. "I highly doubt their wondering." She planted a warm, wet kiss on his lips, but when she felt his arm move, she broke it and escaped before he could catch her.

Mercy felt an unwarranted contentment as she climbed the hill. She'd enjoyed every moment of the afternoon with him—and his family. In her mind, she could see herself settled in this family's relationship, happy and loved. A twinge of jealousy slithered into her thoughts. *It will not be me.* She warned, *this is an act.* Determined, she memorized every minute so she could recall and cherish the memories later when this was over and she was alone.

I Couldn't Protect Her from You

Years had passed since Aurick and Gwen had ventured within the town limits. Usually, they isolated themselves on his parent's estate, completing their business quickly, then left. It had taken both Mercy and Sabria to convince Gwen to go dancing, and it surprised Aurick when she agreed.

The sole night-time entertainment in the one-stoplight town was Barney's Bandstand. When Aurick had left home, it had been a loud, smoky honky-tonk, but as they parked the car, the outdoor speakers thumped with dance music.

Aurick lifted his eyebrow as he helped his sister from the car. "What's that racket?"

Sabria laughed. "You've gotten old, brother. Times have changed. They play all genres now."

Lit by torches in wire cages, the four walked through the congested outdoor patio to the entrance. The overcrowded interior was just as Aurick remembered. There were too many people packing every inch.

There was no rhythm or reason to the deejay's choices as the music slowed to a country two-step from the head thrashing metal. Aurick instructed Mercy through a two-step, and it didn't take her long to catch on. Soon they were dancing across the floor.

. . .

She returned to the table, out of breath and in need of her vodka tonic. A fast polka started and everyone in the building began pounding the tables and stomping their feet—louder than the music. It was like nothing Mercy had ever experienced, but she joined in anyway. Aurick caught Gwen's elbow and whisked her into his arms. Bewildered, Mercy watched the fast movements of their feet as they whirled around. Each time Aurick sent her into a string of turns, she would match and meet him at the end.

When the song finished, Gwen's face gleamed with sweat as she chuckled. It was his turn to be out of breath as he turned her back into her chair and dropped into his own.

"Getting too old for that?" His sister teased. Aurick winked at her and took a drink, reaching for Mercy's palm to hold on his lap.

Sabria was as experienced as her brother, and Mercy took pleasure in watching her pleated skirt swish around her knees as she danced with her partner, returning between songs to drink from the pony-jug paralyzer—a mixture of vodka, coffee liqueur, milk, and cola.

Over the melody, Gwen and Mercy chatted loudly. Aurick entertained himself, freely roaming one hand along her back and over her neck while with his other he held hand possessively for everyone to see.

A slow R&B song started and Aurick pulled her up and into his arms. He ran his palms from the back of her thighs, up her sleek black denims to her waist, then spanned his fingers across her spine and picked her up against his solid body. He planted her heat on his thigh, her feet barely touching the ground, and swayed their bodies to the music. Her scent was intoxicating, and he buried his nose in the hair beside her ear. Savoring her touch and scent, he closed his eyes.

She urged his exploration, burrowing her fingers in his hair. Her thumbs rubbed circles over the cords at the back of his neck and she gave in to the magic of their embrace. She turned her head to brush her lips with his, and as he responded, she demanded more. She opened her mouth onto his, using her tongue to coax his lips apart, then she laced hers with his.

Aurick was oblivious to everything except her. He wanted her—now, alone. They could end this yearning, aching need tonight. She no longer needed convincing, completely pliable. He knew they could find a darkened alley where he could press her against a wall. He'd lift her until she wrapped her legs around his waist. He'd peel her denims down enough to expose her entrance. She'd writhe and constrict her muscles when he roughly thrusted his erection inside.

Her damp denims informed him—she was ready. He rubbed her heat upwards along his thigh, then slowly back down again and again. A small moan gurgled from her throat into his mouth.

Better—the dark park across the street had long plastic tunnels, secluded. Inside one, they could feverishly strip each other naked. Then, as he laid flat, she could straddle his hips, sliding her tight, slick folds over his hardened length. She could grind her button against his pelvis and buck her hips as she wished until they both reached release.

He dragged her again, up his leg. This time, her stomach pressed against the bulge pushing against his jeans, wanting to touch her unrestrained.

In an instant, when a hand tapped his shoulder, he heard the music, became aware of their surroundings, and felt himself soften. He tore his mouth from her—breaking their magic. He turned to face the man who disrupted them.

The two men hugged and slapped each other's

back in a manly greeting as they playfully spared. Aurick smiled at his childhood buddy, introduced Mercy, and held her grip as the three returned to the table.

"So, your fiancée, huh? What about Gwen?" The man winked.

"There was never anything between us. Only friendship." Aurick replied.

"The way George tells it you swooped in and abducted her from him." The man offered, then continued. "When Gwen walked in tonight, I noticed she's looking better than ever. I even mentioned it to George when I bumped into him twenty minutes ago. An 'eat your heart out' dig. He grinned and agreed with me. You know–"

"George is here?" Aurick demanded, his face becoming serious as he stood and pulled Mercy to her feet. "Sabria, check out front, then head for the car. We'll meet you there." She got to her feet, rushing towards the exit.

"That's what I just said–"

Aurick didn't hear any more as he questioned Mercy, towing her behind him. "Where did she go?"

"The bathroom." Mercy stammered by the abrupt change in his behavior. He changed their direction, and she struggled to keep up with his pace.

Gwen emerged from the washroom and walked straight into the wall of someone's broad chest. She lifted her gaze to apologize, and instantly closed her mouth, recognizing her ex-husband. Without a sound, he clutched her arm and forced her out through a side door. Her instinct to fight was stronger than her fear as she threw punches with her loose hand and kicked her feet into his shins.

"Let go of me!" She screamed, realizing that her effort was worthless. The deserted alley was empty and the music from the bar covered her cry. No one was going to hear her.

George propelled her body across the alley as he let her go, and the forward momentum sent her crashing into a brick wall. Her head connected, and she slid to the ground. As quick as her body would react, Gwen used her palms to clamber back to her feet, keeping her eyes on him. The alley was black except for the single bulb above the door. It back-lit his silhouette, casting shadows, and made it impossible for her to gauge his expression.

"How've you been Gwen? Have you missed me as much as I've missed you? I've waited all this time for you to return and the first words you utter are 'let go of me'? You've forgotten your manners. Let me remind you." He strode to her, and she tried to get around him, but he was faster. His hand shot out, gripping her neck while his fist connected with her temple, shooting a buzz through her ears. Her head rocked to the side, and the iron taste of blood filled her mouth. She drooped, praying he wouldn't deliver another blow. Fear built, and she shook, hoping his abuse would end soon.

"That's better," he jeered as he squeezed her chin in his grip, forcing her eyes to stare into his. He smoothed the hair from her face and his mouth settled on hers, mashing her lips into her teeth. She fought against him. This invasion was more than she could take.

"Let me go," she shrilled. She bit down as hard as she could on his lip. He reared his face away, balled his fist, and drove it into her jaw. Someone yelled as her limbs gave out beneath her and unconsciousness took her.

It only took Mercy a glance to check the bathroom while Aurick waited impatiently outside the door. When she came back alone, he knew Gwen wasn't in there and he vaulted out the nearest exit, eager to find her.

Aurick exploded through the door with Mercy in pursuit. It took a few strides to reach George, his back to the door. Aurick grabbed the man's arm, spun him around, and sent a powerful blow into his nose. The sound of breaking bones crunched loudly in the otherwise calm alley.

"Get Gwen!" Aurick commanded over his shoulder to Mercy and lifted his arm high to block an attempt by George, then delivered his own in an upward force, connecting with the man's chin.

Mercy hadn't noticed Gwen, but she scanned the area and discovered her lying against the dirty building. She rushed to the woman's side, using her body as a shelter from the fight taking place nearby.

Mercy was now with Gwen, and Aurick used his strength to capture George, forcing him away. Aurick spent the limited time, placing himself in front of the girls. The man recovered and rushed headfirst into Aurick's abdomen. He anticipated the move, hooking George's leg, and they both tumbled to the ground. Aurick sat on his chest and struck him repeatedly.

Gwen moaned and screamed out as she came to, struggling to fight off her attacker. Mercy's voice tried to soothe her and Aurick quickly came to her side.

Mercy rested Gwen's head in her lap as blood seeped from a cut above her eye and tears fell as she wept. Aurick's fury left him, now worried by her battered face. He ignored the man lying behind them.

"I should have killed the bitch when I had the chance. I'd be a widow instead of the discarded ex-husband everyone enjoys gossiping about." George, now standing, sneered through his split lip and he spit the blood from his mouth at Aurick's feet, then turned to stroll down the alley away from the scene.

Uncontrollable rage surged through Aurick as he leaped up, pounced on George, and flung him down. Aurick kicked him and stomped on him with the heel of his boot. Mercy screamed for Aurick to stop. Her frightened voice sent a shock through him and he spun away, retracing his steps to them. Gwen had lost consciousness again, and Aurick lifted her limp body, settling her head on his shoulder. Aurick strode from the shadowy space towards the street, and Mercy had to run to keep up. As Aurick passed George, he spit on him. Sabria saw them coming towards her, and she opened the rear door.

"You drive," Aurick ordered his sister, slipping into the backseat with Gwen still held against him. Mercy hurried to the front passenger seat and locked the door, worried the man could follow them at any moment. Sabria gunned the gas, traveling at a fast pace until the lights of town were far behind and the security of the ranch ahead.

"Call the house. Let mom know what's happened and tell her we're on our way." Aurick ordered. Sabria dictated the number and with shaking hands, Mercy punched the numbers and relayed the details. She heard the agonizing pain in Aurick's whisper while he soothed Gwen and helpless tears streamed down Mercy's face.

A flurry of activity followed their arrival. Every light in the downstairs was on when his sister skidded to a halt in front of the home. Mick bounded down the stairs. He flung open the door as the car came to a stop and took Gwen's lifeless body from Aurick. Amanda waited at the entrance for her husband and quickly followed him into the house, dialing the phone as she moved.

Sabria rushed around to help Aurick out, but Mercy reached him first, and the two tried to assist him.

Still enraged, he shrugged them aside. "I don't need you. Leave me alone. Get away from me." He roared, his eyes crimson from the blood streaming into them from a gash on his forehead.

His sister swung away, knowing her brother's temper, but Mercy's gentle tone tried to reason. "You're bleeding."

"What don't you understand? Stay away from me. This is your fault!" Aurick's shout accused her and it was like being splashed with cold water as pain distorted her expression. Her heart jolted against her rib cage and her stomach heaved.

Aurick spun and stomped off into the darkness without as much as a glimpse backward. Mercy's body quaked in despair when she felt someone's arm around her. She accepted the support but said nothing.

"It'll be all right," Sabria reassured her with calming words as she guided her into the house. Mercy wasn't as confident. He blamed her, but she didn't know for what. She didn't understand the anger directed at her.

"Where's Aurick?" Amanda called from upstairs.

"He didn't come in. Is Dr. Mathews coming?" Her daughter asked.

"Yes. In the interim, I washed her face. She's going to require stitches. Where's Mercy? Is she okay?"

"She's shaken up. If you don't need me, I'll help her?" Sabria offered.

"No, I've got Gwen covered. Go ahead, help Mercy."

Aurick's sister helped Mercy up the stairs and into the bedroom she shared with Aurick as silent tears rolled down her cheeks. Sabria withdrew, leaving her to deal with Aurick's accusations alone. Balled up tight in the bed, her emotional floodgate burst and she sobbed until the blackened exhaustion consumed her.

Mercy was alone when she awakened during the night. She listened for any noise which might have disturbed her, but none occurred. Aurick hadn't come to bed, and she decided she had left the bedside lamp on long enough. She twisted over onto her other side and reached out to shut it off as she glanced around the room. Before she clicked the switch, her eyes discovered him. His broad frame leaned back in a chair while his elbow rested on the table, his cheek rested in his hand. His eyes were glossy as they reflected the light, and he was studying her. She didn't know what to say when their gaze met, so she remained silent. After a few minutes, Mercy realized he wasn't going to say anything, and she reached for the switch.

"It wasn't your fault," Aurick's hoarse voice was barely a whisper, filled with despair, and it reached her as her hand touched the lamp. Her palm dropped to her side without turning it out, and she waited for him to continue. "It was mine. I let this happen to her again. What kind of man allows that?"

Mercy heard the guilt and self-contempt in his tone. Her heart ached for the misery he was going through and she wanted to go to him but feared his rejection. Instead, she sat up on the bed's edge and listened.

Tears marred his expression, and Aurick momentarily buried his face in his sleeve to wipe them away. "I know I've never defined it but she's my best friend." His tone shifted with contempt, and he sneered. "Thirteen years ago, I left her here. I all but gave her away on her wedding day to George, who beat and tormented her every day."

With coiled anger in his movements, Aurick stood and stepped to the open window beside the bed. "For years, I didn't have a clue what was going on. How could I be so stupid? Why didn't I keep closer tabs on her if she meant so much to me? How did she ever forgive and trust me again?" Mercy tugged on his arm, drawing him to the bed, and she withdrew farther onto it, creating space for him. His glance sought hers while she settled her hand on his jaw, caressing it.

He noted her small tears while she listened. "When she's finally doing all right for herself, I led her back here. I promised I wouldn't let anything happen to her, and she believed me." His hand brushed the wetness from her cheek and his painful, guilty whisper declared, "But, I couldn't protect her from you."

She wrenched her face from his hand, losing her balance, and found herself on the flat of her back, looking up at the ceiling.

Immediately, his hard face framed her vision when his rough hands tightly gripped the flesh of her arms, forcing her to stillness, and he used his knees to steady himself above her length. His wavy curls brushed her skin as his eyes scanned her face. His husky tone accused. "It's like nothing else matters and no one else exists. How do you control me like that? How does it work? Do you realize what loving you has cost me—or Gwen? You invade my every dream and haunt my every thought. The scent of your perfume." He dropped his head into the curve of her neck, inhaling her aroma deeply. His breath tickled her skin, and she fought to control her racing pulse as he whispered. "The flavor of your skin." His masterful tongue blazed a trail of goosebumps across her jaw, on his way to her full mouth.

"The touch of your body against mine." He relaxed his muscled limbs and let his weight settle on her scantily clad frame as a fire ignited in her midsection. "I lose myself in loving you." His eager mouth crushed her lips, forcing them to part and surrender to his impassioned kiss. His love words sang to her, and her tongue deepened its exploration, seeking to give his suffering release.

Their mating—the give and take—of their sensual mouths continued until they were both dizzy. He dragged free of her panting mouth, allowing her to gulp air into her deprived lungs. His firm grip released her delicate arms and found sanctuary in her disheveled hair, pulling to force her chin upwards. Gently, his teeth scraped her collarbone, stiffening the pliable flesh. His wet lips nibbled her throat, tasting her intoxicating vanilla fragrance as his breath nuzzled her earlobe.

Her slender fingers explored his taut ribs as she churned her hips beneath him. The thrill of his attention built through her veins and she sunk her nails into his back as her longing body demanded more of his glorious weight.

Reaching through the fog of his lust-filled mind, her harsh breathing and passionate purrs sounded. His pointed tongue stifled her, entangling hers so no one else would hear. Her fingertips skimmed along his broad shoulders and buried in his hair, urging his soft mouth to take more from her. She heard a rough growl escape his throat in answer as his lips cruelly devoured her, seeking her solace.

His long fingers pushed the strap of her white nightie down, exposing her chest to the cool night air. When his hot palm wrapped over the fullness of her breast, his appetite strengthened and his athletic hips rocked against her thigh. The effect of their passion bulged against her. His talented hand caressed the globe of her breast as his fingertips circled and pinched her nipple. His tongue, wanting its share, started a downward course.

He latched his lips over her pink-colored center, swirling his tongue around its stiffened peak. Gentle flames flowed down through her abdomen and into her aching loins, and she ground her moistening nub against his cloth-covered thigh, searching for release. As he lifted his clothed body from hers, her grappling hands reached for him, wanting his assault to continue.

When the cold air touched her exposed skin, her swollen lips parted, and she uttered a small, negative sigh. Under the guidance of his fingers, she heard the snaps of her lingerie tear apart and strongly he clutched her ribs, pushing the material up the length of her body and over her head. Mercy helped dispose of the obstacle as he kissed her navel, dipping his tongue into its center, a preview of what was to come. She snaked her hands back into his hair and pulled, bringing his face back up her body. His mouth nipped along her quivering ribs, then hesitated as he suckled her puckered nipples, where his rough palms greedily kneaded.

He wasn't the only one who was greedy. Her hands shifted their attention to roam between their bodies, and her fingers grasped the front fabric of his shirt, pulling him to attract his teasing lips to her waiting mouth. As he obeyed, her hands tore his buttons open, gaping the material wide so her touch could explore his contoured torso. Her firm palms dragged his shoulders, urging his chiseled chest to cover hers. The exertion of holding back caused perspiration to bead along his scalding skin as his wispy, coarse chest hair scraped against her satiny flesh.

When their kiss ended, his mouth slipped to her ear and, listening to his erratic breath, she rolled her eager hips beneath him, teasing his erection.

"Let me love you," his ragged voice pleaded.

In agreement, she delightfully moaned as her roving hands drifted down his back, pressing his cloth-covered buttocks and installing his stiff organ against her glistening warmth. His mind gloried when he felt her natural lubrication through the material of his jeans. Through an uncontrollable shudder, his exhale whooshed, bathing her sensitive skin. His mind disciplined his body's hasty urge to climax in the instant. A loud groan left his throat and her mouth found the tightened cord in his neck, tenderly biting her encouragement.

"Tell me," he hissed through his clenched teeth.

Her digits climbed into his hair, pressing his ear to her mouth, and her tongue darted repeatedly over his lobe. Her quick breaths sent shivers along his body's every nerve-ending.

She murmured. "Make love to me, Aurick."

His gluttonous mouth crushed hers, and she was trapped in lust's roaring fire. She felt his weight lift from her naked body, exposing it to the warm glow of the bedside lamp. He pushed himself away before she realized she could protest.

His penetrating eyes roamed over her length and he watched each part tense as if his glance was physically touching her. His impatient fingers split the buttons at his sleeves and without ceremony he shrugged the material from his shoulders, freeing himself from its restraint. Rigidly straight, he stood, bathed in the single light as she appraised his sinewy, broad chest. Her unobstructed, hungry gaze drifted over his brown torso, appreciating his tapered abdomen and his ribcage's muscles stiffening under her bold inspection. He strode to the bedside, planted a punishing kiss on her swollen lips, then snapped the lamp off and backed away again.

The moonlight illuminated his nakedness as her eyes followed his movements. He worked the buckle at his waist, unfastened his button, and dragged his zipper downwards, loosening his jeans. His thumbs hooked his underwear and sent the fabrics down to the floor. Her ravenous eyes tracked upward from the pool at his feet, migrating upwards over his defined smooth legs and settled on his thick rod curled skyward, reaching his navel. Her expression pleaded for him to join her.

Wordlessly, he slowly crawled onto the bed, stalking towards her. His deprived mouth parted her waiting lips as she liberally stretched her hands over his naked body. She heard her pulse drumming violently as he buried his face in her neck. His hands spanned, then massaged the smooth surface of her sides. His warm tongue licked her skin, delivering a surge of pleasure up her spine. Every one of her senses heightened, and she dug her fingers into his muscled back, needing an outlet.

Tenderly, his firm hand tread down her abdomen and along the supple curve of her hip. His thumb skimmed over her delicate, protruding hip bone, then traced a path across and up the inside of her thigh. Her hips crooked upward, increasing the gentle pressure of his touch. Her legs fell wider with invitation when he repeated the motion.

This time, he fluttered his digits against her velvety folds, tormenting her with their caress. She moaned, then captured his hand in hers and drove the pressure of his fingers onto her lust-engorged button. Wishing to satisfy her, he gyrated his slickened fingers in tiny circles against her glistening clit. His teasing built a pleasant frustration within her. Even if she wanted to, she couldn't stop her lifting hips, strengthening his torturous pressure. Out of control and spinning with dizziness, her fluidic body tensed as his ceaseless momentum ignited and fired a myriad of brilliant sparks behind her eyes. His other hand coiled on her side as his mouth engulfed her nipple. His thorough and exhaustive invasion was everywhere at once, and she couldn't discern from one second to the next where his satisfying touch would be as sensations rolled over each other, guiding her through her spiraling orgasm.

Unaware, her raised knees tensed, then fell apart as she panted and whimpered into the darkness. His hand withdrew its pressure, leaving her satiny folds. Wanting to soothe her, his mouth sought hers as he crawled over her leg and rubbed the length of his veiny erection against her pelvis.

Her eager hand seized his thick shaft, and using her gripped fingers, she milked it, causing it to jump with delight. Her pace increased as her teeth zealously sank into his neck. His body quaked and his whirling mind blackened. His desperate fingers caught her wrist to cease its movement, then forced her to let go as he pinned her arm above her head. Gently, he grazed her lips as more sweat beaded on his shoulders, caused by the effort it took to hold himself back, wishing to savor their first coupling. She pulled her restless hips upwards and slid her coated, velvety folds along his hardened member. She was taunting him—motivating him—to find his satisfaction inside her quivering body.

He knew he was unable to deny her much longer, her invitation enticing. He rocked back onto his haunches, and with him, he drew her hips onto his thighs. Her lust-dazed eyes slid open. He towered above her, his back straight, and he dragged her ass to cradle his solid, yet silky rod. His hand wrapped under her waist, hoisting her, while his other shoved and positioned his erection downward to prod the folds of her snug entrance. She felt the heat of him pushing, edging inside her constricted canal. Instantly, the feel of his foreign member thrilled her. She attempted to wiggle closer, struggling to reduce the gap between them. He wouldn't allow her the satisfaction. Taking his time, he flexed his fleshy crown forward, and it disappeared inside her.

Fascinated, he felt her snug tissue encompass him and he retracted, wanting to feel it again. Her voice whispered for more, and she strained the muscles of her hollow, attempting to suck his length further inside.

Again and again, he tormented her and when she thought she would die from the anguish of needing him, he deliberately lifted his sculpted hips, pushing his cap a few inches deeper. He felt her walls narrow and clench over him, demanding he shelter his length within her burning center. She was encouraging him to take his satisfaction from her. Without hesitation or the need of her encouragement, he quickened the pace and lengthened each stroke, feeling her space narrow and tighten against him. He could easily lose himself in this animalistic position, but what he felt for her—what they felt for each other—deserved more gentleness and time.

He withdrew long enough to lie between her legs, then returned his hard shaft back into her opening as her desirous purrs sounded against his throat.

"Mercy," his whisper pleaded in her ear, and she turned her angelic face to stare into his lustful eyes. "We have time."

"No, we don't," she moaned, applied pressure to his straining neck, and forced his mouth to cover hers, justifying her thirst for a quicker pace.

Slowly, he slid his lengthy shaft inside her glistening, heated sheath, stretching the sides to accommodate his further exploration. She writhed beneath him, folding her legs over his ass. Again, he would have withdrawn to intensify and extend their lovemaking, but her hungry need wouldn't tolerate it.

She used the strength of her toned calves to hurtle him deeper into her stretching cavity, and at the same time, she arched her hips, burying his shaft completely inside her. He felt her cervix against his fleshy tip. The heave of her hip's angled lift embedded him to his hilt. A smothered cry escaped her, and he paused, wondering if he had hurt her.

The last thing she wanted was time as she urged him, thrusting her gyrating hips to glide her tunnel up and down over his veined, muscled rod. Recognizing her enthrall, his member thrusted harder, scraping his pelvic bone against her tightening clit. Their lovemaking built into a frenzied rhythm, both searching for satisfaction from their long pent-up desire.

Forward and back—incessantly. He thrust, propelling his pelvis to grind against her. He felt the telltale tingling at the base of his neck.

Harder, more forcibly—he felt his scrotum tightened, preparing. He fought a battle against his rebellious urges, needing to wait for her.

Rougher and deeper—continually. He stroked from hilt to tip, and her hips writhed, curving her pelvis to meet him. She moaned his name as their two bodies became one animalistic rhythm.

His mouth consumed her cries and answered them with his own hoarse murmurs.

She felt her mind lifting and twisting as shivering spasms burst through her body. Tiny shooting stars filled her mind's blackness as her tense body released and jerked beneath him.

Painfully, he felt her tightening muscles convulse around him. He released his tautly coiled control and let himself enjoy the friction of their bodies. Seeking more, his forceful hips thrusted, his length dived, rooting against her cervix, then he drove his sticky semen deep inside her spasming abyss. Her body shuddered beneath his frame and felt his member pulse as his hot spray bathed her walls.

With his strength spent from ensuring her pleasure and the exertion of their lovemaking, Aurick moved onto his side, bringing her with him. He kissed her lightly while he used his feet to bring the blanket up around them. He cradled her head in the protection of his arm, and she nestled, needing to be closer to him.

Mercy knew a contentment she had never experienced before as she laid there, listening to the beat of his heart. *He loves me. What have I done?* She hadn't finished berating herself when her mind drifted off, exhausted.

Aurick passed his fingers through her hair while his mind raced. *This was where we were headed. She wanted it as much as I did. I said it. I told her. Will she run from me now?* His worried thoughts plagued him as he listened to her shallow breathing, and he knew she had fallen asleep.

CHAPTER 12

Call Me Deep Throat

T he mid-morning heat was stifling, and the temperature would only climb as the hours passed. Mercy was thankful for the air conditioning on the jet as she relaxed contently against Aurick's wide chest, contemplating the weekend.

The time had sped by and it seemed impossible they were already on their way home. Gwen had woken this morning with a headache caused by the six stitches above her right eye and the doctor, foreseeing it, had left pain killers.

Aurick had escaped the bed sometime early in the morning, but when Mercy emerged from the shower he was there to kiss her and coax her back into its warm confines, eager to lavish her with pleasure.

I have to confess. He deserves to know how this started, who I am, and why I waited so long to tell him. Will things be this good when we get home? How much of this weekend was an act to him? Maybe his confession resulted from the fake engagement? Two weeks, see where this goes, then I'll tell him. She bargained with herself.

Aurick had his arm draped over her shoulder and his eyes closed as his own thoughts plagued him. *Was what transpired enough to show to her my love? Did I prove this could work between us? Is she going to get back to the apartment and leave me? What will I do if she tries to leave? Her inventive engagement proved useful to my plans. Do I want to marry her? I cannot call my parents and tell them it was a game, but I told her I would. Maybe I'll let it play out before I decide.*

On Monday mornings, the large corporate headquarters of Haggins' Hotel Group felt like a hive, with people buzzing everywhere. On the ground floor, every table in the small coffee shop was full and the line of waiting customers spilled out into the foyer, through those who milled about, talking over projects or catching up on the weekend. With a smile, Mercy navigated her way to the bank of elevators, remembering last night.

On the jet, in the car, in the elevator, in Gwen's apartment—Aurick's suggestive blue eyes roamed over her frame as if her clothing didn't exist at all. His unspoken promise flushed Mercy's cheeks and liquefied her insides with molten heat.

As soon as they were alone in the elevator, his muscled length pressed her pliable body to its wall, his palm cupped her breast and his mouth devoured her, further igniting her hunger.

When the doors opened, noises came from inside, and with a disappointed groan, he pulled her by the hand into their apartment.

Thelma Harper turned from the stove to greet them. "Welcome home," she smiled.

Mercy noted the impatient way Aurick pulled their bags inside, setting them on the floor. It made her smirk as she answered the woman. "Thank you, it's nice to be back."

"Dinner is nearly ready. I've just put in a tray of buns. As soon as they're ready, you can eat. About eighteen minutes."

Under his breath, Aurick murmured for her ear alone. "There's a lot we can do in eighteen minutes."

Mercy blushed when his hands wrapped around her waist, and she pulled to get away. "Thelma, you can go. I can manage taking them out."

The woman sent a knowing glance at the couple as she whisked by, wanting to catch the elevator before it trapped her with the lovers any longer.

The elevator closed. Mercy turned in his arms with a giggle and pushed at his chest, breaking free. Her gaze traveled to his bulging pants, and she teased. "Down boy. Dinner first, then dessert."

At the directed words, his cock jerked. He swallowed, then huskily replied. "I'm not hungry *for dinner*."

She sauntered away from him with a backward smile as she strolled into the kitchen. "If I give you an inch..."

"*I'll* give you eight very hard inches." He playfully growled as he lifted their suitcases and headed in the direction of their rooms.

S he busied herself dishing up their plates while she waited for the time to pass. She heard him unpacking—opening closets, walking from one room to another—returning things to their rightful place.

As she arranged their dinner on the table, his steps sounded down the hall. The hair on her neck prickled an instant before his arm snaked her waist and he pressed his naked length against her back, his thick member twitched against her ass. It was nearly indistinguishable from the dream she'd had.

His warm mouth dipped to her neck, and he

whispered. "Come with me." His strong arms scooped her body, forcing her to relax against his solid chest, and he carried her into the bedroom, their meal was forgotten.

Hours later, they ate a reheated dinner, famished from the extensive workout they'd shared. Afterward, he followed her back into her room, where she noted his empty suitcases beside hers. The significance thrilled her.

There weren't many people left in the elevator when it stopped on the floor, which housed the project managers and their staff. When she reached her desk, she dropped her purse into a filing cabinet and closed the drawer.

Over the interoffice communication system, Connie summoned. "Mercy, my office, please."

She picked up her notepad, pen, and coffee, then strode into her boss's office, closing the door behind her when the woman gestured.

Immediately, she took in Connie's disheveled appearance, the coffee cup laden waste bin, a pile of clothes on a nearby sofa, papers spread out on her desk, thick stacks of open files littered another long table, and the whiteboard against the wall covered in her chicken-scratch writing.

Mercy's eyes scrutinized the woman with worry. "When's the last time you were home?"

Connie sat back, resting against her chair. "Friday morning, when I left for work."

"What's so important?"

Connie eyed her. "Your father has negotiated the purchase of the Macdonald."

Mercy's mind reeled. Aurick and Gwen had talked of little else for months. Every business outing she'd shared with them had steered them towards this goal.

Every file Aurick had pondered and read late at night was another step to secure the purchase. Several rounds of negotiations had occurred, and each time, a few more interested parties dropped out. But Aurick and Gwen were certain the hotel would belong to Power Valley Holdings. What had happened?

She swallowed the disappointment rising in her throat. "How?"

"I don't have the particulars yet, but Bobby had something to do with it." She referred to Bob Paterson, the project manager Mercy had sat in for. "I'm sure we'll hear once everything is final." Connie smiled and stretched her back. "Your father wants another completed project budget before the end of today. Let's get started."

A urick had told Gwen to take the week off and would have enforced it, but she had negated an argument by commandeering his truck and arriving on her own. There was little he could do when he showed up. Regardless of the looks her darkened bruises and stitches received, she was determined not to be George's victim. Aurick needed her at this very crucial time.

After checking her voicemails, her emails, and Olivia's handwritten messages, Gwen, eager to find out if he'd had any success, strode into Aurick's office as he hung up the phone.

His eyebrow lifted with hope. "Anything?"

"Nothing," she shook her head, "You?"

He threw his pen on the desk and leaned back. "Not a returned call or email throughout the entire weekend. I've called several people this morning, and no one's answered."

Worried, she sat across from him. The investment they'd made thus far in this project would cripple his company almost to its demise if they didn't secure the hotel. "What's your take on it?"

He rubbed his temple. He had barely noticed the unanswered emails and phone calls over the weekend. And a couple of hours ago, he'd been incredibly happy coupling with Mercy. Not a single care. What a difference location, time, and company had on perspective. "They're freezing us out. I'd lay money it's Haggins."

"You better not gamble the last of your money. What's our plan?"

His jaw jumped, the only sign of his anger as he stood and shrugged into his fall coat. "I got to walk, clear my head, and figure this out. I'll be back later. If anything changes, text me."

He didn't wait for her response. What the fuck was he going to do? Tens of thousands of jobs—of people worldwide, relied on him for their livelihoods to support their families. He'd ignored everyone's advice. Risked losing everything to make his mark here. How the hell was he going to salvage this?

From inside the car, Mercy watched Aurick take the steps quickly, then strode across the parking lot to where she waited. He hadn't texted or called her all day and any message she sent him went unanswered for hours, then was only replied to by a monosyllable answer.

Her stomach lurched at the sight of his distraught expression as he slid into the passenger seat. He silenced the stereo with unnecessary force, filling the air with tension. It sent a cold shiver down her spine. He barely acknowledged her, his mind obviously elsewhere.

She wanted to comfort him, but she reminded herself she had to pretend. She leaned over and pecked his cheek, but he didn't seem to notice.

. . .

Eight hours had passed since he'd made the realization and still he was no closer to a solution. He couldn't tell Mercy what he'd done to their future, to so many people, and risk seeing condemnation in her eyes. He'd failed everyone—including her. But he wouldn't lie to her either. Therefore, silence was his only course of action.

When the elevator opened into their apartment, he exited first, heading down the hall to their bedroom as she greeted Thelma.

He could hear her melodic voice as he shrugged out of his suit, replacing it with something more comfortable. He picked up his briefcase, then locked himself inside his former bedroom, not able to face her.

It wasn't until Thelma had left, when Mercy checked on him, that she realized his intention. He'd shut her out, leaving his discarded suit crumpled on the bed.

There had to be a way for her to help him if only he'd tell her what was going on. Although she knew a lot of details from Aurick's side, she didn't have many from her father's. And without Aurick confiding in her, she wasn't sure how to help. She paced as she changed. What would Aurick do? What would her father do? Her father. The answer dawned on her. Her father would imbed himself into the equation. He'd source information from someone who could give it.

She checked the time, then hurried to her closet, pushing the long gowns aside, and pulled the duffle bag out. If she hurried and he was alone, she'd arrive in time for dinner. With company present, they'd eat much later, giving her ample time to get there.

As she waited for the elevator, she ensured the stove was off, then rushed out when it arrived.

The large dark glasses hindered her at sunset as she hurried up the sidewalk to her parents' home. She didn't dare glance around but wondered if the private investigator was still watching.

She didn't mean for her knock to sound impatient, or urgent. But it must have. Her father typically didn't answer the door.

His brow lifted as she removed the glasses. He opened the door wider, and she swept past him inside. "Mercy, what's wrong?"

She feigned her brightest smile as she hung her jacket, wig, and purse on the coat tree. "Nothing, daddy. Quite the opposite. I came to celebrate with you. Where's mom?"

He smiled as he hugged her. "She's sleeping. Celebrate what?"

She kissed his cheek as she pushed out of his arms. "The Macdonald. Congratulations. What are we drinking?"

He laughed. "Scotch."

He only drank scotch when others were expected. So, dinner guests, it was. Now, who might they be?

She smiled as she took her purse from the coat tree. "Who are we entertaining?"

"A few board members, a couple of project managers, and an executive from the current company who owns the property."

"Seven-thirty?" she asked, and he nodded as she turned to climb the stairs. "I'll be down shortly."

Mercy checked her cellphone as her father's guests gathered in his study, pouring drinks and welcoming each other. The extravagant clothing she'd left behind at her parents' came in handy. Many of the guests complimented her on the long purple dress she wore, but she was preoccupied with the unanswered message she had sent to Aurick.

She'd texted him an excuse about Carmen needing her and not to wait up.

Bob Paterson, one of her father's project managers, sat down next to her on the leather chesterfield puckered with buttons.

She smiled at him. "I was told this was your doing."

The red hair of his mustache wiggled at his boisterous laugh. "I can't take all the credit, kid. But remember the first rule, it's all about who you know."

She leaned closer to the older, jovial gentleman who she had known since she was a child. She whispered, inviting him to confide in her. "And who did you know?"

"Bonnie, one of Bill's administrators. We dated casually when we were your age." He winked at her. "You can never be sure where someone from your past might wind up."

She wondered who Bill was, but didn't ask. He probably expected she knew her father's associate. She changed the subject, not wanting to seem too eager. Her eyes lit with bewilderment. "Why was there so much competition for this particular property?"

"For most, they wanted the prestige the hotel offered. They couldn't comprehend the thirty-five million dollar building will be worth double when the light-rail system finishes its expansion and the revitalization of downtown is complete."

Her sugary, sweet voice complimented herself.

"Ingenious." Then to him, she asked. "So how did we get it?"

He shrugged. "Bonnie told me what they wanted, and why." He clinked his glass with hers. "We offered five million more than it was worth and a forty-five-day closing, which they needed."

Later, when she left, she knew what she had to do.

Aurick hadn't come to their bed during the night. When she woke, there was a note on the counter with an apology, saying he had left early for the office, which played into her plan perfectly. She scribbled her own note on the bottom. Meeting *Beverly tonight to finish the plans for Carmen's birthday party, don't wait up.*

With the forty-five-day closing, it meant contracts would be nearly finalized and need signatures within the week, if what Bob had said about the sellers needing a quick close. There'd be no hesitation. It didn't give her much time, so she'd have to work fast.

She texted Tom Dunfield, the man she'd arranged for Carmen to date. *I need to see you tonight. 7:30, you know the place.*

There was one advantage to being the boss's daughter. She could show up anywhere in the building and no one questioned it. It was easy for her to gain access to the mountains of paper in her father's *war room*, all she had to do was walk in, feign interest in what her father and his associates were doing and wait until they took lunch, if she hadn't found the information she was searching for beforehand.

Mercy was already seated when Tom walked into the dingy restaurant they'd shared their previous meal at. She'd taken the liberty of ordering the same dishes and drinks. She sipped hers through a straw that her nervous tongue was puckering.

He leaned over her chair and kissed her cheek. "You look well. I feel like we're in a spy novel. Were you followed?" He nervously laughed as he adjusted his pant legs and sat in the chair across from her.

As before, there was no one within eavesdropping distance. One other table sat at the far end of the room and Mercy had tipped the waiter, and asked him not to sit anyone nearby.

Still, she darted her eyes around the room and kept her voice quiet. "You once told me desperation causes a man to consider dishonorable things..." His pupils dilated with shock, but before he could speak, she continued. "Don't worry, I'm not threatening you. I'm only reminding you of when you threatened me. And even though, recognizing your plight, I offered to help you."

He exhaled with relief and relaxed in his chair. "You had me worried—all day."

"I'm sorry, it wasn't my intention." She forked the food as the waiter placed their plates in front of them and scurried away. When she took a bite, she appreciated the food's savory flavor. "Perhaps some advice first. Say you had two friends. One secure, successful and safe, loaded with money. And another, who may be in jeopardy, who possibly may forfeit everything they worked for. Both vying for the same thing and you had the opportunity to help either obtain it without either ever knowing. Who would you help?"

By the lifting of his gaze from his food to her several times, she knew he'd heard her words. Minutes passed, then he took a drink, clearing his mouth. "I'm assuming it's a choice between your father and your boyfriend? What you're saying is your father can afford to lose whatever it is they're after. But, Aurick can't survive without it?"

She clasped her hands, losing interest in her food. "I don't know if Aurick can survive without it. I don't have enough information from him. Whatever his options are, they can't be many. He's tight-lipped about it. Men and their foolish insistence—they must never appear weak."

He crossed his arms over his chest. "You barely know Aurick. You need to ask yourself; if you broke up in a year or six months, could you live with yourself if you betrayed your father's company—ultimately, your company?"

Mercy lifted her glass, swallowing a large mouthful. That's exactly what it was, no matter what spin she put on it. Betrayal. But her father's methods were heavy-handed, and unethical, and affected so many people. Then there was Aurick. He could be heavy-handed, but unethical? Never. Every conversation she'd been privy to, every business interaction or report she'd seen, always revealed one thing. He cared for his people, his businesses, and everyone involved. If she could help him continue, her actions would be worth it.

She withdrew her cell, opened her photos, and spun it around, so Tom could view the screen. "What do you know about this hotel group? Who do you know on this list?"

Bewildered, he skimmed the list, then reached over and permanently deleted the file. "Do you know how much trouble you could get into? Where did you get it?"

She shook her head with a laugh. "I walked it out of my father's building when I left work tonight. Security doesn't check my devices, my things. I'm just the boss's daughter. You didn't answer my question."

"There's a couple, but I have no information to blackmail them with. I'm sorry, I'm no use to you."

It was her turn to be shocked. "Who said anything about blackmail? I don't want to blackmail anyone." She sipped her drink. "I'm not my father. I just need someone to deliver a message. That's all. Simple, precise words. No threats and nothing illegal."

He smiled with excitement. "Call me Deep Throat." He rubbed his hands together. "What's the message?"

Mindlessly, Mercy stared at the centerpiece. She couldn't concentrate on the pretty flowers and smooth rocks. Almost twenty-four hours had passed, and Tom hadn't texted her. What was taking so long?

The night before when she'd arrived at the apartment, Aurick was sound asleep in their bed, still in his suit. She had carefully laid down and covered herself, not wanting to wake him. Soon, though, he'd turned over, spooning her into the cradle of his body.

The florist clicked her tongue, gaining Mercy's gaze before she spoke. "Is this what you were thinking?"

She shook her head, disinterested. "No. Let's go with short vases, crammed with white lilies." She turned her back, walking away. As an afterthought, she lifted her hand and looked behind her. "I don't want to see them either. They're approved."

Her cell vibrated in her hand and she held her breath as she checked the text message. *Delivered, expect a call.*

Now it was up to Aurick to secure the deal.

Thursday, the door to Aurick's office had remained closed for the better part of three days. He rarely left, refusing all phone calls and appointments. A thick tension, which felt like impending doom, hung over the entire building and its staff.

Olivia regarded Gwen with a worried look as she held out the messages.

Reassuring her, Gwen smiled. "We're fine. Aurick has a plan. Don't worry." After saying the words aloud, she realized she'd said them more for her own benefit than the younger woman. Aurick had always saved her. This time would be no different. Mind you—he was taking his time about it.

Olivia whispered. "There was a strange caller fifteen minutes ago."

She leaned in, arched her brow, and mimicked the administrator's whisper. "Who was it?"

Olivia pulled the paper from Aurick's cubby. "Shelagh LaPointe. She had an accent, probably French. She rattled off her number and hung up. She asked for Mr. Aurick Spencer—not *Mr. Spencer* or *Aurick*. Who talks like that?"

Gwen sighed. The younger woman was unaccustomed to big business and wouldn't recognize an important call from any other, even if the person mentioned an emergency. This message was cryptic and needed attention immediately.

In the private lunchroom, the girls ate as they discussed their plans for the weekend. Mercy begged out of their Friday ritual. She wasn't the best company as she waited on pins and needles for the shoe to drop. No, she'd spend tomorrow night relaxing and reading with a glass of wine, curled up in her favorite chair.

Pouting, Carmen blurted. "When's the last time we got drunk together?"

Mercy's mouth quirked. "I signed up for the dating app."

She laughed. "Well, then it's time to do it again."

Beverly shook her head. "You broke–"

The shoe dropped.

Even with the doors closed, Keith Haggins' loud voice sounded as he walked down the narrow hall.

"What delay?" He barked. Mercy pictured the froth forming at the corners of his mouth. "This deal is done. We're scheduled to sign the documents tomorrow… What do you mean another company finalized the purchase today? Who?" More seconds passed and his voice moved farther away. "There's no way Spencer pulled this off himself."

Mercy's cell vibrated in her hand as they picked up the remnants of their food. She checked the message from Aurick. *Meet at our apartment after work. Hurry, I'll be waiting.* She smiled.

Her heart fluttered with anticipation as the elevator climbed. It had been four long days of near silence between them, both busy orchestrating this deal without telling the other. She smiled to herself, replaying her father's final words to the caller. *There's no way Spencer pulled this off himself.* All she did was deliver a message, and he had done the rest.

Votive candles burned in crystal holders on the romantically staged table in the otherwise dark dining room as she shrugged off her shoes. Soft saxophone music played from the surround sound system and a large fire flickered in the fireplace, casting a yellow glow over the carpet and walls in the living room.

Aurick came from the kitchen. In each hand, he held a fizzling champagne flute. As he approached her, she gazed quizzically into his bright, sparkling eyes. Before he planted a quick kiss on her mouth, she noted his wide grin, like a boy who'd received exactly what he wanted on Christmas morning.

"For you." He handed her a flute, then took her hand and pulled her down into the living room as she sipped.

They needed to talk. She couldn't stay in a relationship with someone who wouldn't confide in her.

She stopped beside the coffee table. "Are we celebrating?"

He pushed the table out of the way with his foot, then grabbed the glass from her hand. He discarded them, then wrapped her waist with his arms, dancing her a few steps before he spoke. "We are. I own the Macdonald."

She pushed away, feigned shock, then excitement. "How? When? Tell me everything."

And he did. When he finished telling her about the deal, she still needed more. She needed to understand.

His arm was draped around her as they sat curled together on the couch. Her eyes studied him. "What happened that you aren't telling me? Where'd you go this week?"

He ran his fingers up her arm, trying to entice her with other thoughts. "Nowhere, I was working. That's all."

Her breath heaved loudly as she pushed out of his arms and stood up. "You shut me out like I didn't deserve your trust."

"No," he leaped up and held her shoulders, staring into her eyes. "That wasn't it at all." He fluttered his lips over her forehead as he pulled her towards him. He wrapped his arms tightly around her so she couldn't look at him. "I was afraid to tell you I failed. I almost lost everything, and I was too ashamed to face your disappointment."

Her head rested against his shoulder, and his hand held the back of her neck there. Her steady voice held conviction. "You could never disappoint me. And I could never look at you any different than I do now." His hand moved, but she stayed in the same position. "Don't ever shut me out again."

He lifted her face to his eyes. "I promise." His devilish grin crushed her stern lips with yearning need.

CHAPTER 13

Whose Whore Are You?

Mercy stretched against the mattress as the morning sunlight radiated through the window, bathing her face. She turned over to escape its rays and came eye to eye with Aurick. Since their discussion over a week ago, their relationship had developed further. They made love, fell asleep, and woke up with each other. His boldly spoken advances and continual touches were numerous, and she thoroughly enjoyed them, matching each one with her own.

Aurick recognized the lighter nature of her demeanor as her emotional wall crumbled. Under the effects of their affection, she glowed radiantly. And she sang—not very well, but it was still beautiful to his ears. It was as if he had never witnessed the sun and one day the clouds cleared and there it was, shimmering brilliantly down on him.

She could be very demanding. *Kiss this* and *do that*—and the orders weren't confined to the bedroom. Their relationship amazed him. It felt like home, like his parents' love, and he basked in it. That is what it was—a relationship, no longer a business transaction. She was fascinating and sensuous. Her hunger for him was as insatiable as his was for her.

"Good morning." He huskily murmured, snaking

his heavy palm out to settle on her naked thigh, his fingers kneading her skin.

"Good morning." She snuggled closer to him, resting her head under his chin, and giggled when his hand traveled from her thigh to her buttocks. She lifted her eyes to his and grumbled. "We don't have time for this." He planted a peck on her lips. "You have to work today." Then another. "Remember Gwen?" And, another. "You told her yesterday you would go in and take care of all those contracts."

He grumbled, then stretched. "Doesn't sound like something I want to bury myself in this morning." He pressed his erection into her stomach, lending emphasis to his words.

"We have to leave soon." She chided as she rolled onto her back, throwing off the blankets, exposing her complete nakedness to the sunlight.

He shifted his frame to look down on her while his grip reached for the sheet to cover them again. His mouth began a tantalizing journey over her breasts and down her navel, then he raised her leg over his head, his mouth nibbling on her inner thigh. "Ten minutes?" Taking her agreement for granted, he probed her passion-filled folds with his tongue.

An hour later, Mercy slid behind the wheel of her sedan. The dashboard clock read eight thirty-five as Aurick climbed into the passenger seat. As she drove, the downtown traffic was heavy, everyone was in a rush to get where they needed to be. She'd be lucky if she made it to work on time.

She flicked her signal, waiting for the intersection

to clear before she turned left. "I have Carmen's birthday party tonight."

He groaned as he fixed his tie. "I'll catch up on some things at work. Home around eleven."

After she dropped him off, she winced. It was another lie to dig herself out of when she told him the truth tomorrow. She sighed. It would be a long day with the Children's Hospital charity event this evening.

White satin linens with a small vase of lilies decorated each table as the orchestra played through cocktails and then the meal. Wealthy couples bid on the silent auction items or drank and circulated with other attendees. Mercy worked through both, flitting around in her heels, trying to obtain a higher bid from one guest or another. Her thoughts often drifted to Aurick, wondering what he was doing.

She wore an elegant ivory chiffon gown, one of Aurick's favorites. It caused her more grief than good tonight, as she once again picked it up to move around. Her feet ached, and she appreciated her chair when she sat to concentrate on the speeches being delivered.

Her father thanked everyone for their attendance, generous contributions, and bids. He outlined the role of the children's hospital and its importance to the community. He was a provocative speaker, holding their interest in the serious subject matter, but threw in a few tasteful jokes to liven the speech. People applauded as he introduced Connie Dover, the woman behind such luxurious charity events. Cameras flashed as the reporters covering the affair took a picture of Connie with him, then he walked off the rise where his table was and surprised Mercy when he settled next to Mercy below. Luckily, the press had no idea what she looked like and without a name tag or announcement, they couldn't determine her as newsworthy content.

Connie acknowledged his introduction, then started listing the final bids and winners of the auction items. With one item left, Connie praised her entire staff, the caterers, and the orchestra for their incredible teamwork in creating the successful event.

"Let me welcome Keith and his daughter to announce the winner of our final auction piece. A princess necklace, interwoven with raw white gold and striking sapphires." When Connie finished, everyone stood and clapped their encouragement. Keith drew a shocked Mercy to her feet, then moved his hand under her arm, guiding her to the platform.

Society's manners and expectations were so ingrained—she couldn't dismiss her father publicly, even though she hated the attention. Used to the routine presence of the press, it probably hadn't occurred to him they were there. He wouldn't purposely drag her into their hateful spotlight.

Stunned, she stood nervously beside him as he spoke. "For those of you who don't recognize this beautiful woman, she's my daughter, Mercy. I found it fitting to have her accompany me as we award the princess necklace to the winner." He paused.

"As many of you know, she's headstrong, and we've had our battle lines marked and readied many times in the past." Keith's eyes encountered hers and he winked. "I don't see nearly enough of her since she was in pigtails and stomping through the house with mud up to her ears."

The crowd laughed, and he waited for quiet before he continued. "But I want her to know that I miss her, respect her and appreciate who she has become." His eyes welled with manly tears and he blinked several times to clear them as her mouth gaped open at his very public emotions, uncharacteristic of him.

"I've only demanded the best for you and sometimes I just don't know how to show it." He laughed aloud to break the emotional tension he had created. He cleared his throat and placed an arm around her waist. "Let me share with you the highest bid on the princess necklace, one hundred and twenty thousand dollars... And yes, it stung my wallet!" People snickered at his joke.

"She's my princess—my most priceless treasure." Everyone applauded as he spun her and fastened the jewelry around her throat, then hugged her in a warm embrace.

She smiled, knowing reporters hated *grip and grins*—people wanting attention or recognition for their good deed. It wasn't a good deed if everyone had to know about it. A single flash went off, but her face turned away. If it made the papers, it would be Christmas week, when they had nothing else to print —filler. And no one would recognize her.

"Let me tell you..." a drunken, masculine voice shouted a few feet away from the stage.

Mercy tried to peer down to see who it was, but the lights shining down on her were too intense.

"A princess? Yeah, the ice princess! That dull, stupid bitch..." The statement continued to grow louder as it moved closer to the stage, and shuffled feet mounted the stairs. "She threw away everything I worked for... Me. Not her. I slaved here and pursued the haughty cunt for too long, then *she* threw *me* away?" Suddenly Roger's contorted face passed the light's reflection as he stomped toward her. "Like she's better off without me? Well then, let's toast to your future." He threw the contents of his entire glass— burgundy wine into her face, and the dark red ran down the front of her ivory gown.

It was like a dream in a series of flashes. The entire room took a collective gasp, Keith sheltered his shaking daughter behind him, guarding her against further attack and the tuxedo-clad security team rushed the platform.

Inebriated, Roger didn't fight the numerous hands which forced him face down onto the floor. The Haggins were circled by guards and as they were ushered through the closest door and led through the banquet kitchen, Mercy's father shrugged out of the jacket, draping it over her shoulders.

His long black car met them as they exited the building. She held the jacket closed as the men steered her inside and clumsily she crawled onto a seat. The door slammed closed, muffling the outside noise and blanketing the interior in darkness. Someone thumped the roof, and the tires squealed under the duress of the heavy-footed driver as he sped away.

Several silent minutes passed before Mercy realized she was alone with the privacy screen erected between her and the driver. She pushed the sticky wet hair from her face as she willed her quivering body to the console. She cleared her throat before pressing the button to speak to the driver.

To her own ears, she sounded weak and strange. "Where are we going?"

"My orders are to ensure we aren't being followed, then to take you wherever you want to go."

Followed? She spun her body and her head snapped from side to side, watching the few other vehicles behind them. None were racing to catch up, and she wasn't even sure what else she should look for.

She pressed the button again, giving him Carmen and Beverly's address.

Without knocking, she entered and shot past her confused friends, heading straight for the bathroom.

She showered, ridding the chill and wine from her body. Through the curtain, Beverly handed her two fingers of whisky and left a pile of fresh clothes on the counter. When the scalding water turned luke-warm, she rubbed herself dry, dressed, and ventured into the living room where her friends waited.

The hateful public display left her feeling exposed and defeated. It took a long time for her to recount the humiliating story as her voice faltered and her still numb limbs shook. As she did, she felt a building ur-gency to see Aurick. An overwhelming need for his protection and words in their private world. Where he loved her, and she loved him. Loved? Had she ever used the word and known what it meant until now?

Her eyes sprang wider at the thought. "I haven't told him, I love him."

"Who, Roger?" Carmen's brow furrowed, unable to follow her friend's admission.

"No, Aurick." Her mouth curved into a slight smirk as she pushed up from the futon. "I have to tell him." She balanced from one foot to the other as she strapped on her heels.

Beverly glanced at the clock. "Now?"

"Right now."

Mercy paced the elevator as it climbed to the eighth floor. When the doors cleared, she rushed into the apartment. The dining room light was burning, and the television was on.

"Aurick?" she called, turning the television off, then tried again louder. "Aurick, are you here?"

The bathroom door opened and Aurick stepped

through, a towel wrapped around his waist while he worked at drying his hair. "Yeah." His chin dimpling grin surfaced. "I'm right here, honey." He chuckled as he strolled towards her, standing in the living room.

"You have to sit down." She grinned as he entered the room. "I have something to tell you."

She captured his arm and shoved him down onto the couch, then anxiously she wandered to the windows.

She drew a calming breath as he silently observed her. By her actions, she had something serious to say, and he waited.

Finally, she blurted. "Tell me you love me?"

She whirled around almost accusingly, a strange grin on her face as her adoring eyes traveled over him.

"What?" Confused, he combed his fingers through his hair and continued. "Have you been drinking?" He smirked as he inspected her expression.

"I had a whisky." She admitted. "Do you love me?"

"You know I do. I tell you all the time." He shrugged.

She crossed the room to stand at his feet. "Tell me now."

He lifted his chin, and his eyes sparkled as they admired her. His voice was husky when he replied. "I love you."

She knelt down, planting her hands along his jaw. "I love you."

His vise-like arms circled her waist. He dragged her onto the couch beside him as he climbed over her. Only a breath separated their mouths as he studied her face. She giggled, then sighed as he passed his hand through her hair, catching his finger in the necklace around her throat.

"I've said the words before, but until I found you, I never understood what they meant."

He trailed his tongue over her throat, producing a

wake of goosebumps along her skin. He nibbled her ear as his fingers unclasped the chain and tossed it aside.

"I have more to say." She started, her resolve fading under his skilled mouth.

His hands worked the buttons free on her shirt, then closed over her breasts as he murmured into her mouth. "Later. Let's love now."

He caught her lips with his, then urgently intensified the kiss, igniting a passionate fire between them. Her thoughts vanished when he lifted her, cradling her body against his naked chest, and carried her into the bedroom.

Tomorrow, the last logical thought she had, as desirous waves drove all reason from her mind.

Mercy leisurely strolled down the quiet corridor, on route to her desk. It was typical for a few teams to work the day after any weekend events, cleaning, organizing, and preparing final reports, so they'd be ready for the general meeting on Monday.

It wasn't unusual for her father to be present, rechecking his project manager's work. Though, it was unusual for him to be on this floor, in her chair, at her desk, with Connie perched on its edge.

"Mercy?" His concerned eyes scanned her.

It was pin-drop quiet. The other employees strained to listen.

Noting it, Keith rose, speaking in a discreet tone. "Let's take this into your office, Connie." He flattened his palm on his daughter's back, then ushered her inside.

He stepped around the desk and Mercy sat opposite as Connie closed the door, then sat next to her with a sympathetic look.

Mercy's mouth formed a hesitant smile. "Really," she patted Connie's hand, "I'm fine."

Her father raised his brow. "I called your cell many times last night. I even woke up HR for Carmen's number, but you weren't there. Isn't that where you're staying?"

Mercy hadn't expected him calling to check on her.

"No," she stammered. "I made alternative arrangements."

He cleared his throat. "I'm taking a leave of absence. Connie and Brandon will take over."

Mercy's eyes flew to his face. Upon closer inspection, she saw tired, worried lines and heavy bags under his eyes.

"What is it?" She questioned. "What's happened?"

"When I returned home last night, her nurse and an ambulance were waiting. Her prognosis is grim. Her condition has worsened much faster than anticipated."

"What are you saying?" Her temper flashed. "I'm not a child."

"She has little time left." He announced, and her mind reeled.

She hadn't expected her mother's disease to deteriorate so quickly. Pangs of guilt washed over her. She hadn't dedicated enough time to her lately. She had no words as he continued.

"I've scheduled a leave of absence for you. I assumed you would want to be with her."

"May I leave now? I need to see her." She stood and took a stride towards the door.

"There's more." Her father's words stopped Mercy, and she turned, her expression puzzled. What could be so important?

He picked up the newspaper and angled it so she could see the cover. Mercy appeared on the front, her ivory gown doused in wine. The caption read: *Haggins' Daughter's Demise*. She clutched the chair back, suddenly weak.

What had transpired only last night seemed like weeks ago, and more like a bad dream than reality. But there it was. Her face blushed with embarrassment.

"What do I do?" She clambered, genuinely requesting his guidance.

Keith rose to his full height, towering over her, then stepped around the desk. "This is my fault. You've never been one of those intolerable children who gloried in the spotlight. You should maintain your personal lifestyle and avoid the press."

Mercy nodded. It was what she had always done, anyway.

"But when confronted with no means to escape the press—you should stand taller, a bit straighter, and remember you are Mercy Haggins. A powerful woman with the absolute strength of this enterprise behind you." He smiled at her, seeking to lessen her embarrassment, and planted a chaste peck on her forehead. "Let's go see your mom."

Reporters crowded around the vehicle at the hospital as Keith shielded his daughter and loudly criticized them for showing up while his wife was at death's door. They met with two doctors who repeated the diagnosis but couldn't exact how much time remained. She excused herself, the need to see her mother stronger than her desire to hear their words.

Mercy entered the private room—sterile, white and cold. The window's curtains were closed, casting dark shadows throughout. Her mother looked very fragile and lifeless. She scraped a chair across the floor to sit at her side. A mess of tubes and wires ran over her body, and the steady rhythmic beat of the various monitors and machines were deafening to her ears. As a wave of defeat consumed her, she held her mother's hand and watched her mother's comatose body.

The sluggish hours passed as the pair remained at her bedside, taking turns speaking to her, hoping she could hear them. Once in a while, a nurse would glance inside, but otherwise, they were alone.

Late in the afternoon, Mercy and her father spoke of taking her home. They could care for her there and knew her mother wouldn't want to die in the hospital. He suggested again; she return to their family home, knowing she would want to be nearby.

The elevator climbed while Mercy rested her head against the interior wall. It had been a long, emotional day, and all she wanted to do was curl up on the couch with Aurick. Strangely, the apartment was dark except for a light above the armchair in the living room. She moved toward the light switch but was startled when a hand snaked out, clutching her elbow. She swung her head to find it was Aurick as he dragged her to the sofa, then pushed her down.

He paced to the window, then spun around to stare at her. His skin was red, and the cord in his neck leaped in rage. He hurled his arm, sending the papers from his fist towards her.

She detected the smell of newspaper ink, and she realized instantly what it was as the pages separated and rained down around her.

When she had been told about the newspaper this morning, her thoughts were on her mother, and it hadn't dawned on her to care about it until now.

His voice exploded into the silent room. *"Princess,*

how does a father convince his daughter to bed the competition?"

She winced. "Aurick please–" Her tone sounded like a whisper compared to his shout.

"Please? Please let you explain?" he accused. "No, what can you explain? You're Mercy Haggins—*his* daughter."

"I know you're angry–"

His blood pumped loudly from his chest and coursed quickly through his veins. Too loudly for her words to be heard. "What did he offer you each time I sank my dick in you or were you rewarded by the stroke?" His shout reverberated, his face red from the force.

His words stung as she strode to him. Desperate, she tried again. "Aurick, please," she pleaded, "Please listen to me."

She reached for his arm, but as if it burned, he flung her hand away, causing her to lose her balance. She fell to the floor, and desperate tears slid down her cheeks. "It was never a ploy or a scheme..."

He strode to the elevator and punched the button.

"Wait please." She sobbed. "I love you. Don't go." She shrieked, her mind reeling from his rejection, and desperation seized her as she screamed. "I love you!"

His eyes, icy with contempt, scowled at her quaking body, but nothing pierced his outrage. His loud laugh echoed, and his venomous voice lashed out. "All this time, it turns out you were your *father's* whore—not mine."

He hurt. She *would* hurt.

"You're fired. Get out!" He stepped in and disappeared.

CHAPTER 14
You Don't Even Know Me

NOVEMBER

The weathered gray stone structure with its pitched green roofs, flat gable ends, and protruding square towers looked out of place. A royal castle in a sea of modern architecture. It was breathtaking.

In the black of the cold early evening, with the ground blanketed in freshly fallen snow and light pouring out from each of its windows, it felt as though time had rewound and Gwen was standing in a different part of history.

She wished she had worn a heavier jacket over her forest green gown as she waited outside for Aurick to arrive. As couples quickly climbed the stairs, seeking shelter from the biting wind reddening their cheeks, they greeted her.

She smiled politely at each. "Happy Holidays."

This evening in late November would start the endless string of parties planned for each location of Power Valley Holdings. Aurick had flown out over a month ago and begrudgingly landed an hour ago. It had taken his parents' convincing to get him here, reminding him of his duty to his staff and their children, who looked forward to these events every year.

His truck bucked over a speed bump as it turned into the drive and stopped. A valet rushed around to open his door, but Aurick threw the door open before the valet arrived and strode up the stairs, ignoring everyone around him.

His everyday suit was wrinkled, his longer beard was unkempt, and the lengthy growth of his hair was slicked back into a punishing elastic.

"Don't you look handsome?" Her sarcastic words reached him as she latched onto his arm.

He scowled down at her as they walked into the entrance. "Not here to make an impression. I'm here to make a speech and leave."

He paused as she shrugged out of her jacket and handed it to the coat check.

She adjusted her gown. "I thought you were stopping at the apartment to get ready."

The apartment, where Mercy's memory was everywhere, where her scent still lingered, where visions haunted him. He'd went, but couldn't go inside. Instead, he'd driven to a little dive bar a few streets over and had a drink.

"Speaking of it. Hire a decorator and send me the plans. I want it painted, cleaned, and redecorated before I return in December." He started walking without her.

She caught up and wound her arm through his as they reached the extravagant ballroom. "You're not staying?"

"No. I'm going to South Africa." He nodded at a doorman, who opened the heavy door for them.

"What? Why?" Shocked, she asked as his hand spanned her back, guiding her inside.

"Why not?" He shrugged out of her hold and headed in the direction of the bar.

DECEMBER

She inspected her appearance in the mirror, staring at the startling change which had occurred. Now accustomed, she had stopped trying to suppress the odd stray tear which swelled and darkened the circles under her eyes. Her mouth trembled, no longer having the strength of mind to interrupt it. Her black suit hung loosely from her frame, revealing the rapid weight loss, only eating when prompted.

A tortured sorrow drove her to exhaustion each day while she had taken care of her unconscious mother. She worked until her body groaned with excruciating physical and mental pain, and only then she slept.

At night, desperate nightmares of their breakup plagued her and the echoes of her own screams would wake her. There was an endless ache in her heart and she yearned to hear his voice or feel his hands. Only to herself, she admitted, she prayed for communication from him, but with the passing of time; it became clear it wasn't coming.

Her bedroom door opened, and she glanced through the mirror to see who it was.

Carmen silently entered, her eyes scanning her friend. "It's time. The car is waiting downstairs." She whispered, arranging the black hat and veil over Mercy's face, then reached for her hand and escorted her out.

Three nights earlier, in the blackness of her room, Mercy slept while a nightmare gripped her.

He was standing in their apartment, towering over her as she begged to explain what she had done. The emotions were so real that even in her sleep, she could taste the bitterness rising in her throat. The wrenching agony, like a dull knife stabbing into her, ripped holes and delivered wide slices through her heart.

Her body quaked under his hateful words and the reality of the dream. She awakened with a start, shifting onto her side to vomit on the floor.

She took a few minutes to settle herself, then quietly cleaned the mess. When she finished, not wanting to be alone, she draped a thick shawl over her shoulders and stepped silently down the hallway where everyone else slept.

The door to her mother's room creaked as she entered and closed the door behind her.

The room was wholly lit by the moonlight ricocheting off the snowdrifts outside the window, and she moved closer to the bed. Her mother hadn't regained consciousness, but Mercy spoke to her as if she was alert and listening. She sat on the edge and stared out the glass.

She exhaled. "You understand why I would want anonymity? You must realize what I wanted." She glanced at her mother's still form, then curled up at her mother's feet, lying down.

She berated herself with disgust. "Except, I did to him what every man has done to me. I turned into one of them... I deceived him for my benefit. I will never forgive myself for the pain I caused him needlessly." Her body shook as she sobbed. She rested her head on her mother's thigh.

In despair, she begged. "Tell me how to go on. I loved him so much. I don't know what to do."

Several minutes passed as she gave into her self-pity. She inhaled deep, trembling breaths, stopping another bout of tears from starting. When she had calmed down sufficiently, emotionally exhausted from her confession, she shivered and tried to wrap her shawl more fully around her. She closed her eyes and tried to rest for a few moments before she made the journey back to her room.

Mercy settled her palm against her mother's abdomen, rubbing it for comfort. Her stomach wasn't moving, and she reached up to feel her skin. A frigid coldness met her touch, and she launched herself up, switching on the lamp.

"Daddy!" A piercing scream escaped her.

Her father rushed in as he slipped into his housecoat. He turned her into his arms and the nurse hurried past them, then steered them out.

Mercy surfaced from her memory to discover herself seated beside her father, her hand in his. *It's a good day for a funeral,* she thought. The sky was murky while heavy snow settled around them, seeming to separate each person. The other gravestones were grungy, cold, and unkempt. She glanced at her father. His tears had frozen to his lashes as he listened to the minister.

She concentrated on the scripture, and he concluded by offering. "When overwhelmed here—left alone by our loved ones who have crossed—find comfort in the arms of others until you're once again-"

Mercy burst into grief-stricken hysteria. Carmen and Beverly surged forward, but her father stopped them.

"She's mine. I'll take care of her. Let us through." Not caring what anyone thought about them leaving, he half carried her through the people. He climbed into the backseat of the car, then pulled her head to his chest. Instructing his driver to take them home, his hand rubbed her back as she sank into an exhausted sleep.

"Thank you for coming, Dr. Peterson." Keith offered, standing in the hallway outside Mercy's room.

"I could hardly refuse. Your contributions are generous. I'll be frank." The physician said plainly. "Your daughter, for whatever reason, isn't taking care of herself. I see signs of dehydration, fatigue, and it looks to me like she has lost at least thirty pounds. She couldn't afford to lose ten, let alone thirty. I know her mother's illness and death were hard, but if she cannot care for herself, then someone else has to step in. I have offered her a sedative. She'll be delirious in a few minutes and she should fall asleep soon after. Perhaps your wife's former nurse could take care of her?"

"No." Her father dropped his arms and stood straighter. "I'll do it. You have my word. Can I sit with her now?"

"Of course, I'll let myself out." The doctor nodded and started down the stairs.

Keith entered as she struggled to focus. It was a poor attempt. Sadness clouded her expression, and her lip quivered as tears slid down her cheeks.

He dragged a chair to her bedside. "I'm here, sweetheart. Shh." He crooned softly, encouraging her to settle down. "Go to sleep. I'll make it better, I promise."

Her face swung to his, but she wasn't seeing him at all. "I loved him so much."

Her confession momentarily took him aback. He knew she had been seeing someone when she left home—the signs had been obvious. And, overhearing her cry out in the night, he knew they had broken up. He had made such a terrible mess of things the last time he involved himself in her relationship. She had never spoken of her relationships with him before, and he hoped this was the start of something new between them.

He stroked her hair with his fingers. Eventually, her lids closed and her breathing deepened—she slept.

Aurick's sporadic presence at the office became virtually unbearable for his entire staff. He no longer enjoyed the demand of his position, and his temper flashed at the smallest of hurdles. When speaking, he often clenched his jaw as his patience grew thin from explaining himself. He expected perfection from everyone and when it was unattainable, his anger would boil, leaving someone scarred from a verbal tongue lashing.

He drove his body to the edge of collapsing, spending his evenings in a gym or swimming pool. For the past week, his thoughts found no solace. Tormented by her memory, he prowled the apartment at night.

He would swing his head to see her at the kitchen sink or seated in the armchair, reading a book. In the furniture, her perfume accosted his senses. At least he no longer found his hand reaching for his phone to call or text her, only to hang up or delete the words before he sent them.

Finally, when his body gave into the agonizing plea for rest, she found her way into his dreams. More vivid than reality, he could see her beneath him, her smile and her body's reaction. Aurick would awake in a cold sweat with an aching loneliness.

He'd made every attempt to leave Edmonton behind. Whenever possible, he found reasons to be away, working on other matters. He only returned here when Gwen absolutely demanded it, and even then, he held those business dealings off until they could wait no longer.

Gwen pushed the door open with her hip as she juggled the coffee cups and the briefcase in her hands, entering Aurick's dark office. The only light radiated from a desk lamp. She stepped forward, dropped her briefcase on the floor, and deposited the cups on the surface. Ignoring him, she strode to the wall behind him and pushed open the curtains. Natural sunlight flooded the room, and it took her eyes a second to adjust.

He sat taller, ran his fingers through his tangled hair, then worked to fix the disheveled shape of his suit while she took the seat across from him. He knew he looked like hell and felt even worse, catching the last hour of sleep, laying his head on the smooth top in front of him.

She cleared her throat. Her green eyes appraised his expression to determine his disposition. "Aurick?"

"Yeah?" He scowled, and she silently cringed at her unwanted intervention.

"We need to talk." She hesitated, knowing an argument would follow. "About the future."

"What about it?" His words were irritated at the very mention of *talk*, knowing she'd pull no punches.

"Okay. First, cut the attitude because even though no one else will say anything to you, I will. Your behavior stinks. You're miserable and quickly becoming evil. It's been three months already and if you don't stop, your entire staff will probably quit, including me. Second, you wanted the apartment redecorated, but I've sent you plans repeatedly and you haven't responded. What do you want done?" She rambled, trying to finish before she suffered his temper.

"Get rid of it and move the staff into the hotel." He swept away what she regarded as a problem. He closed his eyes and leaned his head back to rest against the chair, assuming it would end the conversation.

Startled, she shook her red hair. "You can't be serious? You cannot think to move countless families into the hotel with children? Besides, that's an excessive loss of revenue we can't incur on an impulse. Be sensible." She argued, understanding his current heartbreak but needing him to snap out of this stupor to help manage the company.

Anger shot through his eyes when he opened them and settled on her face. His voice hissed at her defiant manner, and he attempted to hold it in check while putting her firmly in her place. "Get rid of it!" He yelled. "And find other accommodations. Better— sell everything we own here. I don't need your permission. Do as you're told!"

"*Do as I'm told*? Nice *boss card*—forget it. You're being ridiculous." She gripped the handle of her briefcase as she stood.

She raised her voice in case he decided to chime in over top of her. "You aren't the first man who's been lied to by a woman, and you certainly won't be the last. Who she was, where she was from—yes, those were lies. Consider, *if* she was planted to work you— ruin you—she did a piss-poor job of it. A pro doesn't walk away from their marks. It was you who chased her." While she was on a roll and he was quiet, she'd keep going as long as he was listening. "Furthermore, they don't fall in love with their marks, either. So which is it; either, she lied for her own reasons and fell in love with you or you started out as her mark and she fell in love with you? *Jesus Christ*, decide already."

She took a deep breath, and quieter she continued. "I don't stay with you because I owe you something. I stay because I want to. At least, you know now, she was staying out of choice."

Gwen walked to the door. "Count your blessings. I'm merely taking today. The next time you ever tell me to *do as I'm told* will be the last words you ever speak to me." She pulled it open. "Get over it, Aurick."

It was a beautiful day, unseasonably warm for the end of December. Mercy allowed the sun's rays to bathe her skin in its warmth through the window. She stretched her cramped muscles, her body's reminder of the hours she had spent reading. She settled again into the chair and opened the book. The doorbell rang, and she moved to answer it, wondering who it could be in the middle of an afternoon.

The housekeeper emerged from the dining room, but Mercy dismissed her and pulled the door open, finding Gwen standing on the step. She was bundled in a heavy coat and hat as she smiled in casual greeting.

"It's nice to see you." Mercy offered the fake off-handed remark, and she fidgeted nervously. Her fierce emotions returned, caused by the other girl's presence.

"I didn't call. I wasn't certain you would see me." Gwen ventured and rubbed her hands together, expecting to be invited in.

"What do you want?" She demanded, ignoring her manners.

"I came by to see how you are? I haven't heard from you." Gwen inquired, tucking her fingers into her pockets, realizing the other was not in a friendly mood.

"Why would you? We weren't *actually* friends, were we?" Mercy's tone was sharp and her rigid eyes made clear she wasn't welcoming her here.

"No, I suppose not." She agreed with a shrug, now uncertain of her choice to come here.

"Well?" Mercy barked.

She nervously blurted. "He's hurting," she placed her hand on Mercy's arm, "and he won't admit it. He misses you." She hesitated, then continued in a whisper. "He's instructed me to sell everything."

A quick pain cut through Mercy. She took a second, waiting for it to pass, then steeled herself. "Take a good look at me. I can't care for myself right now, let alone work up sympathy for anyone else. My mother has died and the man I love hates me. Let him throw everything away. Stay out of my life." She pressed the door forward, but Gwen's hand stopped it.

Mercy glared at her icily, and the girl dropped her hand. "You have no right to judge me, Gwen. You don't even know me."

She swung the door shut, then leaned against the closed door, wrapping her arms around herself for comfort.

H e managed to avoid Gwen by finding places to go where she would never look. The dive on 97th by the Northgate Mall provided just that. He slid the bar across the top of his phone, turning it off—something of a new habit in the evenings, ensuring she couldn't text or call. She was worried. His parents were worried—everyone was worried. If he had to endure another phone call from his sympathetic sister or worse, Bruce's sad attempts to feed him, he'd lose his mind.

He'd learned very quickly, going to bars and picking up women, wouldn't work. Every time he looked at one, he ended up comparing her to Mercy. As sick as it was, she was his measuring stick, and no one came close.

The waiter dropped the bill with another drink on the table, and he downed it. At least the whisky didn't disappoint him. It had been a friend who could numb his body and make his mind forget for a few short hours.

He shrugged into his jacket, dropped some cash on the table, and strode out. It wouldn't be hard to hail a cab on the busy street. A few moments later, a taxi pulled up and Aurick tapped on the window as a group of people emerged.

After securing the cab, he turned and waited for them to vacate. It was odd, he almost recognized them, but couldn't place them from where. And, apparently, by their uncomfortable expressions, they recognized him.

He pushed past them, sliding into the back seat, but when he reached for the handle, a man held the door hunched in, looking at him.

Aurick checked the seats, ensuring they hadn't left anything behind.

The man spoke. "Tom Dunfield, Aurick. We were never formally introduced, but we met at your apartment."

Instantly, the pieces snapped together. One must be Mercy's cousin and this was her boyfriend. Was Carmen even her cousin?

That sparked his temper. "What do you need?"

"I—I need nothing. You, on the other hand–"

What Aurick wouldn't give right now to feel some pain—physical pain. And this guy's tone was asking for it.

He pushed himself from the seat, coming eye to eye with the man.

His voice was steel. "What do I need?"

Tom backed away in self-preservation. He was much too pretty and diplomatic to get into a street brawl with the man who had forty pounds and ten years on him.

He lifted his hands, stopping Aurick. "The truth. How is it you've never questioned how the Macdonald came to be in your possession?"

His eyes narrowed. "I bought it. I know how I got it. It's called skill." Aurick turned to get back into the car.

As Tom backed away to join his group, he called. "Is that so?"

CHAPTER 15
I Don't Need a Recap

The fireplace in the dining room roared as Mercy stroked a match and watched the flames dance over the logs. She surveyed the table set for four, ensuring everything was in place to receive her father's business associates.

Cold, brittle air filled the room as her father stepped into the entrance.

"Did you visit the cemetery, daddy?" Mercy asked as she met him. Their relationship had become much closer since her mother's death a few months ago.

He shrugged the wool jacket off, then removed his fur cap, gloves and scarf, cramming them into the jacket's pocket. His cheeks flamed red from the viciously cold temperatures of January. "It still feels like yesterday. I miss her." Keith wrapped his arm around her and squeezed her to his side as he guided her into the den. When he let her go, she perched herself on a chair's arm and watched him pour a few fingers of scotch.

He took a generous swallow of the amber liquid and it heated his throat as he studied her.

Although still withdrawn and quiet, he could see traces of progress in her physical appearance. The large circles under her eyes had disappeared. She was sleeping better, and no longer cried out in the night.

She ate without coaxing. Her clothes were fitting better, and she had lost the hollowing in her complexion.

"I have to get dressed soon." She spoke her thought aloud.

The ice cubes clinked in the glass's bottom. "Thank you for taking care of the preparations for tonight. It's important."

Her mouth curved up into a slight grin. "It was entertaining. I'm contemplating a return to work."

He set his glass on the table. "Connie's former position remains open." He laughed, then pulled her up. "Time to get dressed. Let's go."

Mercy welcomed the unusual evening ahead. Since her mother's death, she'd found solace in her father's home, isolated.

The reporters had quickly established another outlet for their enthusiasm, and she was thankfully forgotten.

A new routine had developed. Together, Mercy and her father spent their evenings reading or watching television, then very late they would retreat to their rooms. She received her friends occasionally when they dropped by to check on her. Although content with her father's company, tonight would be a pleasant variation.

She could tell by the way he watched and questioned her, he had worried about. Her father had dealt with his grief and she recognized she had wallowed in her self-pity long enough. She went to considerable lengths to improve her behavior. The results were rather satisfying as she examined her reflection.

She listened as a vehicle pulled into the drive and gave her father a few minutes to greet his guests before she joined them. She had piled her hair on top of her head in soft curls, held by pins and wisps hung loosely from the back, tickling her neck. Her makeup was flawless, adding intensity to her blue eyes, and enhanced the startling effect of her dress. The long gown of emerald green swept the floor while white lace flowed over her neck and arms, then down over her torso. It rustled as she swung to admire herself.

She descended the stairs, hearing ice cubes against glass while her father's voice described the painting above the mantel to his guests. *This will be good for him,* she thought and smiled.

"The blues and reds, obviously enthralled the artist, as you can see. They're smudged over the entire background." Keith finished as she reached the door-frame. Her father leaned his hip against the bar, drawing the attention of his guests.

"Fascinating." A familiar, deep tone answered.

Mercy's heart skipped, and she froze to listen to the exchange, recognizing it immediately.

"I hate to change the subject so abruptly, but Gwen assured me we wouldn't be here long. We appreciate the offer you made for the building. It's a solid investment, Keith. Furthermore, I'm glad you were available this evening to sign the documents. I'll be leaving the area tomorrow and I'm not sure when I'll be back." Aurick allowed the older gentleman to refill his glass.

Mercy hadn't listened to the words, only the caressing tone she had missed and she silently tread over the floor as if he had been calling her name to come forward.

Aurick's back was to Mercy, and it was Gwen who watched her slowly inch across on the floor.

The mesmerizing look in Mercy's eyes pleased Gwen after all this time. Not revealing the girl's presence, Gwen silently prayed his response would be the same.

"Our company has completely remodeled the building, and it includes a live-in cleaning staff. You should be very happy with it. Aurick has been adamant about selling." Gwen stated, informing Mercy of the reason behind their visit.

Mercy's mouth dropped at the revelation, and she turned to leave. *He isn't here for me. He hasn't come to find me.* Her thoughts raced with the embarrassment she had nearly caused herself.

"Mercy." Her father transferred his attention to her, and she froze in her cowardly tracks.

Mercy heard the swiftness of glass meeting the tabletop, and she felt Aurick's eyes on her back. She heard his feet approach before he gripped her arm and spun her around to face him. Her head snapped back by the force, and she found herself looking into his cold blue eyes.

"What is this?" Aurick's voice demanded as he narrowed his gaze, his fist clamped heavier on her arm. "Another game? Did you arrange for me to come here? Did you expect to change how I feel? Maybe I'd admit I want you back?"

Mercy's face whitened, and she struggled to pull away from him. Her voice was indignant when she reacted. "I could ask you the same thing, couldn't I? Let me go."

Aurick ignored her. Her attempt to escape was no match for his strength, and he easily held her.

"Let her go." Keith grabbed her arm to tug it loose from Aurick's hand.

He released her, but her father and Aurick now stood toe to toe, glaring at each other. Keith's voice raised in anger. "What is the meaning of this? Do you know my daughter? I invited you into my home to sign documents and if you cannot control yourself, then you can leave. We'll forget the entire deal."

Mercy took the few seconds she had to survey him. Her anger melted.

Aurick's temper flared, and he fought to keep it in check. "Not a problem. Excuse me." His gaze flickered past Keith, pausing on Mercy for a second. Then he strode out into the foyer.

Desperation went through her, and she rushed to follow him.

Gwen rose and caught Keith's arm, keeping him with her.

As Mercy entered, he zippered his jacket. "Did you know I was here?" When he didn't respond, she demanded. "Answer me!"

He turned his back to her and reached for the doorknob. "If I had, I wouldn't have come."

She shouted as tears formed. "I don't believe you! You're lying. You knew he was my father."

A breath of cold air entered as he stepped outside and silently shut the door. As if her words hadn't reached him at all.

She ran to the door and went out. He slammed the door of her sedan and started the engine. She tried to gain his attention. Anger or otherwise, it would be better than nothing.

"Aurick! Please stop. Please. Don't you miss me at all?" Her screams were lost as the engine revved and he sped away.

Footsteps sounded behind her, and a pair of hands grabbed her shoulders, guiding her back indoors. In turmoil, she cried as her stomach twisted.

She heard Gwen's muffled voice but couldn't understand it through her racing thoughts until the other girl's hand swept forcibly across her cheek.

"Listen to me... Do you still love him?"

The stinging sensation lifted her out of her emotional fog and she searched the other's face as if noticing her there for the first time.

She whispered. "Can't you see it? He hates me! I thought maybe he would calm down and we could talk. Seeing me didn't even faze him."

Gwen grasped her shaking hands. "You're wrong. He came here, didn't he? He had to have known you would be here." Mercy's head snapped up in realization as she continued. "Go to him while tonight is fresh. Before he's able to steel himself against you again."

"Where–"

"The apartment and don't leave until he shows up. I'll find him and send him there." Gwen reached for a jacket to drape around her shoulders as Mercy dried her face. "Use my code. It's fourteen-ninety-two. Columbus sailed, blah, blah, blah. Easy to remember but if you forget, call me."

A movement behind Gwen caught Mercy's eye, and she focused on her father, who stood back, watching the exchange.

He offered. "If you love him, go. Take the Tahoe." He tossed her the keys as Gwen shoved her outside, not giving her a chance to change her mind.

When the door closed, Gwen spun around and her red hair bounced around her shoulders. Her mouth smirked as she met Keith's eyes. "Do you think it worked?"

"We'll see." His expression lifted into a grin. "Let's drink. This could be a long night."

He turned, retreating into the study as she accompanied him with a laugh.

Aurick stormed past the living room, down the hall, and into the bedroom, striping his black tie and coat as he traveled. In his anger, the buttons of his navy shirt became a frustration, and he tore the shirt free in one motion. Buttons flew as his phone rang. He searched the jacket he had flung on the bed, battling to regain control.

"Hello dad, how are you?" He greeted his father casually as he ran his fingers through his hair and sat on the bed's edge.

"I've been busy," Aurick responded to his father's remark. "No, it has nothing to do with Mercy. Why do you always bring her into our conversations?" His temper flashed at his father's question. He wasn't ready to talk to anyone about her right now.

His father pressed, and Aurick begrudgingly answered. "She deceived me, made me a joke in her game, and played me for an idiot. How can I forgive her, or for that matter trust her again?"

"Yeah, I saw her tonight actually." Aurick paused for a moment, exhaling a deep breath, then conceded. "And I'm a fool because nothing's changed. I still love her."

The elevator doors opened and Mercy stepped out into the apartment. She cleared her throat to call out but hesitated when his husky voice declared.

"And I'm an idiot because nothing's changed. I still love her."

Her heart leaped at his words and she wandered into the living room, sitting in the armchair so she could watch him when he appeared in the hall. She patiently waited while he continued talking.

"Look, I know you're all concerned about me, but

don't be. I got to go. Gwen just showed up. I'll talk to you later. Good night." He hung up and then raised his voice.

"I'll never sell to her father? Do you hear me?" He yelled from the bedroom. "Her showing up tonight was orchestrated. I know it."

He continued his rant with a little less volume. "I don't know which one of you arranged it and truthfully, I don't care. If seeing her tonight was supposed to prove something, then congratulations—all it proved was I'm still stupid because I know nothing about her and I still can't shake these feelings for her."

He yelled louder. "Jesus, Gwen! Do you have anything to say?" He strode into the hallway, his eyes turned hard and accusing as they found Mercy there.

Her senses were overwhelmed and her heart's pace quickened when his half-nude body appeared. The lamp light caressed his tan skin as he moved, and his rippling torso became rigid when he discovered her intrusion. His eyes steeled and a muscle in his jaw jumped, revealing his anger.

Aurick stopped when his eyes reached her image. She was settled in the armchair, wearing the same gown she wore tonight, but makeup smeared her face. He rattled his head, demanding he rid himself of her memory.

But she didn't fade. She was real and had heard his confession. He became livid over the knowledge she had just gained.

His eyes inspected her as he accused. "Go ahead, laugh. It's what you came here for, right? Or was it to feed me more lies?"

Bracing herself, Mercy sat straighter in the chair. "Keep it coming? I can take it. You must have so much more to say. It has been three months." She encouraged his malicious words. It was better than the silence she had endured all this time.

"Don't, you're no martyr." He strode to the windows on her right, towering over her.

She raised her head to him, and his eyes snapped to her when she spoke. "Are you finished? Ready to listen yet?"

His proximity frayed her nerves, and she stood, putting distance between them as she perched on the couch's arm. She coldly waited for him to speak, but silence met her.

Her gaze passed over his back. "I'm sorry, I understand how you feel. I went through countless relationships where I was the one who was lied to. Believe me, when I say, I never meant to do it to you."

She shook her head, trying to shake away her nerves, then sighed. "At the time, we didn't know each other, Aurick. This started as an escape from my father's name, an escape from the countless men who used me for money or power. An attempt to find someone who *wanted* just me. And you—you *wanted* me."

He swung from the window, stepped around the armchair, and sat on its edge. His anger subsided as she spoke. His eyes noticed her disheveled appearance and weight loss. A lump formed in his throat and he cleared it with a cough. He pressed her. "Now?"

As if she hadn't heard him, she admitted. "By the time I realized it, our relationship was so deep. I tried to tell you—so many times—but I kept losing my nerve or we would get sidetracked. They aren't excuses, it's just what happened. I had every intention of telling you the night of the charity event when I came home and when I didn't, I made plans to confess the next day. You found out before I could tell you and your anger wouldn't allow me to explain." She hesitated, then hung her head and hair fell, covering her face.

She whispered into the silence. "I begged you and you walked out. You left me on the floor."

"I was there. I don't need a recap." His voice was sharper than intended as he recalled the scene. He didn't want to think about how hard it had been or how much it had hurt him. "I ask you what now, what's changed? You lied to me. How can I ever trust you again? How can I live down what you did to me?" His mind rushed to find answers, to find his own solution so he could be with her.

Mercy raised her face and used her hand to shove her hair aside. "I never lied about my feelings for you. I'm still the same woman you claimed to love, only with family and money."

"I appreciate your honesty." Aurick snapped sarcastically, then turned back to the window. "In the spirit of honesty, tell me about the Macdonald."

"The Macdonald?"

Exactly what he thought. "Come now, searching for a lie already? You want to know if I can trust you again, yet you're pretending to know nothing about the Macdonald." He spun around and walked to the elevator.

She sat in the armchair. This time, she wouldn't chase him. She would fight for them, only when he did.

"I'm not searching for a lie."

A pregnant silence ensued as he retraced his steps and sat on the couch across from her. He relaxed against it and propped his feet on the table.

"I'm listening."

She took a deep breath. "I knew nothing about my father's deal when we left for Ontario on Thursday night. It wasn't until Monday morning, when I went to work, that I heard the news."

He questioned. "Monday night?"

"Monday night when I picked you up. I knew. I wanted you to tell me but you didn't." He looked like he would interrupt. "I'm not blaming you." She wrung her hands together in her lap. "I went to my parents' home to see what I could find out."

"That's something I've wondered about. When and how did you come and go from your parents' house? I had a private investigator who swears you were never there."

She cringed, another lie she needed to explain. "I came across the file you had on my family as I was cleaning. I shouldn't have opened it, but it was about my family. It was the one and only time I ever opened any of your work. I bought a disguise, took the bus and knocked on the door. I hoped your investigator wouldn't connect the dots that way."

"The lies have piled quite high, haven't they?"

She ignored him to finish answering his original question. "I went to my parent's home where he was having a dinner party."

"By stealing?"

She clicked her tongue. "Try to remember, I'm a liar, not a thief. I asked some questions and found out they offered five million over asking and a forty-five-day close."

"Tuesday?"

She took another long breath. "On Tuesday, at work, I took a picture of the list of shareholders. Then, I told you, I was meeting up with Beverly. But, it wasn't. I met with someone who owed me a favor and I asked them to deliver a message to those he knew on the list."

"And that was?"

"You had offered more, with a shorter closing window." She stood. "That's it, that's all I did."

When she finished talking, he moved to stand in front of her. "Does your father know what you did?"

His closeness tempted her. She walked to the windows and stared outside at the city lights. "No. The reason I did what I did was to prevent either of you from finding out. You couldn't afford to lose the property and its loss would not endanger our company's future."

He turned, following her with his eyes. "If I asked you to tell him, would you?"

Spinning around, she faced him. "Why? What would it prove?"

"It would prove your confession isn't another lie."

She dropped her eyes. "It would hurt him."

It startled her when he lifted her chin. "It's the only way to prove what you've said."

His touch softened, cupping her cheek. It stole her breath and her pulse surged. Every rebuttal and every thought abandoned her. Of its own volition, her mouth turned into his palm, craving the part of herself that had gone missing all those months before.

With her pliant to his touch, Aurick explored her body further, placing his other hand on her side, pulling her solidly against his length. His groping hand roamed freely over her back, reconciling itself with his memories.

He whispered. "God, you feel good." His hands traveled over her sides and back, fitting her more tightly against him. His warm mouth moved to her throat. "Prove to me, I can trust you."

She opened her mouth to protest, and he seized the opportunity to hungrily taste her. Her flavor was intoxicating, and he deepened the kiss to lace his tongue with hers.

His rough tongue stroked hers and heavenly sensations pitted her stomach and flooded her mind.

He pulled his mouth away, offering her a chance to breathe or protest, finding it hard to control the fire burning through his veins. Would it be so wrong to find a single moment of peace in each other's bodies?

He ran his hurried lips along her cheek, nuzzled her ear, and sucked her lobe. His hoarse voice begged, revealing his need. "Ease my pain."

The anguish she heard in his tone matched the

visceral ache in her incessantly pitted stomach, and with his every touch, hers diminished. It felt urgent and promising. His heart leaped when her hands crept timidly up his hot chest and her delicate fingers massaged the knotted cord of his neck, surrendering. He walked her backward, guiding her down the dark hall and into their bedroom.

CHAPTER 16

It Could be the Jailer

The curtains blackened the room. It was hard for Mercy to tell if anything had changed, but as she felt the frame on the back of her calves, she noted it was in the same position. Her pulse quickened when he pushed her body down, then covered her with his own.

His thickening member was cradled in the vee of her gaped legs, basking in the heat emanating from her sex through the satiny material of her dress. He flexed his eager hips into her soft body, and a throaty cry escaped her when she felt his need pressed against her pelvis. His heartbeat raced, and he answered her plea by covering her wet mouth with his hungry lips. She laced her tongue with his and her breathing labored as their excitement heightened.

All of it—their touches, their urgency, his returning feelings—were too much for him to endure. He didn't want to feel love, didn't want to witness hers either. This was a means to an end—a reprieve from his torment. He broke their embrace, repositioned himself at her side, and rolled her onto her stomach as his mouth feasted on her bare neck.

His fingers encountered the gown's zipper, and they balled into the fabric, forcefully splitting it open. The slider bounced off the footboard. Impatiently, he ripped the white lace covering her shoulders from the green of the gown, exposing more of her flesh to him.

As he straddled her waist with his thighs, her mind shattered, going blank. All she could do was feel —his anger, his carnal need, her love—it offered her hope for their future.

"Love me." Her digits reached over her shoulder, raking his hair, inviting him to continue. Her body quivered with anticipation from the harsh, rough touch of his hand on her exposed back.

The last thing he wanted to feel was her invitation. His hand seized her wrist, and planted her arm on the bed, then moved his body lower so she couldn't reach him.

As his rigid frame inched down her pliable body, his fingers tore apart the threads of her dress's seam and his teeth nipped her spine, sending waves of yearning through her.

When he slid from the bed, the entire length of her gown had been destroyed, and she was nearly naked. Aurick positioned his frame behind her and used his heavy arms to pull her upward, onto her knees. He flexed his engorged member against her buttocks through his pants.

Need burned through her and dampened her thighs as she ground her ass against his groin. His body trembled as she pressed harder against his swollen length. She reached behind to grope him, her hand searching to hold and massage his stiff flesh, but he backed away.

He didn't want to feel her eagerness, but he did, and his mind spun wildly. He leaned forward and his teeth bit into her soft shoulder as his impatient hand loosened the pants at his waist, freeing his hard shaft. One of his hands urged her ass backwards, positioning her, then his thumb hooked the wet fabric of her panties and pulled it aside.

This time when their bodies connected, his hand

pushed his thick, veiny member down, slickening it in her passion. He twisted his harsh fingers into her hairstyle and pulled, arching her back into the air. Without preparation, he plunged his cock forcefully inside her, impaling her violently. He heard her satisfied cry, and for him, it felt like heaven. She gyrated her hips against him, encouraging him.

Wanting to punish his feelings and hers, he lunged his hips forward again, and their strength flattened her stomach on the mattress.

Yes, this is what he wanted, her unable to participate, unable to encourage him. He was in control as he fell with her. He drove his shaft deeper, feeling her cervix, her muscles contracting and narrowing her walls to sheath him. One of his arms brushed against her throat, as he pushed its way over and beneath her, immobilizing her arm as his palm roughly kneaded the fullness of her breast. Against the bedding, her cheek laid and his labored breathing teased her ear, his face poised above it. His other arm circled her waist, his hand slid down her abdomen and over her pelvis bone until his fingers found her budded, wet nub. His thumb and finger swirled over it, working its velvet against his coarse flesh.

Her grunts answered each of his as his vigorous penetration hammered her feverishly, his cruelness propelled her body causing it to slide further across the mattress. She managed to free her arm and over her head, her hand reached his back, digging her pointed fingernails into the solid flesh of his bronzed shoulder.

To her, their animalistic union and his desire were thrilling. His slicked digits rotated over her clit and caused the steady, pressure-building heat in her loins to intensify. It reassured her he still meant for her to find pleasure. She cried out when the tension burst and cascaded through her, numbing and mindless.

He felt her body shudder and her muscles tighten

over him in convulsions, milking him. He heard her whimper his name, and with incessant, rapid, brutalizing jabs he propelled his length further and rougher inside her narrowing cavern. Uncontrollable spasms traveled through his body and labored groans escaped him. With a final heave, he sent his hot sticky liquid frothing inside her and he let his weight collapse further onto her.

Immediately, he rolled their bodies to the side, and he twisted away from her. She turned onto her back—her eyes now adjusted—to look at him. He paused and glanced down at her, his naked torso glistening with beads of sweat.

Her questioning eyes met his as she reached out to grab his hand and pull him back into the bed.

It took all of his self-control not to return to her. He shook his head as he took an additional step backward. His impersonal voice explained. "I'm not staying."

Her body turned icy with the realization that their act had changed nothing—a purely physical release. Her eyes misted, and she blinked into the darkness, averting her face from him.

He reached for his pants. "You have a decision to make and I don't want my presence to influence you." He explained, then strode to the door, opening it. "I'll expect your answer in the morning."

She heard the quiet sound of the door latching behind him as he left.

She raised her head to see the time on the dresser, nine-fifteen. The sun accosted her eyes, and she turned away.

She had hardly slept, her mind returning to the decision she needed to make. Could she tell her father? The passing of time had developed a caring friendship of trust and consideration. He had allowed her to see his vulnerability and emotions. How could she tell him? He was the only family she had left.

She shoved back the sheets. Words would need to be spoken before she could leave and find her father. She found a pair of Aurick's gray jogging pants and a t-shirt, then fixed her hair back with a rubber band she found on the dresser. She checked her face in the mirror and scrubbed the remnants of the makeup away. Lifting the bed skirt, she removed an envelope, then ventured from the room.

Mercy heard the whispered voices before she could see who they belonged to as she padded down the hall to the living room. Unaware of her presence, Aurick sat on the sofa. With his hair tousled, he wore the pants from the night before and a white t-shirt hung loosely over his torso.

She rounded the corner to make herself known and found her father sitting in the armchair.

When she entered, both stood.

Aurick scrutinized her, hoping she would reveal her decision. Mercy's father smiled at her and she strode to his side for support, reached up, and pecked his cheek.

"Daddy?" Her eyes scanned his face. "What are you doing here?" Her gaze ran between the two men. Aurick's expression was blank.

"When you didn't come home last night, I decided to check on you. Are you all right?" Keith asked and ran a caring look over her.

"I'm fine." She turned and tossed a thick envelope down. The slippery bills of red and brown slid out, cascading across the smooth table. "Everything you paid me is there." Aurick eyed it, but his gaze snapped back to her when she spoke. "Am I to tell him now? With you present?"

He muttered under his breath. "I didn't plan this."

Her father's eyebrow lifted in question, and he sounded confused. "Paid you? For what?"

"I'll get to that. Please sit daddy." As he sat back down, she took a slow breath and turned to Aurick. "I understand humiliating me. But him?"

His gaze darted between her angry and her father's confused eyes. "What happened never has to leave this room."

Mercy started from the beginning—the very beginning—signing up on the app. She nearly felt guilty telling her father of how Aurick had misinterpreted her career choice and some of his subsequent behavior. She reddened when she told the story of their engagement and nearly broke down when she told him about her betrayal.

Her father and Aurick never spoke or interrupted her and once she finished, a heavy thick tension laid directly between all parties. The only sound was the ticking of the clock.

Mercy's body jumped and her heart nearly stopped when her father's sudden loud, hysterical laugh echoed. Between his bouts, he managed. "You outsmarted me?" He clapped his hands together. "Humiliated?... Why would I be humiliated?... Proud...—so damn proud." He paused long enough to look at Aurick and jab. "I knew you didn't have it in you to accomplish this on your own, Spencer." Then more laughter.

Mercy's mouth gaped and the cord in Aurick's neck jumped with anger, but neither said anything.

Keith was laughing so hard, he had to wipe tears from his face. "My poor little girl—with what domestic skills?" He tried to take a deep breath, but his laughter still cut through the muffle as he looked at Aurick. "Jesus Spencer, I thought you were smart. Apparently, I was wrong." Then he howled and turned to his daughter. "Answer me this, what's a colander?"

She knew she shouldn't be irritated by his reaction, but she couldn't stand his questioning her ability to pull it off. Defensively, she crossed her arms and lifted her chin higher. "It's a spice."

Again, he clapped his hands. "A spice. Did you hear that? She's completely clueless and God, are you dumb, buddy. This is great. You played my security, played my staff, played me, and played him."

She wished he wasn't being so jovial and pointed about it. She was supposed to be making amends and paying for her lies.

"Daddy, please stop." She darted a glance at Aurick, who looked miffed. She tried again. "Daddy, you must be angry over something I did? Anything?"

He pulled himself together and cleared his throat. "Yes... There's one thing I'm angry about."

"Good, what is it?" Whatever it was, she was ready. She deserved it.

"You should have spent his money and maxed his credit cards," he slapped his thigh, finding it all too amusing. "Given him a real lesson."

He was making this worse by the minute. She pulled him to stand and pushed him to the elevator as he continued to chuckle.

"I can't wait to tell every–"

"No." Both she and Aurick yelled in unison as she pushed the button.

When the doors closed, she turned and bumped into Aurick's solid chest.

She started to speak, but Aurick gagged her with his hand, waiting to hear the elevator move before he dragged her back into the living room.

Her apologetic eyes met his gaze. "I'm sorry, he wasn't angry."

"Mercy–"

She wrung her hands together and walked past him. "And, I'm sorry, he laughed at you."

His hand snaked out, grabbed her arm, and spun her around to look at him. "You can't control how he reacted. And, I deserved some of his mockings."

She scowled. "But it wasn't a punishment."

His hands circled her waist, and his chin dimpled when he grinned. "You want to be punished?"

"What are you doing?" She straightened her back, stiffening away from him.

His arms tightened around her, molding her to his length. "I'm punishing you." When she opened her mouth to speak, his head dipped and his tongue delved between her lips.

Not able to move, her toes curled into the carpet when her abdomen warmed. She wiggled against him, and he dropped his arms, allowing her hands their freedom.

Her fingers splayed against his chest, gently pushing, and her mouth broke from his. "This doesn't feel like a punishment either."

He lifted one of her hands, kissed its wrist, then threaded her fingers into the nape of his neck. "Trust me, it will. Ever seen someone sentenced to life?"

Her other hand joined the first. "It could be the jailer." She smiled as she ran her tongue over his lip.

As his breath washed over her face when he whispered into her parted lips. "I love you."

No further words were needed as he carried her to the couch. Both lost in their desire to love.

Epilogue

They had erected a semi-cylindrical structure of white lattice on the back lawns of the Haggins' home. It was painted white and trimmed with deep green ivy runs. Laced through were sparkling white lights and large lilies. Large pedestal vases filled with red roses and baby's breath lined the walls. A long satin rug of fabric, littered with red rose petals, divided the room. Its length invited the wedding party to stroll down it.

Surfaces were draped in floor-length ivory tablecloths. And at the center of each, matching smaller cylinder vases were placed. Black iron vines climbed them, and a few loops stuck out to allow small candles to be lit up their sides. Ebony pebbles weighted the bottom while white lilies hung out over the top. Black china, with hand-painted white petals along its edges, completed the elegant effect.

Mercy stood in her father's study, peeking out the glass door overlooking the beautiful structure filled with guests. In the early evening twilight, it looked magical. The soft glow of the twinkling lights danced through the night like miniature stars.

Impatiently, Mercy sighed and allowed the thin curtain to fall into place, then turned.

"You okay?" Beverly asked. Her brown hair was

curled and pinned with free-hanging wisps. Her bright green eyes searched Mercy's.

"She's nervous about her wedding night." Carmen teased. Her short black hair shook with laughter as she turned to inspect the bride.

"Come stand on the stool so I can bustle your train." Aurick's mother prompted her.

Mercy's traditional sheer gown had a scalloped bodice covered in sequence and tiny faux diamonds. A soutache accentuated the length and trimmed the empire waist. A chapel train with lace flowers detailed the hem. The elaborate beading continued down the long sleek sleeves, which tear-dropped over the back of Mercy's hand and fastened around her pointer fingers. When she moved, the large stone on her ring sparkled.

The long veil draped backward over Mercy's hair was where Aurick had left it. She'd refreshed her makeup and her blue eyes shimmered with anticipation for the evening to come.

The door burst open, and her new sister-in-law rushed in, out of breath. "You look breathtaking."

Gwen turned, playfully scolding the intruder. "Do you ever plan on slowing down, Sabria? You move around like you're on speed or something."

The bride smiled and continued to stare in the mirror. *Mrs. Mercy Spencer.* The words replayed in her mind as she studied herself, looking for a change in her appearance, now that she was married. The four bridesmaids surrounded her, their rich burgundy A-line dresses sweeping around them.

"We're ready for the reception. It's almost time to make your way down, but I came to tell you that your father would like to walk you out." Sabria explained her sudden entrance.

"What a delightful idea. You four girls go ahead and Mercy and her father will follow, just like at the ceremony." Amanda interjected.

A ringing sound interrupted the conversation, and everyone checked their cell phones.

"It's mine," Sabria announced as she walked a few paces away and quickly brought the phone to her ear. "Hello?"

"Amy?" a deep voice asked.

"No, sorry." She hung up. "Let's go girls."

T he stringed orchestra played a beautiful melody as Carmen, Beverly, Gwen, and Sabria descended the veranda stairs and onto the white fabric, which led them into the stunning white structure.

Mercy stood beside her father, watching the girls' procession.

Keith ran his hand over hers, drawing her attention.

"Are you happy?" He asked.

"Ecstatically daddy." Her brilliant smile made the confirmation almost unnecessary. "We should start our way down."

"I'm so proud of you. I wish your mother could see you today." He cleared his throat. "I love you." He whispered.

Mercy murmured as a tear slipped from her eye. "I love you too, and I'm positive she can see us. She's shocked to see how close we have become."

Her father led her through the dimly lit structure to where Aurick restlessly waited for his new bride on the dance floor. Keith raised her hand, delivering her to her new husband.

Her husband's fingers locked over hers as he used his other to shake her father's hand.

Aurick swung her into his arms. Her hands spanned his chest, while his fingers intertwined behind her back, pulling her closer to him. His eyes lovingly wandered over her as he dipped his head to taste her. Her lips were soft under the pressure of his, and she opened her mouth, inviting him inside.

He raised his head, moving his lips to her ear as they swayed and the music played. "Remember this song?"

Mercy lifted her eyes quizzically. "Should I?"

"It was playing the first night we met when I asked you how much." His chin dimpled under the force of his grin as he gazed down at her. "So let me ask you again, how much?"

She smiled as her fingers crawled up his chest, around his neck, and pulled his mouth closer to hers. "It will cost you your heart." His mouth overtook hers and they lost themselves in each other, except for the distant, muffled ringing of a phone.

A few accusing eyes shifted to Sabria as she answered her phone and in a hushed voice answered. "Hello?"

"Is Amy there?" The same caller from earlier.

"No, I'm sorry." Her mother sent her a silencing glare, and Sabria quickly continued. "I don't know any Amy. You must have the wrong number. Please stop calling."

The male voice chuckled loudly. "I doubt it. Whatever game she's into, I'm not playing. Tell Amy, Jake called."

Before she could rebuke his remarks, the line ended.

She watched her brother affectionately caress his wife as he whirled her across the dance floor. The awe of their beginning took Sabria's breath away, and she wondered what her own happily ever after would look like.

Thank you for entrusting me with your time. I hope you enjoyed reading about this couple as much as I enjoyed writing it.

Visit www.friendswithpensauthorgroup.com to receive a FREE bonus scene from Mercy and Aurick's honeymoon.

About Friends With Pens Author Group

Like an old familiar friend, characters confide in us. We take their narratives, add them to a blank page, then create an intricately woven world for them to discover.

Because we're bound to those characters and their stories, each world and genre can be completely different. We can fill them with breathtaking magical fantasy, delicious romantic liaisons or excruciating pain.

www.ingramcontent.com/pod-product-compliance
Lightning Source LLC
Chambersburg PA
CBHW031945110726
47902CB00001B/304